THE BIG
SHOW STOPPER

Also by Ken Dalton

The Bloody Birthright

THE BIG
SHOW STOPPER

Ken Dalton

For more information concerning *The Big Show Stopper*, email the author at ken@kendalton.com

ISBN 978-0-578-05459-9
1. Humorous—Mystery—Fiction. 2. Pinky—Delmont (Fictional character)—Fiction. 3. Bear—Zabarte (Fictional character)—Fiction. 4. Quebec City—Canada—Fiction. 5. Needles—California—Fiction. I. Title.

ACKNOWLEDGEMENTS

This novel came together with the help and assistance of the following;

To Steve Marshall who kindly allowed me a peek into the secret world of the big-time, multi-million dollar American concert tour world.

To my son, Hugh, and the his smashingly creative crew for another outstanding cover. To learn more about his great adventure be sure to read the Author's notes following *The Big Show Stopper*.

To Dr. Nussbaum for his quick and spot on diagnosis.

To Wendy Maxham for another exceptional picky, picky job of editing.

To my friends and family who encouraged me to complete *The Big Show Stopper,* even though a few had some problems with the language in the first book.

To Dr. Ye, and all the staff, nurses and Pharmacists, that dwell in the magical land of room 170, also known as the Kaiser Infusion Center, for keeping me alive while I completed this book.

To the long suffering members of my writer's group:
Editor-in-Chief Mary Madsen Hallock
Jon Gunner Howe
Norm Benson
Thea Howe
And the divine Sarah Andrews

Finally, to my wife Arlene, for remaining my lover and best friend while she stood by my side during the long summer of infusion madness.

This book is dedicated to the memory of my two cousins, Bud and Brian Marshall. To our precious few rounds of golf and to those glorious days, when as happy-go-lucky boys, we ran through Grandpa and Grandma's ivy covered front yard during Bardeen family gatherings.

ONE

Bear Zabarte—Carson City, Nevada

When Flo barfed her birthday dinner all over the floor, nobody, not even my chicken-shit boss, Pinky, would have gotten pissed-off —at least not if they'd known what led up to it.

Saturday was Flo's thirty-something birthday. All day I'd treated her like she was the Queen of Sheba 'cause when Flo's the center of attention, she's happier than a pig standing belly-deep in mud.

For dinner I took her to the High Roller's Buffet at the Nugget Casino, the best all-you-can-eat spread in northern Nevada. Flo loaded up her plate with some king crab legs, a chicken enchilada covered with that spicy green sauce, a few jumbo shrimps, and a giant heap of green salad. I followed behind her, grabbed the same, except I dumped less salad on my plate to leave room for a thick hunk of roast beef, and a slab of barbequed spare ribs.

After dinner, some of the "Three Card Poker" dealers serenaded my babe with Happy Birthday, and then for the big finish, I drove her to the new Carson City Expo Center so Flo could see the Brady Blackstone concert.

Shit, if it hadn't been Flo's birthday, I wouldn't have wasted my time or money going to a Blackstone concert. The tickets started at sixty bucks, and that was for a hard seat in the nosebleed section. Besides, watching Brady Blackstone prance around the stage didn't turn me on anymore. Don't get me wrong. I used to be a big fan back in the days when he played his guitar and sang so sweet. Then he got to be a Country-Rock star with hit records, and a big-time concert tour. I didn't go for the new Brady,

1

but I had to admit that taking in two million a concert wasn't bad money.

According to Flo, in the history of the whole damn world, there were only two performers worth paying money to see—Elvis Presley and Brady Blackstone. She was so crazy about those two dudes that when she moved into my place the very first thing she did was stick up two 8x10 photos over her side of the bathroom sink. And every morning, before she jumped into the shower, she'd light a candle below the pictures of her two heroes. So when I heard that the Brady Blackstone concert tour was coming to Carson City, I knew, one way or another, she'd be there. Sure enough, Flo came up with two free tickets.

The big question is why am I so damn broke that I can't scrounge up two Benjamins for a pair of concert tickets?

Everything started out okay after Flo moved in. I'd pick up a few days of work for Pinky and then I'd tend bar three or four nights around Carson City. Pinky paid me more than tending bar but I still wasn't bringing in enough to keep Flo happy.

What did she need? Shit, a list of what she didn't want would be shorter. One of the first things Flo did when she moved into my place was to find a beauty parlor and make an appointment to get her hair done and a manicure every damn week! I got my hair cut four times a year and looked okay. So her hair-do every week seemed like a lot of wasted scratch to me, but Flo promised me that a weekly trip to the beauty parlor was something all broads did.

While tending bar, I'd cover some of my shortage through tips and skimming a bit from the register, but now I'm broke all the time 'cause Pinky put the screws to me. He found out I was doing some bartending on the side and he didn't like that. Pinky told me to quit bartending or he'd fire me. Shit, I was between a rock and a hard spot. With Flo around, I needed to bring in three thousand a month just to keep my nose above water.

2

Pinky paid me a hundred and fifty a day, plus expenses, so I had to work five days a week to make my nut.

So now you know why I was a little short on cash and had to depend on Flo to come up with the Blackstone concert tickets.

How'd she pull it off? It turned out that Alice Spurlock, the broad who did Flo's hair every week, had a son, Jack, who worked in Brady Blackstone's backstage crew. That was all Flo needed.

"Omigod!" Flo shouted to Alice. "Except for Elvis, Brady is my all-time favorite singer. I'll do just about anything to see him before I die."

Flo told me that Alice stopped right there, in the middle of washing Flo's hair, dried her hands, grabbed the phone, and called her son. Then she handed Flo the phone and inside of thirty seconds my babe had conned Jack Spurlock out of two free backstage passes to the Blackstone concert.

I tried to get out of going with her, but Flo let me know that if I stayed home and watched a baseball game on TV, our sex life would dry up faster than a fence post in the desert. So I said sure I'd go and now after a great dinner, I pulled into the Expo parking lot ready to see Brady Blackstone, in the flesh, in style, and for free.

Being as I come from a long line of dumb Basque sheepherders, I didn't have a clue just how good backstage passes are, but as soon as we drove into the parking lot, I learned real fast. The parking dude took one look at the tickets and said, "Yes, sir, just follow the VIP signs on your left." I did and pretty soon another guy waved us over to a parking place about twenty feet from a door. Jack Spurlock was waiting inside, and he showed us all around the backstage area—even the bathroom where Brady Blackstone himself had once parked his royal butt on the throne. When she heard that, Flo's eyes lit up like a pinball machine. I figured that before the evening was out, she'd find a way to get in there—sashaying along in Brady's footsteps, I guess you'd call it.

After showing us the rack that held all of Brady's guitars for the show, Jack glanced at his watch and said, "Before I take you to the hospitality area, I'm going to let you in on a little secret concerning Brady's entrance. Before we open the arena, Brady and I go inside a black box sitting on the ground floor located in the center of the audience. We wait there and he drinks wine until the warm-up acts are over. Once the band starts his entrance music, I help Brady onto a chair that carries him over the audience to the stage."

Seemed kind of weird to me, but Flo said, "Wow, I can hardly wait."

Jack's tour ended up at the hospitality spot where all the people with backstage passes could get free beer and free guacamole and chips. But the best part was that our backstage pass got us into 'Brady's Corral', a roped-off section between the rest of the audience and the front of the stage. Flo told me we were standing where a fancy orchestra would be if we were going to watch an opera—like I'd ever go to an opera!

Brady's Corral was cool. I could drink beer and rest my elbow on the stage. Before he left, Jack gave us earplugs and warned us to use them, 'cause the giant speakers were so close that the pounding noise might melt the fillings in your teeth.

The warm-up acts? They weren't so bad, but they weren't great either. I was on my third beer when the band started to play and a cute redhead bounced onstage. I had heard her name once before, because she had won one of those stupid TV talent shows. Her back-up band was okay, a little too loud, but okay. Once the redhead hit her first note though, I'd heard enough. I put in the earplugs Jack gave us and headed back to the hospitality spot for another beer. I knew warm-up acts were generally second rate, but the redhead couldn't sing her way out of a wet paper bag. For the next ten minutes I kept my earplugs in, drank beer, and concentrated on her bouncing boobs.

After the no-talent babe, the next act up was Kyle Roubidoux. He was a young good-looking dude in a pair of jeans so tight that I thought his zipper was going to explode. I could tell all the women thought Kyle was sexy. He sang a bunch of pretty good songs, and Flo went wobbly-kneed every time he flashed his baby-blues in her direction.

The audience was pretty charged up when it was finally time for Brady to make his grand entrance. The lights went out. The band got real loud. The crowd screamed. A spotlight caught Brady Blackstone as he cruised over the heads of the audience toward center stage. About the time I thought the thing he was riding on should be slowing down, it seemed to speed up and Brady crashed head first into a metal beam holding up one side of a giant TV screen. A chunk of something flew across the stage and smacked Flo on the arm. She gave me a nasty look, like she thought I'd done it.

I yelled over the band, "Didn't touch you, Babe."

She brushed at her arm, like she was trying to shoo away a fly, then stared at her hand. It was covered with blood, a wad of brain, and some black hair.

Her mouth fell open and she looked down on the floor where a super-sized burger hunk of Brady Blackstone's scalp had ended up. The color in Flo's cheeks drained away faster than a toilet could flush, and she hurled her High Roller's Buffet dinner all over that hunk of head lying there. Flo started to crumple, like her backbone had turned to Cream of Wheat. I caught her before she hit the deck and pulled her away from the bloody mess on the floor.

I said, "You'll be okay, Babe. Hell, if that nasty thing had hit me in the arm, I'd have barfed, too."

I looked up just in time to see the rest of Brady Blackstone's body slip to the stage. That was when the whole place went nuts and twenty thousand Brady fans started to scream and yell out their hero's name as they figured out Brady lying there might not be part of the act.

Finally the band stopped playing and a deathly silence settled over the arena.

A guy in a suit ran onstage and bent over Brady's body. He whispered something in Brady's ear, nodded, and then grabbed a mike.

"Ladies and gentlemen, Brady's had a little accident, but don't worry, he told me he's okay."

Two guys rolled a stretcher onstage and the suit blocked the view of most of the audience as they lifted Brady's body on top the stretcher.

The suit stood up and said, "As a precautionary measure, an ambulance will take Brady to a nearby hospital where he'll be checked out. I'm sorry, folks, but the concert is over. Please exit the arena in an orderly manner."

I looked at the slab of brain on the floor. "Babe, the suit's feeding the crowd a crock of bull. Nobody could lose that much of his head and live."

The suit followed the dudes as they pushed the stretcher off stage and the house lights went up. The stunned audience stood and started to clear out. Some of the women were sobbing as they inched their way up the aisles toward the doors of the arena.

Flo looked at me. "But he said Brady's okay."

"He had to say that or he'd never get the crowd to leave this place."

The color slowly returned to Flo's face. "So you're pretty sure Brady's dead?"

I wrapped my arm around her. Flo wanted me to say no, but I'd rather she heard the truth from me. "I'm afraid so."

Her lip quivered, she took a deep breath, and flicked a tear off her cheek with her finger. "I'm okay now. Let's get out of here."

Out of the blue I heard a man's voice say, "If it isn't Bear Zabarte. I should have known you'd be hanging around. You and dead people just seem to go together."

Shit, it was Detective Ice Conner, the lowest of all Carson City's cops. Me and that bastard never got along

6

and I wanted to punch his lights out, but I knew this wasn't the time or the place. For Flo's sake, this being her birthday, and now in mourning for Brady, I tried to be nice. "What are you doing here, Ice?"

"Picked me up a good paying moonlighting job. I'm in charge of security for the concert." He stepped closer and his eyes bugged out as he took his sweet time casing out Flo. "Who's the broad?"

I growled, "She's no broad, damn it. This is my lady friend, Flo."

Ice turned his head and smiled, "Pardon me, ma'am, I think Bear forgot to introduce us. My name is Detective William L. Conner."

Flo dried her eyes and said, "How do you do. My name is Florence Sonderlund."

I stepped between them and said, "Ice, got any idea what happened to Brady?"

"Don't have a clue. Looked to me like some kind of chair malfunction. Hell, I just read last week that every year there's a pot-full of skiers accidentally killed riding those damn chairlifts." His eyes locked on Flo's massive rack. "Pleased to meet you, ma'am. Excuse me, but I've got to head to the lobby to make sure all the doors are locked after everybody leaves."

I said, "See you around, Ice."

He flashed me his high-power death stare. I don't think he liked me calling him Ice in front of Flo.

Before the bastard walked up the aisle, he leaned toward me and whispered, "I hear you're working for that shrimp shyster, Pinky Delmont. Bear, I know we've had a few disagreements in the past, but if that chicken-shit lawyer throws more work at you than you can handle, I'm available to pick up some of the excess."

"Oh sure, I'll call you."

I closed my trap before the rest of what I wanted to say flew out—yeah, I'll do that when elephants fly! Shit, Ice Conner couldn't solve a murder if the killer strangled his victim while the two of them stood between first and second base during a World Series baseball game.

Eventually, Ice figured out that I knew all he was doing was staring at Flo's boobs. He turned, licking his lips, and walked up the aisle toward the lobby.

TWO

Bear Zabarte—Carson City, Nevada

Flo said, "I don't understand why you insist on calling that friendly police detective, 'Ice'."

"It's simple, Babe. The dude's been on the Carson City force for three years, and in that time, he's iced three suspects after he arrested them. There was an investigation after each killing, but he was able to convince the review board that he shot in self-defense. According to the scuttlebutt around town, the bastard ended up in Carson City because he had to leave the Spokane force after he killed a bunch of suspects there. Now do you understand why I call him Ice?"

She jabbed her elbow in my side. "I'm surprised that you place so much stake in gossip. Just the other day—"

Flo was interrupted by a voice over the loud speaker.

"Attention. Attention. All members of the Blackstone tour will meet center stage at once."

Flo said, "We should stick around. I have to convey my appreciation to Jack for the backstage passes."

I glanced at my watch. If we left now, I could still catch the last few innings of the game. "Flo, I don't know. It sounds like the meeting is just for members of the tour."

She frowned. "Expressing our gratitude to Jack Spurlock is more important than rushing home to watch another stupid ball game on TV. Jack treated us real nice, like we were members of his family. Remember, before the concert started, he took us backstage and I got close enough to touch Brady's arm. Damn it, we're staying!"

I don't know how she knew I was thinking about watching the ball game, but I had to give Flo credit, she had nailed me again. "You're right. We'll stay."

We hung back and waited as the staff gradually filled the stage. I spotted Jack up there and waved. He waved back.

The man in the suit, who came on stage after Brady hit the deck, was now wearing a cool cowboy hat. He grabbed a mike and said, "It's obvious to everyone that due to Brady's untimely death, the Blackstone tour is finished. In honor of our fallen comrade, I want everyone to give Brady a moment of silence."

The suit took off his hat. Everybody stood around for almost fifteen seconds before one of the medics grabbed the suit by the arm and handed him a note.

The suit read the note, crumpled it up and tossed it over his shoulder. "I've just been informed that a representative from The Division of Industrial Relations of the Nevada Department of Business & Industry is sending an agent from Reno to investigate the accidental death of our fallen hero. My question to you is this—are we going to stand around and wait, or are we going to load the trucks and head to Portland as scheduled?"

Why go to Portland without the star attraction? I wondered. The guys and gals milling around the suit seemed confused by the question too— like they were used to doing, not thinking.

The suit said, "My answer to the state of Nevada would be limited to five words—this show must go on!" His voice started to rise, like he was one of those tent show preachers. "Now, from this very moment, we will be known as The Kyle Roubidoux Sunrise Tour. The tragedy of Brady's untimely death will be the top show biz news story all over the world, and if we take full advantage of the publicity, I predict we will sell out the rest of our concerts. Any questions?"

To me, the suit's comments came off as pretty damn cold, but what did I know? Maybe this was the way all unexpected deaths were handled in show business.

The suit said, "Good. Now get your asses in gear. We have to strike the set and be on the road in less then an hour."

10

The group bunched up, put their hands together, yelled go, and scattered like those damned dandelion puffs floating on a spring breeze. In all the commotion I lost sight of Jack. Me and Flo climbed onto the stage and for a few minutes, we dodged speakers, hunks of the set, and soundboards as they were being rolled out of the arena and into a bunch of waiting eighteen-wheelers.

I finally found Jack standing by a metal chair. "Jack, Flo and me wanted to stop by and thank you for everything."

Flo elbowed me. "And extend our condolences."

I said, "Yeah, that too."

Jack said, "Flo, I'm sorry you didn't get to see Brady do his—"

Flo said, "That's okay. I got to touch his arm before he died. That's a lot more than I got to do with Elvis."

I said, "What's the name attached to the suit who took over the stage and did all the talking?"

"The tour manager? His name is Rene Gagnon."

"Is he always that cold?"

"Rene? I never thought about that, but I guess he is. Why?"

"Just nosing around. Jack, have you got any idea what went wrong out there tonight?"

"Don't have a clue." He held up the metal chair that took Brady to his death. "This has worked perfectly all year. The chair and cable rig were custom built for the tour by one of those big name ski-lift companies."

I shook my head. "Brady's entrance looked risky to me."

Jack said, "But there shouldn't have been any risk. The chair was equipped with a dead man brake, like the ones they had on the old steam locomotives."

I looked at the chair. There was a seat, and attached to the right side of the seat was a steel bar that came up about two feet. The bar crossed over to the left. In the middle of the bar was a black box with a white button.

Jack pointed at the white button. "See this? All Brady had to do was let go of the button and an automatic brake would stop the chair."

He pushed at the button and it didn't move.

"I don't get it" he said, sounding puzzled, "I just —"

"Jack," said a voice from behind us. "Get that crap into the truck and move your skinny ass out of here. Your bus hits the road in two minutes."

"Okay. Sorry folks. I have to leave. If we come back next year, I'll give you a call."

I yelled to Jack as he headed toward the exit. "Did anyone check the dead man brake to be sure it worked?"

He stopped and turned. "Bear, that was one of my jobs. Every night, just before Brady climbed onto the chair, I tested the dead man."

I said, "And you checked it tonight?"

"Of course I did." Jack's right eye twitched. He turned and ran out the arena door.

Flo said, "If I understand what Jack just told us, Brady's chair should have slowed down as it approached the stage. Am I right?"

I was pretty sure that Jack's twitchy eye told me he had just lied. "Yup, but it didn't slow down."

Flo grabbed my arm. "Are you thinking what I'm thinking—it's possible that Brady's death wasn't an accident?"

"Yup."

She said, "But that puts us in a delicate situation, doesn't it?"

"Yup."

"Bear, I know you don't like that Detective Conner. And I'll never find anyone who can do my hair as good as Jack Spurlock's mother, but we can't just stand here and let the guy who murdered Brady Blackstone get away."

The last thing I wanted to do was tell Ice what Jack had just told us, but Flo was right. I said, "We may hate ourselves for this later, but we have to find Ice."

We checked out the lobby, then the bathrooms, finally, after about fifteen minutes of wandering around the empty arena, we found him sitting on a chair behind a dark bar sucking down a brew.

I said, "Ice, Jack Spurlock told me about a dead man break button on the chair. I tried the button and it was stuck. I know this sounds crazy, but we don't think Brady's death was an accident."

I think Ice must have been on his fifth or sixth beer because he belched a sour one and said, "Do tell."

That's when Flo got pissed. She pushed me aside and said, "Detective Conner. Bear just gave you some information that makes Brady Blackstone's death look very suspicious. Some might even call it first-degree murder."

Ice blinked a couple of times, like he hoped doing that would help open a path to his brain.

Flo grabbed his arm and the rest of his beer ended up on the floor. "Look, while you've been sitting here getting drunk, the whole damn tour, fifteen to twenty trucks and busses just left. Damn it, you let the murder leave the scene of the crime."

Ice sat up, clenched his right fist, and for a second I thought he was going to deck Flo.

I stepped between them, "Hey, don't get pissed off at her because you've had too many beers. Check the arena out, this place is as empty as a whorehouse on Christmas Eve."

Ice belched a couple more times and pulled out his cell phone. "Highway Patrol? This is Homicide Detective Conner with the Carson City police. A murder suspect by the name of Jack Spurlock just escaped with a convoy of Brady Blackstone trucks and busses heading north on Highway Fifty. I would appreciate if you would arrest Mr. Spurlock and remove the chair and cable rig he used to murder Brady Blackstone."

Ice sat back and smiled. "Does that make you happy?"

The bastard doubled over like he was going to barf so I took him into the men's room and watched him throw up. Then he tossed some water on his face. After he dried himself off, his cell phone buzzed. He listened, nodded and said, "Thanks."

Ice returned to the lobby and said, "Ms. Sonderlund, I just received a call from the Highway Patrol. They stopped the tour caravan five miles south of Reno. They have Jack Spurlock and the requested evidence in custody. Thank you. I owe you one."

Flo said, "You're welcome."

Ice got real close to me. "Bear, like I told you earlier, we need to work together more often. I'll call you soon."

I still wanted to punch the bastard out, but it was getting late and Flo was starting to look a little antsy. I said, "Ice, we worked with you tonight because we were afraid a man would get away with murder if I clammed up. I can't speak for Flo, but I'd shoot my right big toe off before I'd ever talk to you again."

Ice sobered up real fast and his hand moved toward his shoulder holster, like he was trying to figure out if he could shoot me, and then claim I was Jack Spurlock's partner.

I don't think Flo had a clue what his gun hand was doing, but she probably saved my ass when she grabbed my arm and dragged me toward the exit door. "Detective Conner, have the vendors left?"

"I think so, why?"

"I didn't get a Brady Blackstone concert tee-shirt."

I said, "I'll see what I can find tomorrow."

Ice staggered forward and walked out of the empty stadium.

We followed him, but just before Flo pushed the door open she stopped. "Hold on. After the accide . . . the crash, when we walked up on the stage, I saw a small piece of Brady's smashed guitar sticking out from under the curtain by that steel I-beam. That would be better than a tee-shirt."

"I don't know, Babe. That's evidence and Ice would just love to have me do something that stupid."

Flo gave me the stink eye. "Did you forget it's my birthday celebration?"

Shit!

"Let's go back and take a look."

It was real dark inside the stadium. I got to the stage, jumped up, found the curtain and got down on my knees. After a minute of feeling around I found a six-inch piece of splintered wood with a string attached to one end.

"Got it. Now let's get out of here before you think of anything else."

As we walked to my truck, Flo patted my butt. Damn, I thought. Hope there's more of that to come later. "Babe, I know things didn't work out the way I had them planned, but did you have an okay birthday?"

She smiled, and brushed away a tear. "I guess so, as long as I know that Brady and Elvis are together, and they're strumming that big guitar in the sky."

I opened Flo's door and the light on the roof of the cab turned on.

"Bear, look. You found me a real piece of Brady's guitar with one of his guitar strings attached. As soon as we get home I'll wrap the string around Brady's picture." A couple of tears trickled down her cheek. "This was the best birthday I've ever had."

Ohmigod, I thought. From now on she'll need to light two candles every morning!

"Hey, it's just a piece of a crunched guitar. Sorry you had to con those tickets out of Jack. I'm going to stop by Pinky's tomorrow and try to get him to give me more work."

Flo said, "You tell that little pipsqueak that if he doesn't, I'll call the newspaper and tell them what a cheap bastard he is. And another thing—"

"Babe, calm down. It's your birthday. My Pop told me people shouldn't say anything bad about other people on their birthday."

Flo looked at me. "Did he really tell you that?"

"Yup. On my fifteenth birthday. Right after I blew out the candles on the cake." My Pop was a great guy, but he never said anything like that to me. Flo liked stories about my Pop and me growing up and I knew she'd like to hear one, even if it was pure bullshit. "Now put your head back and start working on sexy thoughts. We'll be home in ten minutes."

THREE

Pinky Delmont—Carson City, Nevada

I arrived at my office promptly at nine and found Mabel, the gray-haired major-domo of my business affairs, sitting behind her desk, sobbing softly.

I approached and gently asked, "Mabel, what's wrong?"

Between snivels I picked up, "Have . . . . you read the . . . . morning paper?"

"I have, and frankly, that story concerning a proposed increase in the capital gains tax truly upset me. However, I wouldn't say that the discouraging commentary concerning the difficulty of decreasing my wealth moved me to tears."

Mabel pulled a handkerchief from her purse and dabbed at her red eyes. "I was talking about the tragic death of Brady Blackstone last night."

"You have my deepest sympathy, Mabel. Blackstone? Excuse me, is there some reason that I should be familiar with that name?"

"Are you telling me that you don't know who Brady Blackstone is—was?"

I considered lying to Mabel to end this ridiculous conversation and get us both to work. However, I was concerned that if she discovered my duplicity, this inane discussion might continue beyond lunch. "Not that I can recall, and I fear that no one in my inner circle of friends, or acquaintances goes by the name of Brady Blackstone. Who is, pardon me, who was the aforementioned Mr. Blackstone?"

"Just my all-time favorite country-rock singer. I have all his albums. Besides being a great performer, Brady played the guitar, and he was so good looking. But most of all, Brady was a true gentleman. He was the kind of man you'd trust with your daughter on a date."

"I am profoundly moved by the news of his death. Now, we both need to get to work. I assume you've printed out my—"

Mabel sobbed again and her ample frame shuddered. I decided that was her way of informing me that she hadn't quite worked her way through the grieving process.

"Pinky, I don't think you understand. Brady Blackstone is dead!"

"As I was about to say—"

"Damn it, I should know better than to expect empathy from you." Mabel took a swipe at her tears. "Give me a second to compose myself . . . " One final sniff, then she blew her nose and tossed her lace edged handkerchief into her handbag. "Bear just called. He'll be here any minute."

"Pardon me, Mabel, during your histrionics my concentration drifted. Did you just inform me that Bear Zabarte was on his way to my office?"

"Yes, and he didn't give me a reason."

I glanced at my watch. I had not had the opportunity to peruse my morning schedule, but I was positive that I had neither the time, nor the inclination, to discuss who was leading the American League East Division, or any of the other mindless drivel that my part-time investigator spent his conscious hours worrying about.

However, before I could find a quick escape route, Bear burst through the front door.

"Pinky, we need to talk."

"My good man, that was precisely what I had on my mind. Please step into my office."

On my desk lay the printout that detailed every hour of my day in half hour increments. As Bear and I sat down, I glanced at the morning portion and noted that I was free for the next hour.

I said, "I will have to leave in five minutes due to a trial. You of all people know that once a trial begins, the

18

judge takes a dim view if an attorney is tardy. If my memory serves me well, Bear, the charge I rescued you from was second degree murder."

"Yeah, and we both know that you got me off, and that I'm eternally grateful. But for some reason you don't want to remember what you told me after I fingered the real killer in the Page murder. Damn it, Pinky, you said that you'd give me five days a week of investigative work. I don't want to come off like a whiny bastard, but I can't get by on two or three days of work and you don't like me working part-time as a bartender."

"Of course not. I am a respected attorney. If the word ever leaked out that my investigator worked part-time dispensing alcohol, my professional reputation would be put to the test."

"But Pinky, I'm dying here. Flo drops more than a couple of hundred a month on her hair and nails."

"Bear, I understand your concern, but you need to remember that I warned you about living with that woman. My good man, contrary to popular belief, my life as an attorney is not all fun and games. I have a lot of personal expenses—a huge overhead—and multiple ex-wives. And at this moment, I don't have any investigative work for you. Bear, we both know that you are a proud man and I was concerned that you would be uncomfortable getting paid for doing nothing."

Bear stood and leaned over my desk. He was a huge man, and he was so close that I could smell the brand of toothpaste he had used that morning. At that moment, I thanked my lucky stars that we got along so well.

Bear growled, "Pinky, there's a rumor around town that you took down a million on the Page case. Stop acting like a cheap bastard. The interest you'd make on that would more than cover my full-time salary."

Actually, I had cleared closer to five million, a salient fact that will remain under Bear's radar. But how did he find out? A rumor around town? I could not afford to have gossip of that ilk floating around Carson City. In the very near future, I might set out a few mousetraps to see who takes the bait.

"Bear, my good man, I am up against a time constraint. Perhaps we can continue this fascinating discussion at a later time."

Bear clenched his ham-sized fists, but backed away and started toward the door. His retreat both surprised, and alarmed me. Something was out of place. Bear's quiet withdrawal did not follow the usual modus operandi of my ursine comrade.

He placed a paw on the doorknob, then he stopped and turned, making sure his immense frame blocked my only exit. "By the way, did you hear about the death of Brady Blackstone?"

"Yes. Mabel informed me a few moments ago. Why?"

"Mabel doesn't have all the inside skinny on what went down last night. I was there and saw the whole thing. Brady's death wasn't an accident. He was murdered. The police have a suspect in custody, and guess what? The guy that killed Brady asked me to find him a good attorney. Pinky, I think it's time we agree on a permanent deal. Starting today—no wait, yesterday—you'll pay me a salary of two hundred bucks a day, five days a week. Flo told me that would come up to fifty-two thousand a year, plus expenses. If you don't agree to my offer, Charlie Erickson—he's the new hotshot attorney in town who got that rapist acquitted—Charlie Erickson, not Pinky Delmont, will be the name of the lawyer I recommend to the poor bastard sitting in jail."

In my gut I had known there was more to this meeting than Bear complaining about Flo's excessive beauty parlor expenses. And I had suspected that the she-witch was the brains behind his demands, but this was neither the time nor the place to argue that point. "And I assume that the murder suspect has sufficient funds to cover my initial sixty thousand dollar retainer?"

"Yup. His mom will put it up. She owns the beauty parlor where Flo spends all my money."

I did a quick calculation. If I agreed to Bear's terms, I would be out fifty-two thousand. However, my initial retainer was sixty thousand. I would end up with an eight thousand dollar profit, an imperfect, but satisfactory arrangement from my point of view. "My good man, from this day forward, you will receive an annual salary of fifty-two thousand, plus expenses. I will instruct Mabel to pay you one thousand dollars each Friday, plus any expenses that you can back up with a valid receipt. Now, I assume that clears up any confusion concerning your recommendation to the suspect?"

"Yup, and now that I'm working again, Boss, you need to know that the cops have the chair that carried Brady to his death, but the rest of the murder evidence has gone to Portland."

"What? I don't understand."

Bear explained to me that after the ambulance removed Brady's corpse, the concert tour had moved on and the Arena was an empty shell. That situation was going to present a problem for me, but a major one for the prosecution. "What's my client's name?"

"Jack Spurlock."

I checked my schedule. "I have a spare hour at eleven. I'll roll by the jail and talk with Mr. Spurlock. You check with the police and see what you can find out concerning evidence. We'll meet at noon at Ling's. With your newfound riches, you can buy me lunch while we compare notes. And stop calling me Boss."

"Right! Okay, Boss, lunch at Ling's."

The instant the door to my office closed, I grabbed my phone and called the Carson City jail.

"Henry?"

"Hi, Pinky. What can I do for you?"

"Henry, I understand that you have a man in custody by the name of Jack Spurlock. He is being held for the murder of Brady Blackstone. I called you this morning to clear up any possible confusion concerning Mr. Spurlock's legal representation. The man in custody for the Blackstone murder is my client. If anyone, including that young whippersnapper, Charles Erickson, starts to sniff around, you will not, under any circumstances, allow him access to my client. I'll stop by at eleven to talk with Mr. Spurlock. Do you have any questions?"

"Nope. The Blackstone murder suspect is your client, and don't let Erickson near him. Pinky, on another subject, I'm starting to run a little low. Do you recall the name of my favorite brand?"

"Henry, your last allusion cuts me to the quick. I would never forget the desires of someone so close to my heart. A case of Scotland's finest will be delivered to your home within the hour."

FOUR

Bear—Carson City, Nevada

Life couldn't get much better than this. Now I had enough scratch to let Alice Spurlock fiddle with Flo's hair every week, but even better, I had a new murder to investigate.

I jumped in my truck and headed back to my apartment.

When I pulled into the driveway, I noticed an unmarked cop car parked at the curb. That didn't make any sense because—

"Bear," Flo yelled at me from the pool area. "Detective Conner is out here on the deck. He was in the neighborhood and stopped by."

Shit! Except for last night, I hadn't seen, or talked to Ice Conner since he arrested me on that trumped-up murder charge a couple of years ago.

The whole town knew that Jerry Butler's head got stuck between my fist and a brick wall. And everybody knew that Jerry had hit me first. So anyone with a brain bigger than a tomato seed would understand that a human as dumb as Jerry wasn't going to live long enough to make kids.

I opened the gate to the pool area. Flo was lying on a lounge chair and she was wearing a new bathing suit with so much skin showing that a charging bull would stop to take a closer look.

Ice sat next to her, and he wasn't staring at Flo's manicured toes.

I shouldered my way between them and said, "What do you want, Ice?"

"Bear, I stopped by to get a statement from Flo. Now that you've arrived, I can take your statement too."

"Ice, you aren't holding a note pad or nothing to write with. What are you going to do, remember everything Flo tells you?"

He looked surprised to see that his hands were empty. "You're right. Actually, we were just shooting the breeze when you arrived." Ice reached into his jacket pocket and pulled out a notebook and a fancy looking pen. "Now, Flo, let's take it from the top."

I reached down, grabbed the pad and pen, and threw them into the pool. "Whoops, how stupid of me."

"Hey, I could arrest you for obstruction of justice."

"You and what army?"

Flo jumped up and said, "Come on you two, stop joking around. I'm going to get me a cup of coffee. Anyone else want some?"

Ice carried a piece in a shoulder holster, under his jacket, on his left side. If he was going to make a move, it would be with his right hand. I locked my gaze onto that hand and said, "Thanks, Flo, a cup of coffee sounds great."

Ice said, "I appreciate your offer of hospitality."

"Good. Now both of you sit down and talk about the good old days. I'll be back in a couple of minutes."

Me and Ice glared at each other.

Flo disappeared around the corner.

I tightened my left hand into a fist. I was damn sure I could clip his jaw before he could pull out his piece. "Ice, we both know your story about taking a statement from Flo was pure bull-shit. You're here to sniff around my woman. Now clear out before I kick your ass all the way to the Nugget Casino."

The tips of Ice's fingers toyed with the lapel of his jacket, a few inches from cold, blue steel. "Bear, I have every legal reason to take a formal statement from Flo and you. In fact, for the destruction of my official police note pad, I should place you under arrest. And that pen you threw in the water was a birthday present from my mother."

"Ice, if your hand moves any closer to that holster I'll have to deck you."

24

"Bear, if you touch any part of me, I'll have to blow you away."

"Sounds to me like you've used that line before."

His voice shook a little. "Don't make me kill you."

"Is this how you iced those other poor bastards? You tricked them into making the first move and then you shot them?"

I knew that accusing a cop like him was dumb, and hitting him was even dumber—worth at least a couple of years in the slam, but we were both way past backing down. In a couple of seconds all hell was going to break loose and I was glad the pool area was empty, so no innocent sunbathers would catch a stray bullet. I shifted my weight to the balls of my feet and came within an ant's eyelash of slugging the slimy bastard when Flo waltzed around the corner and stopped me and Ice from doing something really stupid.

"Here's the coffee, and I brought some of my favorite butter cookies from that wonderful Danish bakery downtown."

Ice slowly lowered his right hand from under his jacket. He stared hard at me, but talked real nice to Flo. "You really didn't have to go to all that trouble."

Once the chance of crushing his jaw had passed, I started to relax and opened my fist. "Yeah, Babe, the cookies look real good."

Flo smiled, "It's the neighborly thing to do, what with you two being old friends."

Flo poured the coffee and handed Ice and me a cookie. Then she said, "Now where were we?"

Ice took a bite of his cookie and crumbs dribbled all over his pants. "Flo, as you know, the night of the concert we arrested Jack Spurlock for the murder of Brady Blackstone because it turned out that he was the person who was suppose to check the chair that carried Brady to his death. Yesterday, we figured out how the dead man button was rigged so it failed."

I said, "How come the button didn't work?" As I chewed a cookie, I decided that Flo's coffee and cookie thing was her way to get me to be friendly to Ice Conner. As I said earlier, if Flo wants something, give it to her or get out of her way. And who knows, I might pick up some important information from this dumb-shit cop.

He laughed. "Super glue! All Spurlock had to do was to place a couple of drops of super glue on the button, hold it down for a few seconds, and that baby was stuck there for all eternity, or until my guys at the lab freed it."

While I crunched another cookie, I came up with a sure-fire way to find out more of what the cops had. "You know, I heard somewhere about a murderer needing three things, but I don't remember what they are. I'm new in this murder investigation game. Can you help me out here?"

Ice set his cookie down, took a noisy slurp of coffee, and stared at me long and hard, like he wasn't sure if I was really asking for help, or just putting him on. "Bear, I'm going to be frank with you. If you're going to make it in the modern world as a homicide investigator, you'll need to understand that a murder is like a triangle with three identical legs—the means, the opportunity, and the motive. If you can't grasp that simple concept, you'd be better off working behind a bar."

Now I knew I had the dumb-shit. "Thanks for the advice. Let me see if I understand what you just told me. We know that Jack had the opportunity. He was the man in charge of the chair and he tested the dead man brake every night before Brady used it. You just told us that he had the means—two drops of super glue and a couple of seconds. The part I still don't understand is do all murders need all three parts of that triangle?"

Ice stopped chewing his cookie. "I don't get what you mean."

"That motive part." I stood up and towered over him. "What was Spurlock's motive, you dumb-shit?"

"Who are you calling a dumb-shit?" He jumped up and we sort of bumped into each other. Ice's big gut hit my solid abs and he bounced backward a little. No harm, no foul, but the crazy part was that the heels of his shoes were hanging over the edge of the pool. Ice Conner, Carson City's nastiest homicide detective, lost his balance and fell backwards into the blue water.

Flo dropped her cookie and screamed.

As he dog-paddled toward the pool ladder, Ice looked a lot more like a wet cat than a tough cop.

I said, "Don't worry, Flo, I'll make sure the bastard doesn't drown. I think he jumped in to pick up his favorite pen before he went back to his office."

FIVE

Pinky—Carson City, Nevada

Six years ago, the discerning gentlemen of Carson City were blessed when Bruno Battista, a world-class men's hair stylist, moved his salon into town thus providing the astute males who lived and worked in the capitol of Nevada the opportunity to purchase a decent haircut.

Every Tuesday, at 10:00 am sharp, I had a standing appointment with Bruno—to maintain my perfectly coiffed hair—a weekly visit to guarantee that I never seemed in need of a haircut.

Bruno's salon was discretely located—sans crass signage—behind an unmarked brown door, along the regular walking route between my office and the County Courthouse.

I entered the salon at 9:58 am, and before I could sit down, Bruno said, "Pinky, I heard on the grapevine that you are the attorney of record for that scoundrel who murdered my favorite performer, Brady Blackstone."

Could it be possible that I was the only person on this earth that didn't know, and revere, Carson City's latest resident of the local morgue?

I said, "The grapevine, as you so aptly put it, was correct. Now will you be so kind as to help me out with some information? What attributes of performing did Mr. Blackstone display that made him so desirable to a man with your elevated love of the arts?"

Bruno said, "Please sit down and I'll answer your question while I trim your hair."

With a razor in his hand, Bruno was not a man to be trifled with, so I did as instructed.

He draped a mauve silk wrap over my shoulders, and after a few tiny slashes with the razor near my right ear, he said, "Brady was more than a common performer. He was a generous human being. In my opinion, the man was a saint. And why do I feel that way? At the conclusion of each Blackstone concert, he would select a deserving child from the audience and present the youngster with a brand new, personally signed, Brady Blackstone guitar."

For a moment, I considered informing Bruno that the Brady Blackstone guitar was at the very least a tax write-off, if not a freebie, given to Blackstone by the manufacture of the musical instrument. However, I kept my opinion to myself because Bruno wielded a very sharp instrument in his hand.

Bruno said, "Now that I have answered your question, let me tell you why I'm not pleased that you are defending the man accused of Brady's murder. I'm fully aware of your perfect record concerning the killers in this town. I fear that one way or another, you'll come up with some tricky way to get your client acquitted."

As tiny slices of my hair fell to the silk, I realized that I now knew two mature adults—people who had generally exhibited good common sense—who had been bamboozled by a simple crooner of western tunes. It was possible that Brady Blackstone was a nice man, perhaps a truly good human being. However, based on my experience, the underlying motives of any performer who generated sixty to a hundred million a year in show business revenues would never be mistaken for those of Mother Teresa.

"Bruno, I'm sure that Mr. Blackstone was an outstanding example of American generosity. All I ask is that you recall that the U. S. Constitution guarantees that each citizen is innocent until proven guilty in a court of law. As Mr. Spurlock's attorney, my job is to make sure that his constitutional rights are upheld and protected."

The razor whistled past my left ear as Bruno said, "I understand all that gobbledygook. Just make sure the bastard gets what he deserves for murdering an authentic American hero."

During the final few minutes of Bruno's trimming, based on his and Mabel's premature canonization of Brady Blackstone, I quietly pondered the difficulty of finding a jury of unbiased peers in Carson City, or anywhere in the country for that matter. However, I was jumping ahead of the game. Based on the financial limitations imposed by my sixty thousand dollar initial retainer, selecting a dispassionate jury would not be a concern. For a payment of that size the best I could anticipate for Alice Spurlock's son would be to negotiate some sort of a plea bargain.

At eleven sharp, with a perfectly trimmed crown, I met Henry-the-guard outside the interview room that contained my newest client.

I said, "Has Mr. Spurlock been briefed concerning my visit?"

"The minute I hung up the phone I pulled him out of his cell, stuck him in here, and told him you'd see him at eleven."

"Thank you, Henry."

I opened the door. "Jack Spurlock, my name is J. Pincus Delmont. According to Bear, between your savings, and your mother's business establishment, my initial retainer is covered. Congratulations my boy, you are now represented by the number one defense attorney in northern Nevada!"

Jack looked to be in his early thirties. His clothing was less than remarkable, but what did I expect from a modern day gypsy who made his living working for a traveling troubadour. Jack's only unusual feature was that his face had taken on the blue-white pastiness of new fallen snow. I had seen the identical pallor during the initial visit with many of my clients. Homo sapiens are only capable of coping with so much, and finding oneself in custody for the murder of another human generally pushes the boundary of sanity.

I decided to calm the man by bringing him back to familiar territory. "Jack, tell me a little about your position with the Blackstone concert tour."

A touch of peach returned to his cheeks. "I'm the lead man with the backstage crew."

"Please excuse my ignorance, I am but a simple attorney. What does the lead man of the backstage crew do?"

Jack shrugged. "I am responsible for everything and anything that happens behind the scenes. Like when Brady needs to change guitars, I'd assign the job to one of the backstage crew. From that point, every night, that crewman has to be at the right spot, at the right time, to make the exchange."

My expression must have slipped into a befuddled look because Jack continued, "Trust me, that's not as easy as it sounds. When Brady and the band are going full force, the stage can turn into a battle zone."

"I see." But I did not see. Three or four times each year I attended concerts presented by the San Francisco Philharmonic Orchestra, and frankly I couldn't comprehend how a few musicians wandering about a stage could become a combat area.

"Could you further explain what you mean by battle zone?"

By now, the color of life in Jack's face had returned. "Sure. Have you ever been to a Brady Blackstone concert?"

"No."

"Any rock, or country-western concert?"

"No."

"Wow! Well, the Brady Blackstone concert would look like this. Brady, and his band, six guys, would run all over the stage while they sang a song. At the end of a song, Brady, or the lead guitarist, or both, might need a different guitar for the next number. While the audience was applauding, a stagehand would run out, hand the talent a new instrument and get his ass off the stage before he'd get run over."

I could see that this was not at all like the classical concerts I had attended.

31

I said, "Jack, at this juncture, we need to discuss the facts of your situation. As your attorney, I am bound by law and the ethics of my profession to provide you with the best possible defense. That means from this moment on, I am the only person on the face of the earth you can trust, or talk with concerning the death of Brady Blackstone. That includes a spouse, girlfriend, mother, brother, or any other lawyer. Do I make myself clear?"

"I can't even talk to my mother?"

"Concerning this case, that's correct! We both know she would never do anything that would hurt you, but how many murder cases has your mother tried in a court of law?"

Jack's eyes started to collect water. This was the stage I had been waiting for. I had seen grown men cry—women scream—total collapse—angry frustration, but this was generally the point when most clients opened up and started to tell the truth.

"Mr. Delmont—"

"Jack, call me Pinky."

"Pinky, I didn't kill Brady. I know things look bad, but I'm innocent."

"Would you care to explain to me why the police think you were responsible for his death?"

He sat up and wiped his eyes. "I'll try. Every night, I would take Brady out to a spot about a hundred feet from the stage. He'd climb on the chair that was attached to an overhead cable. It's sort of like a ski lift."

I said, "I'm familiar how a ski lift works."

Jack's expression informed me that he was gratified that I was listening intently.

"A couple of minutes before Brady would make his dramatic entrance, all the lights in the arena would go off. Then his band would start to play. The stage lights would go up. A spotlight would hit Brady, sitting on his chair, in the middle of the dark auditorium. Brady would wave, that was the cue to me to start the chair moving. Brady would belt out his opening number as the chair carried him toward the stage. Once he reached the stage, the chair would slow down and Brady would step off. The chair would turn to the right and one of the stage crew would grab it and take it backstage. But for some reason, on the night he died, the chair didn't slow down as it approached the stage. Brady and the chair flew across the stage, and his head crashed into the steel I-beam that supports the giant TV screens."

I said, "Was the chair equipped with some sort of fail-safe system?"

"Yes. The chair had a dead man's brake. All Brady had to do was let go of the button and the chair would come to a stop."

"And did anyone test the dead man's brake the night of the accident?"

I watched Jack's lips tighten ever so slightly.

"That was my job and I tested the brake the night of the accident."

He was lying, and not doing a very good job. If we did go to trial, one of Willow's rookie prosecutors would slice him open like a Thanksgiving turkey.

"Go on, my boy."

"Brady and I were friends. I was with him through the lean years. You know, the one-night stands. Things started to pick up when he signed onto the county fair circuit. Five years ago, Brady crossed over from country to pop-rock and now he sells more concert tickets than anyone else in America, and that includes Madonna, Barbara Streisand, and the Rolling Stones."

While I pondered that fact, the door opened and Henry stuck his head in. "Pinky, I need to talk to you."

I jumped up and charged to the door. I hissed, "Henry, you know better than to interrupt a meeting with my client. My interrogation techniques are carefully—"

"Pinky?" Bear growled from the other side of the door.

I looked into the hall. "Bear, what I told Henry stands for you, too. No one is allowed to—"

Bear said, "I know all that crap, but this was something so important you have to hear it now."

33

I sighed. How could I expect more than a modicum of intelligence out of two men that were only a step away from the primordial ooze? "All right, the damage is done. What was so important?"

"The DA doesn't have a motive."

This was good news. "And how do you know that?"

"Ice told me."

Ice Conner was giving Bear classified police information? My God, the next thing he would tell me was that the sun would not set in the west tomorrow evening.

"Bear, I didn't think you and Ice could stand being in the same room for more than thirty seconds, and now you tell me that he's passing on confidential information to you?"

He shrugged. "Yup. I guess that we just hit it off today. But they do know that Jack was supposed to test the dead man every night before Brady used the chair."

I said, "Bear, I am aware of that fact. However, in your maladroit way, you are correct that a murderer requires a motive or—"

My cell phone rang. Damn, my well-planned morning was turning into a three-ring circus.

"Pinky?"

"Willow my love. Just a moment." I covered the mouthpiece. "Bear, Henry, give me a little privacy."

The two backed away. I waited until they were both out of earshot. "Now, beyond expressing my undying love, what can I do for you?"

"Can the bull-shit. By any chance, is Bear with you?"

I glanced down the hall and noticed that he towered a good two feet over the top of Henry's head. "No, I'm afraid not. Why?"

"Detective Conner is running around the county trying to convince a judge that he has probable cause for an obstruction of justice arrest warrant. It seems that your large friend pushed Ice into a swimming pool while he was attempting to interview Flo concerning the Blackstone murder."

34

"Willow, those two have been at each others throats since Ice arrested Bear on that trumped up murder charge."

"That was not a trumped up murder charge. Bear killed a man with his bare hands. He was just lucky enough to hire you for his attorney."

"Come, come, my dear, we both know that my Bear is a peace loving soul."

"Pinky, the only thing I know is that Bear killed a man named Jerry Barber a few years ago."

"And do I need to remind you that he was acquitted of all charges?"

"One of those losses I'd like to forget. Had I stuck to my guns and held out for that right-wing pit boss during jury selection, Bear would be . . . hold on, where are you this very minute?"

"At the county jail talking with a new client."

"Oh my God," I detected a positive change in Willow's voice. "Don't tell me that your new client is Jack Spurlock?"

The joviality of her tone concerned me, but I forged ahead. "My dear, are you aware that your case against Mr. Spurlock contains a gaping hole large enough to drive a school bus through? My client, Jack Spurlock, lacks a motive for murder. In fact he was a long time friend and working companion of the deceased. In my humble opinion, you should save the tax payers of this county a large amount of money and reclassify the death of Brady Blackstone as an unavoidable industrial accident."

"You'd better find yourself a chair because I'm about to pass on a bit of bad news. I just finished going over a report from Ice Conner. It seems that your client and a lady named Lucinda have been carrying on a long-term love affair. Now I realize that in this crazy, immoral world we live in, an illicit love affair isn't all that important. But your client's girl friend wears a gold band on the ring finger of her left hand, and her last name just happens to be Blackstone!"

Since our marriage ended, there had been very few times when Willow surprised me, but her revelation hit me like an unanticipated punch to the stomach. It took all my years of courtroom stoicism to cover my reaction. I was at a loss for words when my cell chirped with a second call. Thank God for technology. "Excuse me, my dear. I have to answer another call. The moment I see Bear, I will inform him that you are looking for him."

I tapped the call button and a female voice said, "Am I speaking with Mr. Delmont?"

"Yes, this is Pinky. What can I do for you?"

"My name is Lucinda Blackstone. We need to talk. No, more than talk. The truth is that I have to decide if you are the right man to defend my man in this criminal matter."

At times the effrontery of some people made me wonder about the future of the human race. "Mrs. Blackstone! You are speaking with the most successful attorney in northern Nevada and the best hope you have for the eventual release of, as you choose to call him, your man."

"Perhaps I jumped to an early conclusion. Can we move on?"

"Mrs. Blackstone, I know I can. Now, please accept my condolences concerning your late husband."

"Save the phony sobs for the press. Mr. Delmont, meet me at my hotel suite this afternoon or risk losing an extremely large retainer."

Click. The phone went dead. Over the years I had talked with hundreds, if not thousands of potential clients, and my snap judgment concerning Lucinda Blackstone was that she was a woman who generally got her way. I have learned over time that an excessively large bank account tends to do that to a person.

Before I had time to think, Bear said, "Bad news, Boss?"

My ursine friend's question snapped me out of my mental apathy. "Bear, Willow tells me that Ice is

36

shopping around town for an arrest warrant concerning an encounter you two had around a pool."

"Boss, there's more to—"

"And I do not have time to listen to you prattle on." I pulled my keys from my pocket. Selected one and handed it to Bear. "This key fits the front door of my Condo next to the lake two blocks west of Harrah's. The address is on the key. Go there immediately and do not go to your apartment. Ice may have the building staked out."

A big grin spread across Bear's basketball-sized face, "Gee, that's really nice of you."

"Nice has nothing to do with it. According to our agreement I must pay you a thousand dollars a week and I will be dammed if I am going to continue that practice while you rot in a jail cell. Now get out of here and wait for my phone call."

"Got'cha, boss."

After Bear left, I said, "Henry, I need to talk with Spurlock for a few more minutes. After I am done, you will return him to his cell, and if anyone asks, you have not seen Bear."

"Right."

I turned and for a moment considered Jack Spurlock through the one-way glass that looked into the room where he sat. I tried to determine what the wife of a multi-millionaire could possibly see in him. Granted, a few nights in jail would drain the vital juices from most, but the man seated on the other side of the window did not come across as the secret lover type. He was more along the line of the solid, next-door neighbor acquaintance that could be counted on to help you restart the water heater pilot light after a heavy windstorm blew it out.

Returning to the room, I was determined to get to the bottom of Jack and Lucinda's illicit relationship. "Jack, that phone call was from Lucinda Blackstone. I'm meeting with her—"

"Lucy? How is she?"

"She sounded concerned. Now as I stated, I'm meeting with her in an hour. We were cut off before she told me the name of her hotel."

"She's staying at the Nugget in Sparks. On the top floor in the penthouse."

"Jack, this would be a perfect opportunity for you to give me your side of the long term, clandestine relationship you carried on with Brady Blackstone's wife behind his back."

Jack slumped, as if he had just realized the magnitude of getting caught going to bed with his best friend's wife. "The way you put it makes our relationship sound so dirty."

I glanced at my watch. Considering the forty-five minute drive, my appointment with The Widow Blackstone was approaching rapidly. "Excuse me for a moment."

I turned my back, called Mabel, and whispered, "Google the name Lucinda Blackstone and call me back with the details."

I returned my attention to my client. "Trust me, Jack, the shame over an illicit love affair is the least of your problems. It is time to summon Henry. He will return you to your cell, but don't think you are off the hook. I will return tomorrow morning and you must be ready to give me your side of the Lucinda Blackstone affair."

After Henry removed my client from the room, my cell phone rang. Mabel said, "Okay, according to Google, Lucinda Blackstone is thirty-three. She's been married to Brady Blackstone for fifteen years. No children. On a hunch, I checked out Forbes richest people in the world and Brady Blackstone was ranked in the final grouping."

"What does that mean in real dollars?"

"More than five hundred million, but short of a billion."

"Mabel, I am leaving the jail and driving to Sparks. In case Willow calls, you will inform her that for some unknown technical reason you have not been able to contact me by cell phone."

A smile tugged at the corners of my lips. The prospect of spending an hour or two with a widow that wealthy caused the tips of my fingers to tingle.

SIX

Bear—Carson City

Jesus, working full-time for Pinky was fun because everything changed so damn fast. One minute I was standing next to him at the Carson City jail, and now I'm waiting for Flo at a back table in the Old Globe Bar, my old stomping grounds.

I knew I had to lay low for a while and Pinky's joint at Tahoe was a pretty good place to hide.

The phone rang and I grabbed it thinking it might be Pinky.

"Pinky?"

"Bear, this is Flo. Pinky got a hold of me and told me to call you, like that little shrimp can tell me what I can and cannot do. Where in the hell are you? This morning at breakfast you told me that this afternoon we'd go shopping in Reno."

"Babe, there's been a little change in my plans. I need you to throw some clothes in a bag for both of us and meet me at the Old Globe. We're heading to Lake Tahoe."

"Why?"

"It's a long story."

"I'm going to need more than . . . wait, did you say Lake Tahoe?"

"Yes. Pinky has loaned us his condo for awhile."

"Something's wrong here. Why would Pinky do that?"

"Maybe it's about Ice getting mad at me because he fell into the pool."

"See, I told you that you can't push a policeman into a pool and get away with it. I suppose the condo is the same place we saw last year with the big hole burned in the living room carpet?"

"Nope. This joint's on the California side at the south end of the lake. Babe, Pinky told me that there's a really nice beach just outside the door where you can lay in the sun."

"Tell me the truth. Why are we going to Tahoe?"

"Babe, you'll think we died and went to heaven."

"I heard you, but I trust Pinky as far as I can throw him. What was it you wanted me to do?"

"Pack us both some clothes. Don't worry about food or booze. I'm sure Pinky's place is stocked. Ask Shelia, that broad who lives next door to us, to give you a ride to the County Courthouse, but don't tell her you're going to Tahoe."

"I can do that, but why all the cloak and dagger crap? Is Ice more than just pissed at you?"

"Yup. He wants to throw my ass in jail."

"That's not nice of him. His fall into the pool was an accident, and I'll testify to that in court."

"Thanks, Babe. Now, like I said, clam up with Shelia on Pinky's condo. I know the joint is on the California side of the border, but if Ice ever found out where I was hiding, he'd hit me on the head, and drag me back across the border. Now, my truck's in the courthouse parking lot. I'm at the Old Globe and will wait for you here. Can you handle all that?"

"Hey, buster, do I have to remind you that I'm the one who did all the heavy work on our first murder case outside of Eureka, Nevada."

"Right."

"And this is a lot more exciting then spending my afternoon in that stupid outlet mall in Reno."

SEVEN

Pinky—Carson City

After completing a couple of brief courtroom obligations, I drove to Reno and headed east on Highway 80. Eight minutes later I pulled off the freeway at the Nugget Hotel. The town of Sparks was originally a distinct entity separated from Reno, but they have both grown toward each other to such a degree that today the border between them is purely political. In fact, they are often referred to as Reno-Sparks.

Like the town of Sparks, The Nugget Hotel/Casino started small, but today it's a high-rise destination resort boasting some of the most desirable suites in northern Nevada. I was not the least bit surprised to find that Lucinda Blackstone was staying in the penthouse suite at the Nugget.

I knocked, and before I could pull my hand away, the door opened and I stared directly into the green eyes of a very attractive woman.

She looked younger than her thirty-three years. Her gorgeous face was topped with straight, shiny, auburn hair that hung down to her shoulders.

"Mr. Delmont, I presume."

I nodded. "Mrs. Blackstone, please call me Pinky. May I come in?"

"Pinky? My Jack's life is in the hands of an attorney who calls himself Pinky?"

"Mrs. Blackstone, my full name is J. Pincus Delmont. I prefer you address me as Pinky, but if you find that unacceptable, then call me what you must. Now, may I enter your room?"

"Pardon me. Please come in and sit down. It's just that your name seems a touch silly for a lawyer."

"I understand." I walked into the penthouse. I had been in one of the lesser suites a few floors below a month ago, and had been impressed with the accommodations. However, the penthouse was obviously the top of the line in Sparks. An expansive sitting area opened to a wall of plate glass with a view of Reno, and beyond to the snow capped peaks of the Sierra Nevada Range.

"Care for a drink?"

"No, thank you."

"How about some coffee, then?"

"Black, please."

"No cream or sugar? You're a real tough guy. I like that in a man."

She handed me a cup. The coffee smelled wonderful. I took a sip. It was so hot I nearly burned my tongue, just the way I liked it. "Mrs. Blackstone—"

"Call me Lucinda."

With no effort on my part I had progressed from the formal Mrs. Blackstone to Lucinda, but I had not yet reached the intimacy of Lucy. Could it be that level of casualness was reserved for lovers? "Lucinda, during our phone conversation you mentioned a large retainer."

She returned to the bar and poured herself a glass, sans ice, of what looked like vodka. "I thought that would catch your attention. Pinky, I want you to represent Jack."

"My good woman, I am enjoying your hospitality, but if that's all you wanted to tell me, you have just wasted two hours of my valuable time. I am already the attorney of record for Jack Spurlock, and I represent him concerning the first-degree charge of murdering your husband."

"But Jack's paying the tab, right?"

"I am not at liberty to discuss—"

"Pinky, I don't want to know where the money is coming from. What I'm trying to say," she turned and stared out the glass wall toward the west, "I'm ready, willing, and able to supplement Jack's original retainer—assuming you find the need for additional funds—up to a million dollars."

Sitting atop one of northern Nevada's finest hotels, I suddenly felt like an old Nevada prospector who had just hit the mother lode in the middle of the desert. I calmly took another sip from my cup.

"Could you use more coffee?" Lucinda asked.

"No, thanks. Now concerning my retainer. Before you make me an open ended offer, you need to understand how much money could be involved to properly defend Jack against the charge of first-degree murder."

Lucinda turned and looked me in the eye. "And that's exactly what I want you to do."

I smiled. "Let me walk you through a few realities. First, the Carson City Police Department has in their full-time employee seven police detectives whose sole responsibility is to investigate capital crimes. I have but a single man, a capable investigator, but he is still but one against seven.

"The District Attorney's office consists of twelve attorneys whose singular duty is to send criminals to jail, prison, or in Jack's case, to their death by lethal injection. On the other hand, I am a solitary humble servant of the law. On top of that, I have other clients, some destitute, and for those wretched souls, I graciously hold out the hand of charity through my extensive pro-bono activities.

"As you can see, the odds against Jack are extremely high—not insurmountable, but very, very high. The limited retainer I have received so far will restrict my ability to successfully carry on a fight against those odds."

She frowned. "So what can you accomplish with Jack's existing retainer?"

"The best I could hope for would be an agreement with the District Attorney for a manslaughter plea."

"You've got to be kidding me!"

"Lucinda, when it comes to one of my clients, I never kid. Jack Spurlock had the opportunity, and the means to murder your husband. All that was missing was a motive.

This morning the DA informed me about your little infidelity and bingo, now Jack has a motive."

"Explain what you mean by, 'Jack had the opportunity.'"

"Jack Spurlock was at the concert the night of Brady's death."

"He and twenty-five thousand other people!"

I considered her statement. She was correct. Everyone in the arena had the opportunity. "Yes, but not everyone had the means. Jack was the singular person in charge of testing the dead man brake on Brady's chair every night."

"Wrong again, Pinky. We've been on the road for most of the year and completed at least a hundred and fifty shows. During that time, a lot of the back stage crew made sure Brady didn't fall off his chair. Jack was the man ninety percent of the time, but not the only one."

I considered this revelation. "How many crew members are you talking about?"

"Could be as many as fifty."

I said, "And you think all of them had a motive to murder Brady?"

"No, but Brady was a miserable bastard to work with, so you've got a lot of possibilities."

That was curious. According to Jack, his boss was a great man. But I guess a wife see her husband differently than the rest of the world. God knows that many of my ex-wives did. "Lucinda, I am going to say something that I fear could upset you."

"As the wife of a musical icon, nothing you can say will shock, or upset me. Every month at least one of the tabloids informs me that I'm a lesbian, or Brady's gay, or he's the father of a starlet's pending baby. Go ahead, I've heard it all."

"Your lover has a rope around his neck, and both feet are balanced on a wet bar of soap. His situation is grim. Jack's only ticket out of jail will be to find someone else who would gain from Brady's death."

She said, "I understand. You need a motive. Someone besides Jack who wanted my husband dead."

"Right, and finding that someone could be an expensive proposition."

She said, "How expensive?"

During the drive from Carson City to Sparks, I had anticipated Lucinda's question. "As I said, I have one full time investigator. I could redirect all his time to this case."

"How much will that cost me?"

"At least one hundred thousand."

"That's nowhere near as bad as I thought it would be."

"Please don't jump to an early conclusion. In addition, I would have to, as much as I could, concentrate all my personal efforts on clearing Jack's name."

"And now we're talking . . .?"

"Four hundred thousand."

"Pinky, are you telling me that it's only going to cost me a half million to get Jack out of jail?"

"No! I said that was the minimum cost to you for me to go beyond a plea agreement. The total cost to you could go higher—much higher— to find that someone who wanted your husband dead, and there are no guarantees of success."

Lucinda stood and returned to the plate glass wall. She stared out at Reno for half a minute before she spoke. "If we were playing poker, you just called me, so I've got to see your call or drop out of the game. Before I contacted your office, I did some checking. As you have so boldly stated, you are the best attorney in northern Nevada. And, according to my sources, the best you can hope to do for Jack would be a manslaughter plea agreement, and most of my expert's thought that would be a stretch.

"That brings me to your offer to look for another suspect, someone who had a motive to kill my husband. Pinky, you may be the top mouthpiece in northern Nevada, but you are not the best in the US. I am a very rich widow—I can afford the best, but I want Jack out of jail now, so I'll settle for you because my sources tell me that it would take them at least a year to duplicate the intricate web you have constructed in and around the Carson City justice system."

My fragile pride was momentarily tested to the breaking point. I jumped up to protest.

She said, "Relax, Pinky. As far as I am concerned, I don't want to know the details of how you get Jack out of jail. Brady's massive success has left me with enough money to feed a lake full of legal piranhas like you, so before you leave here today, I will write you a check for $500,000."

I sat down and suppressed a smile. It looked as if spending a few hours in Sparks would turn out to be financially rewarding after all.

Lucinda said, "Now that we have the mundane business aspects taken care of, if someone else had wanted to murder Brady, the bastard would have to be a member of the tour. No one else would have the opportunity, on a day-by-day basis, to sabotage the chair. Trust me, there are lots of band and crewmembers that my husband had screwed over. That was one of Brady's best attributes."

"A list of names would help trim the odds."

"That'll be easy."

She sat down and scribbled six names on a note pad. Now I had one final hurdle to clear. "Lucinda, before you sign that check, we have to clear up one last detail. You need to understand that as an officer of the court, if and when I uncover the guilty party, I will encourage that person, or persons to turn themselves over to the police."

She frowned, and for the first time since we met, a bemused expression crossed Lucinda's blue eyes. "I'm sorry, did I miss something?"

"My dear, you really don't see the obvious do you? There is one name missing on this list. At this juncture, if I were the police, you would be my prime suspect."

Lucinda slowly shook her head. "I guess you're right, but I'm not worried. Counselor, you've walked into the middle of The Brady and Lucinda movie and it will take you some time to understand what happened at the beginning—what made our relationship work, and eventually fail. But I can assure you that I didn't kill my husband." She sat back and stared at the ceiling. "At one time, our marriage was beautiful. We were childhood sweethearts, married young, and then, it's hard to put into words, the magic vanished. On the tour it was common knowledge that Brady and I weren't getting along—"

"My dear, that knowledge was not all that common, or you would be sitting in a jail cell next to your boyfriend. I'm curious, did the police ever interview you?"

"Why yes. A Detective named Conner stopped by the day after Brady died to tell me that Jack had been arrested for my husband's murder."

"A brief word of warning concerning Detective Conner. Watch out for him. Most of his arrests end up with a dead suspect. He always has a good story about how they tried to escape, or how he had to defend himself, but for whatever reason, the suspect ends up on a slab in the morgue."

She nodded, as if my thinly veiled accusation confirmed her previous perception of the man. She pulled out a checkbook. "If you are going to be offering me advice, I had better pay you. That was five hundred thousand, correct?"

"Yes, I believe that was the sum that we had agreed upon."

She wrote out a check and waved it in the air. "Pinky, are you a gambling man?"

"Occasionally, but I generally limit my monetary risks to a few rolls of the dice at a local casino in Carson City. Why?"

"I'll make you an offer. You get Jack released from jail inside of two weeks and I'll double your five hundred thousand retainer to a cool million."

I had to admit that her offer received my full attention. "And what happens if I fail?"

"It's a simple double or nothing bet."

"I fear that my expenses, and common sense, will not allow me to assume that wager. However, I am willing to make you a counter offer. Tear up your check, and make me a new one for one hundred thousand dollars. That money is not refundable. Once I come up with a viable suspect, a man or woman that the District Attorney charges with Brady Blackstone's murder, and releases Jack Spurlock, you will owe me two million dollars."

Lucinda laughed. "Pinky, playing poker with you has been fun. Hell it beat betting a hundred thousand on number twelve on the roulette wheel. Perhaps my sources underrated you . . . I'll take the bet if Jack is released in two weeks."

"That is not enough time. How about thirty days from tomorrow."

She seemed to enjoy turning our negotiations into a game. "I accept. I'll write you a check for one hundred thousand today, and a second check for one million, nine hundred thousand when you get my man out of jail." She glanced at her watch. "Counselor, you had better get your ass in gear. The thirty day clock starts in eleven hours."

EIGHT

Bear—South Lake Tahoe, California

The first thing Flo did when she walked in Pinky's condo was to put her bathing suit on and head for the sandy beach to soak up some sun. I turned on the giant sixty-inch TV, and was watching a great baseball game between the Red Sox and the Yankees when the phone rang. Damn! I was afraid that sooner or later Pinky would remember where I was, and he'd put me to work.

"Bear?"

"Yes, Boss."

"Damn it, stop calling me Boss. I have an assignment for you. I just left Brady Blackstone's widow. She's—"

"Was she dressed up like a widow with a black dress, dark veil and everything? Like you see in those old black and white movies on cable?"

"Cease asking me those inane questions and listen."

"Okay, Boss."

I heard Pinky sigh, like he was real tired, or something. "Bear, you are going on a trip."

Just then the batter hit a high fly toward right field. The fielder raced back and jumped to catch the ball but it went over the fence for a home run.

"Bear, did you hear what I just told you?"

"Ah . . ."

The ball cleared the fielder's glove by inches and the Red Sox won the game in the bottom of the ninth with a three run dinger.

Pinky said, "What is that noise I hear in the background? Are you watching something on TV?"

I found the remote and hit the mute button. "Nope."

"Please recall that I am paying you two hundred dollars a day and I do not expect you to sit around my condo and watch TV."

"I know that, Boss."

"Now that I have your undivided attention, you are to join the Blackstone concert tour in Oakland, California. They have two shows left before the tour heads east, one in Oakland, and one in LA. I will arrive at my office in five minutes. Then I will fax you the name of the person you are to contact in Oakland along with a list of potential suspects."

"Wow, you've been real busy while I've . . . hold on, yesterday you told me that Jack's mom didn't have enough money to do a big-time investigation."

"At the time that information was correct. As of today, the bereaved widow has agreed to pony-up a few extra dollars."

"How much?"

"Bear, your job is to investigate. My job is to look after the financial details."

"Okay. How long do you think this job will take me?"

"I haven't a clue. You will find the person with the motive in Oakland, or follow the entourage to Los Angeles and find him there."

"But Boss, I didn't bring enough clothes for a long trip and you told me I can't go home 'cause Ice will arrest me."

"You are testing my patience."

I was pretty sure that Pinky would come around if I clammed up and waited long enough. Pinky's real smart, but he gets antsy quick. If he wants something done, he wants it done now. I sat back and tried to lip-read what the announcer was asking the guy who'd hit the home run. If I let Pinky stew for a couple more seconds, he'd—

"All right, stand up and face the big fireplace," snapped Pinky. "Walk to the right side. Put your hand on the mantle and count down three rocks. Pull the rock out. You'll find an envelope with fifty, one hundred dollar bills.

That equates to five thousand dollars. That cash should cover your expenses for a month."

"Sounds good to me."

I stood up, walked to the fireplace, pulled out the rock and there was the money envelope. "Okay, I've found the expense money, but what about Flo? She doesn't have enough clothes to wear, and —"

"Damn it, Bear! I'm not dressing that witch and I don't care what you do or say. You both will have to make do on the five thousand."

"Okay," I sighed, "But what if I run out of money? Do you want me to leave the tour and come back to Carson City, or—"

"Damn it . . . That's not my . . . . . very well. If you run out of cash before you have finished the assignment, call Mabel. She will wire you more."

The phone went dead without Pinky sending Flo his best wishes.

I opened the big, sliding glass door that led to the beach. "Come on up, Flo. We need to talk."

She walked in from the bright sun. Her killer body was all shiny with little drops of sweat. Flo looked so good in her bathing suit that I almost forgot about Pinky's phone call.

Flo said, "Hey, why do I have to come in? I was enjoying myself out there."

"I know, but we just got an investigative assignment from Pinky and we've got to get going."

Her face perked up. "Really, where do we get to go this time? Hawaii? New York City? France?"

"Not even close. Oakland."

"Oakland, California? Isn't that the half-baked town that sits across the bay from San Francisco?"

"Yup."

"Last year Pinky went to Rome while we ended up in Eureka, Nevada. A truly godforsaken place if there ever was one. Where's His Majesty going this time?"

"He didn't say."

"I'll guarantee you that he'll end up someplace a hell of lot nicer than Oakland."

"Come on, Flo. Pinky's not so bad. In fact, he's offered to buy us both some new duds for the trip."

Flo frowned. "You're kidding me?"

I pulled out a fist full of one hundred dollar bills and tucked one under her bathing suit top.

Her face lit up like a pinball machine racking up the leader's new point total. "Hey, we could head to that great mall outside of Reno. I can't wait—"

"Babe, we can't go back to Nevada for a while. Don't you remember that Ice wants to throw my ass in jail? Don't worry, Oakland will have lots of joints where you can pick up some new stuff."

"Okay. Now tell me what we're doing in Oakland."

I said, "We're going to join up with the Blackstone concert tour."

"Oh boy. I get another chance to . . . but wait, Brady's dead. I don't want to sound like an ingrate, but sitting through another hour of Kyle Rubidoux's singing is more than I can take. He has a cute butt, and baby blue eyes, but that kid is no Brady Blackstone."

"I don't think we're going to the concert to have fun, Babe. Pinky's sending me a list of people that he wants me to talk to."

"What about?"

"He needs me to figure out if anybody on the list had a motive to murder Brady."

"Ah-ha, I get it now. Pinky wants us to figure out how to get Jack Spurlock off the hook."

I smiled. Flo's brain can run circles around mine, and sometimes she even thinks faster than Pinky. "Yup."

I heard the phone ring once, then the fax machine started to make noise. "That's Pinky's list. All we've got to do is pack our bags and drive down the hill to the bay."

"How long will it take us to get to Oakland?"

"About three hours."

Flo said, "After we pack, I'll need to go to the bathroom before we leave. I'm not like you. I'm a delicate lady with a small bladder."

"I remember. I'm ready to make all the potty stops you need, just like that time we drove up Highway 99 from Bakersfield."

NINE

Bear—Oakland, California

Usually I don't listen to what Pinky tells me, but I had to admit that there were days when Flo could be a real pain in the ass!

The drive to Oakland wasn't much—one stop to fill up the gas tank, grab a cup of coffee and let Flo spend some time in the ladies room.

I found a motel in Jack London Square that looked good. The joint had a pool, a nice deck with lots of those fancy blue and white chairs, a hot tub, a great view of the bay—everything I figured would keep Flo happy while I did my investigative stuff.

But Flo didn't like the motel. All I heard was, "I didn't lay by the pool today because it was too cold." I tried to explain that it wasn't my fault that the damn sun never came out? I was positive the sky turned blue sometimes, but the damp, gray fog never went away the days we were there.

She didn't like Oakland. Flo went on and on, "I don't care what you heard, there isn't a decent mall within ten miles." She knew that I didn't have anything to do with the building of shopping malls, in Carson City or Oakland, so why take it out on me?

Hell, she didn't like anything about the trip to the Bay area, and by the time we headed south to LA, it got so bad that I hoped that she'd just shut-up or go back to Carson City.

Anyway, the first day I left Flo at the motel and drove a couple miles south on Highway 880 to the Oakland Arena.

From the parking lot entrance I could see a pot-full of eighteen-wheelers lined up at the big round building, but a chain blocked my way, and a big dude, close to four hundred pounds big, sat dozing on a little chair guarding the entrance.

He cracked open one eye and growled, "Can't let you pass. Only crew and cast members of the Kyle Rubidoux Tour are allowed in."

I handed him the paper Pinky had faxed. "That's okay. I'm supposed to meet with Sid Zander."

The giant dude flashed me a cold stare through one eye—like he'd heard that one a hundred times. He pulled a cell phone out of his shirt pocket.

After a couple of seconds he closed the cell. The dude gave me a look that would curdle milk, like he was pissed off at me for having to wake up. Then he lifted his giant ass off the chair and unhooked the chain.

I drove toward a line of big rigs that were parked in a semi-circle. I got out of my pick-up and followed behind a bunch of guys who were pushing dollies loaded with all kinds of expensive looking crap. When we all walked into a dark tunnel it took me a few seconds to see and I bumped into the guy in front of me who was pushing something black and the size of a refrigerator. He yelled, "Hey dip-shit, look out. You got a death wish or something?"

"Sorry."

I jumped to my left and just missed crashing into a line of empty handcarts being pushed back to the trucks outside. I grabbed the arm of one of the pushers and yelled, "I'm looking for Sid Zander."

"Go in about twenty yards and turn left."

I stayed close to the wall, and as promised, found a lighted hall with a circle of people talking at the far end.

As I got closer, they turned and stared at me, like I had green skin and horns sticking out of my head.

I said, "I'm supposed to meet a guy named Sid Zander."

A cute blonde with a great rack pointed at a door and said, "Zander's in there."

I wanted to stay there and stare at her, but I had work to do. I opened the door. The room was empty except for an old guy sitting on a folding chair behind a card table that shook on spindly legs. He wore a big cowboy hat that might have fit when he was younger and had a full head of hair. But now the hat slipped down until it hung just above his white eyebrows, and the damn thing rocked up and down when he talked, like the Stetson was hinged to his ears.

"My name is Bear Zabarte. Are you Sid Zander?"

"I know who you are. Tiny Vaughn called me from the gate. What I don't know is why are you wasting my time?"

"Mr. Zander, I'm the investigator who —"

"Hey, call me Sid. Now let's cut through all the bullshit." He sat back and the hat rocked. "I'll bet you're that investigator guy from Carson City. I know that the Canadian whore hired your boss, and that he sent you to Oakland. What I don't know is what do you want from me?"

For some weird reason, I liked this old coot. I was thinking that with any luck me and Flo could be back in Nevada by tomorrow afternoon. "Sid, I have a list of people I need to talk with. I've been told you are the man who can set up the meetings."

"And just who fed you that line of crap?"

So maybe he wasn't a nice old fart after all. "Look, my boss told me that Lucinda Blackstone had set this up."

"Ah-ha, so it's an order coming straight from the Black Widow. Okay, what the queen wants, the queen gets. Give me the list."

I handed Sid the fax with the names, and for the first time since I had walked through the door, he smiled. "The first two of these names here are going to be tough."

"Why?"

"They ain't here, that's why. Rene Gagnon's gone. He knew we had only two shows left on the west coast so he put the last days of this traveling circus in my capable hands. And Harold Haffner only shows up every couple of weeks, usually when we have some sort of cash flow trouble."

"Where does Rene live?"

"Quebec City."

"Uh . . . where's that?"

The hat bobbed up and down like he was a banty rooster getting ready for a fight. "Jesus, where'd you grow up, kid?"

"Elko, Nevada."

"I don't understand why, but they don't teach kids geography like they did when I went to school. Now listen carefully. I might give a pop quiz later. Quebec City is located in the province of Quebec—in a country called Canada— as the crow flies, that's approximately three thousand miles northeast of where you stand at this very moment."

I was pretty sure he was making fun of me, and if he'd been about fifty years younger, I'd have popped him one on his nose, but my Mom told me that I should always be kind to weird, old farts and this dude fit that bill.

"What's Harold's job?"

"He's the tour controller—that's nothing but a bean counter with a fancy MBA degree. Harold thinks he was put on the earth to be a constant pain in the butt to everyone, if you know what I mean."

I remembered Flo's ragging at me this morning and nodded. "That I do. How about the rest on the list?"

"They're here, but they're up to their asses with load-in work at the moment. How much time will you need with each one?"

"Twenty to thirty minutes."

"Okay, that means you'll need a little more than an hour. Get one of the broads outside my office to take you to the dining area. The first name on your list will be there inside ten minutes."

Now things were looking up. "Thanks, Sid."

"Don't thank me so soon. If we fall behind our scheduled load-in time, I'll pull the bastards back and call off the agreement."

"What scheduled do you have to meet?"

"We must have all the equipment off the trucks and loaded into the arena by noon."

"Do you get behind often?"

He cackled, "Often enough."

I could tell that this was the best I was going to get out of the old dude. I said, "Thanks again."

He grabbed his phone, sort of like that was his way of saying, you're welcome, Bear.

I turned and reached for the door handle.

"One final thought, young fella. I'd recommend you are finished with your talking and out of that dining area by 11:55. I have a crew of eighty starving men and women. By noon they'll trample you like a stampeding herd of cattle if you get between them and their favorite vittles."

The good news for the day was that the first gal I bumped into turned out to be the cute blonde with the nice boobs I had seen earlier. She told me that she'd take me to the dining area.

As we walked through the dark halls, she said, "My name is Betty. Is this your first time?"

"Uh . . . first time doing what?"

"First time backstage, silly."

"No, I was backstage at Carson City."

Her feet stopped so quick that the rubber soles on her fancy yellow tennis shoes made that funny screeching sound on the concrete floor. Her eyes got real wide and I watched her boobs sort of jump up and down real fast. "That was the night Brady was murdered, and I don't remember seeing you there. Is that why you're here today?"

"Yup."

She turned and got real close, like nose-to-nose close. She smelled good, sort of like a lemon meringue pie fresh out of the oven. "Are you a cop?"

"Nope. I'm a private investigator."

"Oh my god, a real private eye! Are you famous? What's your name?"

By now we were so close that I could almost taste the cinnamon flavored toothpaste she had used that morning. "Bear Zabarte. That's Basque."

She giggled. "Wow, a PI and a foreigner to boot. Bear, I get an hour break soon. How about we get together so you can tell me a few stories about some of your other investigations?"

Just like the first time I met Flo in LA, and now Betty in Oakland. The broads really get excited when they find out I'm a PI. And I'd be lying if I told you Betty wasn't a tempting broad. She had all the right parts and she was ripe for the picking. But I had a pot-full of work to finish, and if Flo ever found out, she'd rip out my eyeballs and use them for fish bait in San Francisco Bay. "I'm sorry, but I've got to interrogate a bunch of people before lunch. You know how it is."

I saw a flash of hurt cross her baby blue eyes. "Sure, I understand."

Betty stopped and opened a door. I followed her into a room with a dozen tables and chairs. Along the far wall was an empty buffet table. To the right were two big refrigerated units filled with iced tea, soft drinks and milk.

She turned to leave. I touched her shoulder. She shivered.

I said, "Once I finish the last name on my list, I could interview you."

She turned and pressed her boobs into me. "Bear, I get an hour off for lunch at twelve-thirty."

"I'll meet you here."

"Not here, silly. The food sucks."

"But Sid told me that the crew loved the food."

"Old Sid's taste buds disappeared with his hair. We can eat lunch at my place. I have one of those small motel suites, with a kitchen, across Highway 880."

I was pretty sure what we were going to do in her suite and it wasn't eat lunch. Part of me, the brain part, told me to walk away. But the other part, that part lower down, kept asking why not? Me and Flo weren't married

60

or anything like that and I didn't owe her anything so there were times when I wondered why I always had to be so damn good.

That lower part of me almost won, but all of a sudden my brain part took over. "Betty, I really do have a lot of work to do. There's a man sitting in the Carson City jail charged with first-degree murder. His life might depend on my investigative work today. I'll make you a deal. If I don't get through my list today, I'll have to follow the tour to LA. Maybe we'll catch up for lost time there. Who knows, you might give me some important stuff about who killed Brady Blackstone."

Her baby blues perked up. She flashed her perfect smile, but before she could say anything, the door popped open and a guy walked in.

He said, "Sid told me you needed to talk to me."

"Sit down. I'll be with you in a minute."

He did.

Betty walked out the door, and then she turned, and said, "Okay. Hope to see you in La La land. You know where to look for me. Just outside of Sid's office. I'm his number one gofer."

Her tight buns rolled around like two volleyballs in a duffle bag as she made her way down the hall. That broad was ready and able . . . maybe too ready? I wondered if being Sid's number one gofer meant she did anything more than bring him his morning coffee.

The guy sitting in the chair said, "Hey, big guy, tell me what you want or I'm splitting."

I turned and remembered why I was here. He looked like a regular guy with medium build, gray hair, but his eyes told me he was scared. I tried to act like Pinky and calm him down.

I sat down next to him. "My name is Bear Zabarte, and I'm investigating the Blackstone murder. What's your name?"

He frowned. "Carl Shanks."

I crossed his name off the list. "Carl, we have to get cracking. Sid tells me that there'll be a mad rush in a few minutes to get at the food."

Carl shook his head. "One time old Sid was right, but a couple of months ago, everything started going down hill. First it was the coffee. Brady made sure the tour used his favorite Caribbean blend made especially for him. Then one day we were drinking some black crap that tasted like it had been strained through a pair of dirty socks. Now even the food has turned to shit. Only the broke and starving roadies eat here. Trust me, go down the road and get a burger."

I glanced at the clock. It showed 11:35. I'd better get going. "My list tells me you play lead guitar."

"That's right. Hey, why are you asking me questions? What's going on here?" He stood and started toward the door.

"As I told you, I'm investigating the death of Brady Blackstone. Now sit down and try to remember the night of the murder."

Carl backed toward the door. "Hold on, I'm not answering any of your questions without an attorney present."

Shit, in the old days he'd have told me what I wanted to know or I would kick his ass. Now everybody watches TV! They've all got rights! They know they don't have to say anything if they don't want to. Then I remembered Pinky's old line, the one that never failed to get a client talking. "Carl, you can talk to me now, or you can talk to a judge, under oath, in an open court with reporters and TV cameras. The choice is yours."

Then I did what I'd seen Pinky do. I sat back and waited.

Carl shuffled his feet, and then came back and sat down. "All right. I'll stick around, but you aren't going to hang Brady's murder on me."

"Why would you think I'd do that?"

"Because of what he did to my sister."

"Carl, help me out here. What did Brady do?"

62

"Shit, it's pretty much common knowledge around here. I caught that bastard screwing my sister. My God man, she was only fifteen."

"That's called statutory rape in Nevada!"

Carl put his face in his hands and sort of whimpered for a while. Between sniffs he said, "My Mom trusted me to take care of Grace when she joined the tour for a couple of weeks during her summer vacation. Brady saw her and jumped her bones. He told me if I went to the cops, he'd make sure I'd never get another job in the business."

Was this the same Brady Blackstone that Flo thought walked on water?

"So what happened then?"

"I'm embarrassed to admit that I caved. The music business is a tight group, and if you ever get blackballed, you're through. I sent Grace back home, but the damage had been done. I know what happened wasn't all Brady's fault. He was a bastard, but he didn't force her to do anything she didn't want to do. Bear, this is just one of those tragic things that happen. Something you want to bury forever. You know what I mean? Jesus, if I had to testify in court, my Mom might find out what I let happen to my little sister."

"Carl, I'll do what I can to keep all this stuff out of the trial."

He stood, wiped the back of his hand across his eyes, and said, "Are we done?"

"Yup, we're done."

The next two stories came from the same pile of crap. Brady had used his position as the Big Kahuna to take some kind of advantage and then threatened to do more than get even if anyone went to the cops. No matter how I cut it, Brady Blackstone was not a nice guy.

At the end of the last guy's interview, he told me that Sid had to call off the last interview because the crew had fallen behind the load-in schedule for tonight's concert.

I left the Arena and the minute I walked in the motel room, Flo started to go on about the shitty bay area weather.

I did my best to change the subject. "Babe, I got a lot done today along with some help from a cute blonde."

"A blonde? What kind of help?"

Jesus, why did I have to bring that up? "I was just kidding. The broad showed me the way to the dining hall. That's all."

Flo flashed me her nasty look. "Bear Zabarte, you'd better be telling me the truth."

"Cross my heart and hope to die."

She thought about what I'd promised for a minute and then said, "For your sake I hope you're telling me the truth. Now, I'm damn near starved. Let's see if there's a place in this burg where we can get something decent to eat."

After a long day I finally got lucky and found a killer B-B-Q place about a block from the motel.

Feeling a little sick, like I just ate most of the whole pig, I burped and said, "Flo, before we hit the hay we need to send Pinky an email."

"Can't it wait? I'm tired."

"Babe, I did my part of this partnership while you laid around the pool."

"But the sun never came out, so I don't think you can count that as a day off."

Like I've told you before, Flo could be a real pain in the ass! I growled, "Sun or no sun, the day counts. Tomorrow, after breakfast, we have to follow the tour to LA. I have one more interview and then we can go home."

She walked to the little desk and turned on the laptop. "At least LA will have sunshine. Besides, I can use the visit to list my house for sale with my old real estate friend."

"Good. Now start typing. This is what we need to send to Pinky."

The whole job took no more than three minutes of Flo's valuable time. As I said, there were days when her nastiness was beginning to piss me off.

```
Pinky:
I met the tour at Oakland and interviewed
three names on the list. Big surprise, all
had damn good reasons to kill Brady, but I
don't think they did it any more than I
think Jack Spurlock did. Turns out that
Brady was a real bastard, but if all the
real bastards got murdered, the population
of the world would get cut in half.
We're heading south to LA to talk with the
last guy on the list.
The other two names you gave me were not in
Oakland.
Rene Gagnon, the tour manager, has gone home
to Quebec City. I hear that's some place up
north.
Harold Haffner, the tour controller, has an
office in LA, but he might be at his home in
Needles, California.
Other news. We're damn near out of money.
Will need another five thousand real soon.
I'll call Mabel and give her the address of
the motel in LA so she can wire the cash to
me.
Bear
```

Flo said, "I like the new clothes, but even Pinky will figure out that there's no way to spend five thousand bucks after two days in Oakland."

"Babe, just send the email. What Pinky doesn't know won't hurt him."

"I'll send the email as long as you promise me that you won't spend one dime on that blonde bimbo."

I growled, "Just send the damned thing."

"Whatever."

TEN

Pinky—Carson City

I had been struggling over a few key words of an important closing argument when Mabel's knock on my office door interrupted my deep concentration. Damn it, once I start to compose one of my legal masterpieces she knows better than to disrupt me unless it is a matter of life or death.

"I know I shouldn't bother you, but Bear's on line one. He's driving south on Highway 5 and holding for you on his cell phone."

I growled, "Damn it, Mabel, that is not his cell phone. That instrument belongs to the practice."

She snapped, "After all the years I've spent slaving in this office I would expect you to treat me with more respect. You need to recall that you are the one who hired that criminal as your full-time investigator. And you are the one who pays him what I consider to be an excessive salary. And you are the one who supplies him with what any fool would consider to be an unwarranted expense account."

My investigator's call seems to have hit a sore spot with my matronly secretary. "Mabel, I apologize and stand corrected."

"Apology accepted. Now, do you want me to tell him to call back later?"

"No, my focus has been irreparably defused. I will talk with him."

Bear said, "Hi, Boss. I tried to talk to Mabel about this, but she said I had to kick the deal up to you. Okay, I'm asking for more expense money."

"I sent you to Oakland with a list of six names. All you had to do was find me a legitimate murder suspect. I

66

have a judge who is willing to issue an arrest warrant once you provide me with a name."

"Look, Boss—"

"Stop calling me boss."

Bear said, "Okay, Boss. I don't have the name yet because I don't think the three guys I interviewed killed Blackstone."

"Bear, I don't pay you to think. All I need is a name."

"They all had good motives, but those sad-sack bastards couldn't squash a mosquito if the damn thing was sucking the last drop of blood out of their veins. I didn't talk to the tour manager, or the bean counter, so I guess they both could have killed Brady. One more thing, I bumped into a blonde who came on a little too strong. Something about her just wasn't right so I'm going to try and interview her in LA."

Cute blondes were Bear's meat and potatoes. There might be more on his mind than a murder investigation.

"Just be sure all you are going to do is interview the woman. I do not have the time to defend myself from a sexual harassment suit because a man in my employ conducted himself in a manner that is unbecoming a gentleman."

Bear growled, "Hey, I don't need you to start ragging on me too. I'm getting enough of that kind of crap from you-know-who. Anyway, I called because I need five thousand more for expenses. Mabel said I'd have to talk to you first, so I'm talking. After we hang up make sure Mabel wires the five G's to the Staples Center Inn."

I had to give Bear credit where credit was due. The man had more balls than brains!

"My good man, there is no way that two human beings could have gone through five thousand dollars of expense money staying in an Oakland motel for two days. I'll instruct Mabel to wire you two thousand, and not a penny more."

The phone line was quiet for a moment. "Boss, between you and Flo, I don't know which one is the bigger pain in the butt."

Before I could respond, I heard Flo say, "Don't worry. I won't be a pain in your butt much longer."

"Bear, what did she mean by that remark?"

"She wants me to drop her off at her house in LA."

"And?"

"Boss, she's pissed off at me and I think we could be through. She thinks I did something with that blonde. I told her that all we did was talk, but she won't believe me."

Flo's voice got louder. "Give me that phone." There was pause and then, "I've told you before that it's illegal in California to talk on a cell phone and drive a car."

There was a flurry of words between the two and then I heard Flo's voice cut through the receiver of my phone. "Pinky?" The sounds of the wicked witch burned my ear. "I don't care what you did in Italy, or who you did it with. My God, everyone in Carson City knows you're a philanderer who will jump into bed with any female who is breathing, but I won't stand for that sort of activity from my man."

I had to admit that Flo's accusation had cut me to the quick. After my return from Italy, I had spent countless hours trying to convince my ex-wife, Willow that nothing of a carnal nature had happened between Christina and myself. The whole affair was no more than a little too much Italian wine combined with a full moon over the Mediterranean. Now, after many months, Willow and I were talking again, and I did not want Flo to rekindle the pain of my past indiscretion.

"Flo, now that we are laying our cards on the table, I want you to know that your moving back to the City of Angels would not cause me to lose any sleep."

"Harrumph."

A loud noise, akin to the rushing of air, suddenly assaulted my ear.

I said, "What, pray tell, was that noise?"

"Flo tried to toss my phone out the window and she left the window open."

"Let that be a lesson to you. Do not allow that woman to touch my cell phone again."

Bear said, "Right. Now, what about kicking up my advance?"

"Bear, negations are closed on that matter."

"Boss, we'll get to the Staples Center Inn in a couple of hours. I don't want to sound like I'm not grateful that you gave me a great paying investigate job, or anything like that, but if those five big ones aren't waiting for me at the motel desk when I check in, I quit!"

Was my illiterate Basque friend threatening me? Well, two can play at that game. "Bear, guess who just walked into my office?"

"I don't know, who?"

"Your old police buddy, Ice Conner. Excuse me, Bear. What did you say, Ice? . . . How fortunate you happened by, I might be in the position to hire some part-time investigative work."

I listened to the pant of the Bear's hot breath for a moment. "Boss, is that bastard really there, or are you just pulling my chain?"

"He is leaning against the door frame, just like you do. Would you care to talk with him so you can verify that?"

"Ah . . . I'll tell you what, I guess we can squeak by on four thousand, but if the cash is not there when I check in, I really do quit."

It was time for me to back down a notch. I had to come up with a viable suspect to collect the rest of the most generous retainer from Lucinda Blackstone, and God knows Bear was the only person who was in position to come up with a name.

I said, "Calm down, my good man and consider what you will be throwing away. As soon as I hang up, I will instruct Mabel to wire you three thousand dollars. I know that's not the amount you requested, but you must admit that it is a fifty percent increase over my initial offer."

"Sorry, Pinky, three's not good enough."

"All right, I will make it thirty-five hundred, but that's my final offer."

"Hey, LA's more expensive than Oakland. I don't think we can get by on thirty-five hundred."

"Bear, these negotiations are closed. Take my final offer or be ready to turn your cell phone and laptop over to Mr. Conner."

I sat back and waited for Bear to sort through his alternatives. From my view he had two—take my last offer, or throw away a job that paid him three times more than he would ever make tending bar.

"Okay, boss, but we'll have to get by on three meals a day at McDonald's."

"That, my good man, is not my problem. Now, before you hang up, is the she-witch truly upset with you?"

"Yup."

"Generally I abhor involving myself in domestic unrest such as this, but I have a piece of advice concerning your relationship problems with women. By now you must know that I cannot bear your female companion, but years of experience have taught me this simple truth—even the simple three-toed sloth deserves a moment of bliss during his or her mundane existence. To that end, I recommend you take a couple of hundred of the excessive amount I'm sending you and sweep the woman off her feet. Buy her two-dozen roses. Take her out to an expensive restaurant. Surprise her with a pearl necklace. In my vast experience, there is not a female on this planet who can resist an unplanned event or an unexpected gift."

"Boss, I don't understand what you're doing."

"I am offering advice concerning your relationships with women."

"Like Flo?"

"If the shoe fits."

"I don't know what my shoes have to do with Flo's silent treatment, but thanks for the heads-up. God knows you've been around the block with a bunch of wives, so I guess you know how to handle women a lot better than I do."

Over the rush of air I heard Flo demand to know if we were talking about her.

Bear, in rare a moment of sanity said. "No! And close your damn window. I can't hear Pinky."

"My boy, wine her and dine her, but don't forget, while you play the big spender in Los Angeles, an innocent man is rotting in jail."

"Got it, boss."

The phone went dead.

Mabel knocked lightly and entered my office. "I hate to interrupt a second time, but Lucinda Blackstone is holding for you on line two."

It never rains but it pours!

"Not a problem. Bear just hung up. Before I pick up Lucinda, you have my approval to wire him thirty-five hundred."

I picked up my phone and pasted a smile onto my voice. "Lucinda, and how is my grieving widow today?"

"Pinky, I'm still waiting for Jack to get out of that hell-hole you call the Carson City jail?"

"I was going to call you in an hour with a complete report. I just talked with my man and at this very moment he's approaching Los Angeles to complete his investigation. When he—"

"Damn it, I gave you a list of names. Your man was supposed to interview them all in Oakland. What happened?"

"Lucinda, two of the men, Gagnon and Haffner were not with the tour group. In fact, we're tracking them down as we—"

"Cut the bullshit. You have $100,000 of my money and all you have to do is get my man out of jail and you clear a couple of million. Did I make a mistake hiring you? Is your organization up to this job?"

"I am appalled at your insinuation that my team is incompetent. I need to remind you that a mere two days have passed since I agreed to take you on as a client."

"Don't bore me with your lame excuses."

"Lucinda, I would venture a guess that the vast resources of the FBI would not have made more progress in that amount of time."

She paused, perhaps a sign that her vitriol was waning.

"Pinky, all I want is the bottom line. How long will I have to wait before I can feel Jack's warm body next to mine?"

"You have asked me an unanswerable question. However, I will give you my best estimate. This scenario is highly unlikely, but my man could come up with the suspect by tomorrow. So the earliest Jack Spurlock could be free would be the day-after tomorrow. If we have to track down Gagnon or Haffner then we are talking a week or two on the outside. I understand that Gagnon lives in Canada somewhere, and Haff—"

"Gagnon lives inside the walls of old Quebec City."

That was a curious piece of information. Why would Lucinda know, or care, where Brady Blackstone's tour manager lived?

I said, "As I was saying before you interrupted me, Haffner lives near Needles, California. To interview either of those men will take more time."

"I thought you told me that your man was in LA?"

"He's on his way there to interview the last backstage crew member you had on your list. Then, if he hasn't found a viable suspect, he will travel to Needles to interview Mr. Haffner."

"Okay. But don't forget, you have twenty-eight days left. If Jack is not out of jail by then, you'll be out nearly two million and I'll hire another team of legal beagles. And don't think you will walk away with my hundred grand. I'll sue you for malpractice faster than you can write me a check."

"We will do our best to complete the task at hand within the —"

"Twenty-eight days and not a single day more. Au revoir."

I set the phone down but before I could return my thoughts to my closing argument, Mabel walked in. She had the look of a woman who was not to be denied.

"Mabel, I can see from your expression that you have something on your mind, but I need to talk with Bear first."

She sighed, "Fine, I'll get him for you, but you're correct, we have something very important to discuss."

"Right."

A moment later Mabel buzzed me. "Bear's on line one."

"Thank you."

"Bear, earlier, we spent so much time talking about your expense money that I neglected to reiterate the vital objective of your trip to Los Angeles."

"What's that, Boss?"

"You must come up with the name of a viable suspect."

"And what happens if I don't?"

"When you return to Carson City, have Flo, or what ever female you are cavorting with at the moment, stop by my office to return my cell phone, laptop and to pick up your final check."

"But, Boss—"

"No buts. I am on a tight timeline and need results. If you cannot produce those results, I'm sure there is someone in the area who can, and will, come up with a name."

I counted to thirteen before Bear growled, "Are you telling me that you want me to open the LA phone book, close my eyes, and pick a name?"

"No, damn it. The definition of viable in this case means the name of a person who had the opportunity and a damn good reason to cause the untimely death of Brady Blackstone—someone the DA will eagerly trade for my client, Jack Spurlock. Now get to work."

Before I gave Bear the opportunity to respond, I hung up my phone, sat back, and realized that Mabel had never left my office.

She said, "Pinky, I've worked for you for a long time. During that time, I've been a loyal employee. Am I correct in that assumption?"

Oh God, I had too much on my plate at the moment. Where was she going with this?

I said, "None better, Mabel."

"As requested, I wired the funds to Bear, but I cannot contain myself any longer. Why are you giving in to that man? Don't you understand? He's stealing you blind. There's no way he could have spent five thousand dollars in two days on legitimate expenses."

Ah, now I understood. Greed was rearing its ugly head.

I said, "I am well aware of that fact."

Mabel stared at me, as if her boss had slipped into the final stage of dementia. "Then why did you authorize me to wire him more money?"

"Because I needed Bear to do this job and thirty-five hundred was a little bonus to finish the task promptly. Why is what happens between Bear and myself so important to you?"

Tears burst from Mabel's eyes. "Pinky, over these past years I never made any demands on you. Now the moment I question what you've done for Bear Zabarte, a man we both know killed another man, you wonder about my motives. Just remember, what's good for the gander is good for the goose."

"I think you have reversed your metaphor."

"I don't believe so. If Bear deserves a bonus, then I deserve one too."

Mabel's bold demand surprised me. Frankly, I didn't think the old girl had it in her.

I hesitated for a moment, to allow Mabel to briefly bask in her glory, and then I said, "Fine, consider it done. Make out a check to yourself for thirty-five hundred and I will sign it. However, don't think this is something you can ask for on a regular basis. Based on our history, your next scheduled bonus will not come due for at least ten years."

She wiped away a tear as it trickled down her puffy, rouged cheek. "Pinky, I wasn't sure I could muster up the courage. Thank you for listening to me, and for your generosity."

I forced a smile. "You are welcome. Now, if we are done, I still have a closing argument to finish before I can go home."

Mabel turned and closed my office door.

I sat back and considered my morning.

My employees' demands were extortion, pure and simple—the sort of behavior I expected from Bear. But what had happened to Mabel—the lady who scrubbed my desk with Lemon Pledge at the end of each workday—the woman who never took a day off? Was I to expect more of the same from her?

A seed of irritation germinated as I considered the monetary adjustment I had been forced to make, but then a feeling of calm replaced my budding anger. After I included Mabel's 'bonus' into the equation, I would only be down a total of $12,000 from Lucinda's original $100,000 retainer. Forget the slave's revolt. Regardless of the final outcome I would still retain a tidy sum.

ELEVEN

Bear—Los Angeles

Between Flo's clamming up, and Pinky's advice on how to handle females, I had to stop a couple of times and pretend the truck had a low tire, or something. All I really did was walk around and kick the tires as hard as I could so I wouldn't get more pissed off than I already was.

As we got close to the Kettleman City off-ramp, the air inside the truck started to smell like there was a humongous pile of steaming cow manure piled between me and Flo. I opened the window but that made the smell even worse.

Flo put her hand over her nose. "My God, what's causing that stench?"

Those were the first words she said to me in over an hour. Maybe she was perking up!

"There's a big feed lot on the left. That's just the smell you get from old cow crap. By the way, did I ever tell you about my first trip to LA?"

Flo grabbed a handkerchief from her bag and blew her nose like there was no tomorrow—like she thought the harder she blew, the faster the smell would go away.

"I know you never liked LA, but are you trying to tell me that there is some sort of relationship between your first trip there and odor of rotting animal waste?"

Hot dog! Flo was starting to talk again. "When I went to Elko High, I played in the marching band."

She stopped pouting. "Really, I never knew that. What instrument did you play?"

Aha! I'm right. She's back to normal. "The tuba."

Flo slumped down and looked out the window. "Now there's another example of why this relationship is going nowhere. When I was in high school, I also played in the band, but I played a real instrument, the flute."

"What do you mean, a real instrument?"

"The tuba players sat in the back of the band next to the drummers, and from my view all they did was try to hit on the girls in the flute and clarinet sections."

"Hey, I took private lessons for a month."

"Bear, enlightened instrumentalists, and I include myself in that category, do not consider tuba players to be true musicians—never did and never will, end of discussion. So what did going to LA have to do with your band?"

Damn, she was a pistol. "Of all the crap I learned at school, playing in the band was the only thing that I thought was any fun. Anyway, when I was a senior, our band was invited to march in a special parade at Disneyland. We did car washes, sold candy, held cake sales, everything we could think of to raise money for the trip."

Flo frowned. "That's weird. My high school wasn't thirty miles away from Disneyland and we were never invited to play there."

I almost told her that it was because she didn't play her flute good enough, but I was trying to make up with Flo, not get her more pissed off. "It was quite a trip for a kid from northern Nevada. We left Elko on a bus at noon and the drive to LA took all night. This was the first time in my life that I'd left my hometown and I was so stoked that I couldn't sleep. Just as we hit downtown LA the sun came up and I remember watching the light bounce off the windows of the big buildings."

"Was the traffic as screwed up as it is today?"

"That's funny, but I don't remember the traffic, just the sunlight on the giant skyscrapers. I was just a big Basque kid from the wasteland of Nevada and even today, when someone says LA, that's the only thing I remember."

Flo said, "LA must have seemed huge to you back when you were a kid, but now it's like that big mountain of cow crap, only instead of cows, LA's filled with people and cars."

Damn, she has a nasty way to bring me down. I snapped, "To you, LA may be nothing but a mountain of manure, but I won't let you screw up my good memories."

"Harrumph."

Now we were both pissed off and we didn't say another word to each other until I pulled into the parking lot at the Staples Center Inn. The three-story building was stuck below the Santa Monica Freeway, hemmed in by buildings, and surrounded by the usual crap that clutters up the streets of a big city.

The motel looked pretty good, in fact it looked damn good, but maybe not good enough for Flo. On one side of the motel was an old brick building that was all boarded up except for a Mexican taqueria on the ground floor that looked okay. After I parked, I got out of the truck and picked up some great smells coming from that taqueria.

Flo got out, stuck her arms over her head and stretched. Wow, she was a sight for sore eyes. I never had a doubt that Flo was an ass burner, but she had the best body I'd ever seen. I knew she really was hard to get along with, but if we split up, I was pretty sure that I'd never get to bury my head into that great rack of Flo's, and . . .

"Hey, I thought you were going to drop me off at my place."

If I was going to change her mind about splitting up, I had to talk fast. "Babe, before we left Oakland, I picked up a brochure for this joint and it looked pretty cool."

If Pinky was feeding me the straight scoop about how to handle a broad, that should give me a boost in the right direction.

Flo squinted in the hazy sunlight and glanced at the motel.

I said, "They've got a great pool, nice deck chairs, and I'll bet people sitting under blue umbrellas sipping glasses of wine. All the kind of stuff you like to do. And it's a lot warmer here than Oakland. And the sun's out. At least I think it's out on the other side of that brown, hazy sky. After you get settled in, we could go out to a fancy restaurant. Your pick."

She stopped stretching and stared at me. She didn't smile, or touch me, nothing like that, but after what seemed to me like a long, long time, she said, "Okay, I'll take a look at the pool, and then the room. If this establishment meets, or exceeds my standards, and the pool water is crystal clear, and this warm weather holds up, an afternoon by the pool sounds like an acceptable way to pass some hours before dinner."

Well, I'll be damned. Pinky was right. All I had to do with a woman was give her something she wanted, and something she didn't even know she wanted!

I said, "I'll get a key from the guy at the desk so you can check out the room. Then we'll see what the pool looks like."

Later, after Flo stuck our stuff in the drawers, and she let me watch her change into her bathing suit, I headed to the Staples Center.

At the main entrance, the same sort of hulk I ran into at Oakland stopped me, but this time he checked his list and my name was on it.

I dodged through the now familiar line of roadies loading the crap in and made my way through another dark tunnel to Zander's office.

It looked like Sid was wearing the same shirt and his head was camped out under the same hat that he had on in Oakland. "Howdy, young fella. Heard through the grapevine that you didn't get finished with your interviews up north."

"Right! I got one left, unless Haffner or Gagnon have come back."

"You got something wrong with your ears young fella? I told you in Oakland that they were gone for the rest of the run."

"Yeah, but—"

"No buts. You didn't ask, but here's a word of advice from one of your elders. Get your mouth gears to mesh with your brain before you ask me another dumb question or I'll get one of my roadies in here to chuck your sorry ass into the parking lot."

79

That was it. Old fart or not, I was ready to deck him. I pulled my right fist back and said, "Sid, for an old guy, you have a nasty way. Give me a good reason why I shouldn't knock you one on the nose. "

"Calm down, kid, it comes with the territory. Now get out of my office. I've got a lot of work to do."

I started to leave and then I remembered Betty, the cute blonde. "Sid, is Betty going to take me to the place for the interview?"

"Betty? Don't know a Betty. Who are you talking about?"

"Betty, you know, your number one gofer."

"What does she look like?"

"Cute—blonde—big boobs."

"Young fella, you just described ninety percent of the females running around backstage. I don't recall one named Betty, and I don't have a number one gofer."

"Sid, thanks for all your help. If you ever come back to Carson City, stop by the Old Globe and I'll buy you a drink."

If I was a betting man, I'd take the odds that Sid's smart-ass mouth would get him kicked from here to Sunday, or he'd just die from old age long before he got back to Carson City. Besides, I didn't work at the Old Globe anymore so if Sid did get there, and found the Old Globe, the thought of my nasty boss telling him to pound salt made me smile.

Outside Sid's office I glanced around and he was right. There were four cute blondes, they all had big boobs, but not one of them was my Betty. I grabbed the nearest one and said, "Sid wants you to take me to the interview room."

This blonde had a tattooed spider web complete with a one-inch black widow crawling across the top of her right boob. "This way, big guy."

Me and the tattooed broad walked through the back of the Staples Center to a dining room that looked a lot like the one in Oakland.

Inside an hour I had heard the last dork's story and decided he wouldn't swat a fly, much less kill Brady Blackstone.

At this point, I had interviewed the four guys and in my opinion none of them killed Brady. That was great for them but not for me. Pinky had told me that I had to come up with a name today or I'd lose my job, Flo, and spend the rest of my life cleaning up spilled drinks.

There were the other two guys, Gagnon in Canada, and Haffner in Needles, but there was no way I could get to either guy in the next couple of hours. I was up shit creek without a paddle, but on my way back to Sid's office, I spotted Betty walking down the dark tunnel.

In Oakland, Betty was really nice to me, maybe too nice to the son of a Basque sheepherder, but there was something else about her today that didn't fit . . . that's it! . . . she was all dressed up in a fancy skirt and shirt, like she was somebody's secretary or something. And Sid told me she didn't work for him. I didn't know what to do, but right then Betty was the closest thing I had to a possible suspect and God knows, I needed a name to give to Pinky before midnight tonight. But I knew Pinky wouldn't fall for Betty-the-Blonde. I had to figure out her last name.

She reached the exit and disappeared into the bright sunlight. I ran close to a line of guys who were heading outside for another load of concert equipment. I grabbed one of the guy's arms. "Do you know the name of that good-looking blonde who just walked by you?"

He looked toward the sunlight. "I don't know her name, but I've seen her before. I think she belongs to one of the suits."

"Do you know which one?"

"Nope. All suits look alike to me."

"Thanks."

As I ran down the dark tunnel, I remembered the suit I saw the night Brady was murdered. He was the tour manager, Rene Gagnon. According to the old fart, Sid, Gagnon was in Canada. But what if Sid was wrong?

What if Betty was Gagnon's broad and he was picking up Betty in the parking lot?

I cleared the tunnel just in time to see the rear end of a bright red Porsche reach the exit gate.

I ran to my pick-up, jumped in, and slammed the pedal to the metal. It didn't take me long to figure out that following a car around a chicken-shit burg like Carson City was one thing, but trying to follow anything through the freeways of LA was another kettle of fish.

The Porsche shot up a freeway on-ramp heading east. I ran a red light to keep the Porsche in sight. Once I got on the freeway it took me a couple of seconds to spot the Porsche as the car veered left through what looked like a thousand cars trying to merge right to get onto another freeway going somewhere else.

The sun was behind me, so other than heading east, I didn't know where the Porsche was going. There was so much traffic moving past my truck that it seemed like I was in one of those old Sci-Fi movies where the world was about to end and everyone was trying to escape to the mountains.

The Porsche darted across four lanes of metal, rubber and plastic, and shot onto another freeway. I saw a highway sign flash by that I think showed the number of the freeway, but I was so busy trying to catch up with the Porsche, and avoid crashing into the cars all around me, that I didn't have time to look. Other than heading northeast, I still didn't know where I was going, but at that point, I knew I had to stay close to that Porsche or get ready to mop the barf off the men's room floor at the Old Globe.

The Porsche jumped a lane to the left. I cut off a guy who gave me the finger and in a few seconds me and the Porsche both ended up on a different freeway. I almost got close enough to see who was driving when my cell phone beeped.

"Bear, I have just completed my daily tan. Have you finished your morning interviews?"

"Uh . . . I have one more thing to do and then —"

Suddenly everybody's stoplights went red and I had to jump on my brake pedal with both feet.

"I'm sort of busy right now, Flo."

"Humph! As soon as you're finished fooling around come by and pick me up. Before we go to dinner I need to drive by my old house. I have a few personal things to grab and then we can stop by the real estate office. I'm going to list my house and sell it."

The Porsche suddenly darted into an opening in the right lane. Shit, I thought. The lanes on the right are heading onto another freeway and I'm stuck in the center lane. I glanced at my mirror, closed my eyes and cranked the steering wheel. My truck slipped into an opening just big enough for my pick-up and a small box of corn flakes.

Flo yelled, "Earth to Bear, did you hear what I just told you?"

"Yeah, I heard, but like I told you, I sort of busy at the moment."

"So I can expect to see you in ten to fifteen minutes?"

"Uh . . . "

That's when I heard a siren, checked out my rearview mirror, and saw a highway patrolman on his motorcycle. The siren wailed again and he waved at me to pull over. As a general rule, I don't get along with cops. I knew that bullshit line that all cops were not bad, like Ice Conner, but to me most of them were nothing but losers hiding behind a badge.

"Shit!"

"Was that remark directed at me?"

"Flo, that wasn't for you. A highway patrolman just pulled me over."

"What? I thought you were at the Staples Center!"

"I was."

"Bear Zabarte, is that blonde bimbo with you?"

"No! I'm . . . a . . . I'm trying to follow one of the guys I interviewed a few minutes ago."

"And what did he say that made you feel the need to follow him?"

By that time I'd made my way to the shoulder. The cop was off his bike and on his radio, probably calling in my Nevada plate for any outstanding warrants. Then I noticed the Porsche stopped in what had suddenly become the world's biggest parking lot. If I could get rid of the cop, and grab a little luck, I could still catch up with the Porsche.

I rolled the window down.

The helmet said, "License and registration please."

Flo yelled into my other ear, "Answer me, Bear. How do I know you are telling me the truth?"

"Damn it, Flo, I'm the only one in my truck."

"That's not good enough. Let me speak to the officer."

The helmet leaned forward and said, "Sir, I told you to give me your driver's license and registration."

I shrugged my shoulders at the cop, and said, "Flo—"

She said, "If you're not lying to me, and a highway patrolman did pull you over, then he should be standing outside your truck at this very moment. Let me talk to him at once or we're through forever."

I looked up at the helmet and said, "Officer, my . . . uh, my girl friend doesn't believe that I'm in my truck alone. Would you tell her what you see in my truck while I dig out my license and registration?"

He stared at me for a second, took my cell phone and started to talk to Flo. I guess he got that sort of request a lot because he didn't blink, at least I don't think he blinked, 'cause I couldn't see his eyes on the other side of his one-way sunglasses.

I got out my license and registration and traded him the paper work for my cell phone.

I said, "Okay, Flo, did the cop convince you I was telling you the truth?"

"Yes, but frankly, I'm not one hundred percent sure that I should believe him. You men are all alike. I don't—"

"Damn it, Flo—"

"All right, get back to the motel as soon as you can. I'm tried of sitting around doing nothing. I'll call the real estate agent and ask him to meet us at my house so I can sign the listing papers before dinner."

The cell beeped and went dead. I set the phone down and the helmet handed me my truck registration.

"Everything okay with the little woman?"

"I guess so. Why did you pull me over? What did I do wrong?"

"You were talking on your cell phone while operating a motor vehicle."

Shit! Flo had told me about that when I was talking with Pinky on the way to LA. The line of cars stacked up on the connector started to move. I watched the red Porsche shoot ahead and disappear around a bend.

"Damn."

"Hey, I can understand. You're from Nevada. What do you know about our new cell phone law?"

"Officer, I have a question."

"I hope your question doesn't concern your woman. Solving domestic problems is out of my jurisdiction, but if you want my opinion, she must be great at something besides talking to highway patrolmen over the phone."

"Yeah, she is. But sometimes she can be a real pain in the ass."

He looked at my driver's license. "Benate Zabarte. Is that French?"

"Nope, it's Basque."

"Mr. Zabarte, because you're from another state, and at the moment, your plate is full of domestic difficulties, I'm going to let you off with a warning this time. Now what was your question?"

"Those lanes up ahead that go right, what freeway does it link to?"

"That takes you onto the San Bernardino Freeway, also known as Interstate 10. You can follow Interstate 10 all the way to the Atlantic Ocean if you're inclined to take the southern route across America. Mr. Zabarte, enjoy your visit in our golden state, but stay off your cell phone while you are operating a motor vehicle. Okay?"

The helmet gave me a wave, got on his bike, and slipped into the river of metal flying by my left elbow.

I checked my side view mirror and looked for an opening in the solid wall of cars that flashed by at sixty miles an hour. Then it hit me. Even if I found an opening, now that I'd lost the Porsche, other than drive east on Interstate 10, I didn't know where to go. In fact, I didn't even know how to get back to the Staples Center. I slammed my fist into the steering wheel and figured that maybe mopping smelly floors in a men's can wasn't so bad after all.

TWELVE

Bear—Los Angeles

A lot of the jerks I used to hang with had nothing good to say about their father, but not me. Back when I was just a kid my Pop would take me with him on an overnight camp out whenever the herd got close to Elko.

Pop was a sheepherder and he knew how to handle most anything that came up in the wastelands of eastern Nevada.

One summer after breakfast, when I was around twelve, Pop walked me a couple of miles from camp and spun me around until I was real dizzy. Then he showed me how to use the sun, and the lay of the land, like the creek beds and things, to find my way back to camp.

After the freeway cop left me sitting by the road, I got out of my truck and looked around.

"Okay, Pop, which direction do I go?"

The only thing I was sure of was that I had gone a pot-full of miles on the LA freeways. Then I noticed that the shadow of my truck leaned to the east. I jumped back in the truck, grabbed the first off ramp, turned right, and followed the building shadows back to the Staples Center Inn parking lot.

I opened the door to our room and Flo was watching another one of her dumb quiz shows on TV. She didn't wave or say anything so I guessed she was still pissed off at me. I checked my watch and was sure the Red Sox were playing an important game 'cause all Sox games were important, but half the season was over, and now they were even more important than usual. I reached for the remote but Flo slapped my hand.

"Not so fast. After I set the phone down, I realized you never answered my question."

"Huh?"

"Why did you feel the need to follow him?"

"Who?"

"Damn it, the man you interviewed. The one who jumped in his car and left the Staples Center. Why did you follow him?"

It had been a couple of hours since I had talked with Flo on the phone and I couldn't remember which line of bullshit I had fed her.

"I don't know what you're talking about."

Flo jumped up from her chair and flashed me a look that would knock the scales off a snake. "I knew it. You were lying to me. Bear Zabarte, you have one, and only one chance to save this relationship. Start telling me the truth, the whole truth and nothing but the truth, or we are through."

Shit! If I told her the truth, she'd leave me. And if I told a lie, she'd walk out the door and never come back. I needed some quick advice from Pinky on how to handle a woman.

Flo grabbed her suitcase. "You think I'm kidding? You have five seconds to start talking or I'm out of here. One—two—three—four—"

She had me between a rock and a hard spot. Then I remembered what I did during my murder trial when Pinky found out I didn't have the money I owed him. I dropped to one knee. But this time I moved too fast and my knee bone hit the floor real hard. A hot pain shot up my hip and I had to grit my teeth to keep from screaming. "Flo, we both know I'm not a perfect catch, but since we've been together, I've never cheated on you—not even once. Stop packing and listen to me."

Flo closed her suitcase and sat on the edge of the bed. For a second it looked like my drop-to-your-knees trick still worked.

She shook her head. "Now there's cheating, and then there's cheating. Are you telling me that you've never eyed those two bikini clad bimbos that lay around our pool back home?"

My knee hurt so bad that I had to get up. "Jesus, Flo, I didn't tell say I was blind, I just said that I never cheated on you. That means I haven't . . . you know . . . done it with anyone but you since we met."

Flo stared at me for a minute. I know that when most people say a minute they mean a couple of heartbeats, but in this case, Flo's cold eyes stayed on me for at least sixty seconds.

She nodded. "Okay. You have one more chance. Tell me exactly what happened."

I confessed and told her that I was really following Betty-the-blonde, the babe with the nice set of boobs.

Flo sat down, like she was trying to figure out if I was still shining her on. Then she shook her head and tossed her suitcase back on one of those cool, metal suitcase racks that all the good motels have.

"Bear, I have to give you credit. If that was a lie, that was the dumbest one I've heard. Now where do you suppose the bimbo was going?" She grabbed her purse and started to root around. That gave me a second of peace so I punched the remote and turned on the ball game. It was the bottom of the sixth. The Sox were ahead seven to . . .

"Hey, turn that damn game off and get over here. We've got work to do."

I muted the sound.

Flo had spread out a map on the motel table.

She said, "Okay. Here's where our motel is, and here's where you got on the freeway." I watched her finger slide around and stop. "If you ended up at the connector to Interstate 10, my guess is this is about where the cop pulled you over. Now I think the big question is where was Betty-the-blonde going?"

Her finger pointed to a fat blue line on the map, Interstate 10, the main highway that went all the way to Blythe, where the road crossed the Colorado River, left California, and went into Arizona. That was super if I wanted to go to Arizona, but . . . I glanced at the TV. The Sox had a guy on second with one out.

"Bear, didn't you tell me that one of those guys you wanted to interview lived in Needles?"

The batter hit a solid line drive to right. The Sox runner rounded third and was going to score.

"I told you to turn that damn TV off. I'm not going to do all the work on this investigation."

I hit the power button. The screen went dark.

Flo took the remote from me and stuffed it in her purse. "Damn it, I asked you if the guy you wanted to interview lived in Needles?"

"What about him?"

"That's what I just asked you. What about the guy in Needles?"

"Needles?"

"Jesus! Wipe that stupid ball game from your brain and follow my finger on the map."

Flo's little finger slid along the blue line to Blythe and then turned north. That's when it hit me what she was going on about, and I was glad Flo had brains along with her boobs.

About a hundred miles due north of Blythe, on Highway 95, sat the town of Needles—the home of Harold Haffner—one of the dudes I had pegged as a possible suspect.

THIRTEEN

Pinky—Carson City

"Slow down, Bear. And run that scenario by me again."

"Boss, I don't know for sure, but I was pretty sure that I was following that Rene guy, you know, the tour manager, driving a red Porsche, on the freeways of LA."

"Did you actually see him?"

"Well, no. Not exactly."

"So what exactly did you see?"

"I saw Betty-the-blonde get in the passenger side of the Porsche. Then I followed the Porsche to Interstate 10 where I lost the car."

"And this Betty-the-blonde was the same woman who had aroused your, uh, suspicions in Oakland?"

"Yup."

Bear was an uneducated clod, but his instincts in circumstances such as this were generally correct. "But according to Lucinda, Rene Gagnon presently resides in Quebec City."

I listened to Bear's hot breath rush past the telephone transmitter and wished his brain functioned as quickly. Then he said, "So maybe it wasn't the tour manager. But I know for sure that I saw Betty get into the car."

"So someone else besides Gagnon could have been behind that wheel."

"I guess so. I got as close to the Porsche as I could, but trust me, driving a car on these freeways is like trying to run through a herd of stampeding cattle."

I snapped, "Bear, shut down your quaint homilies and let me think."

At least I had the name of a suspect I could give to Lucinda. But if one name was good, two or three had to be better.

I said, "If I remember correctly, you told me that the tour comptroller, a man named Harold Haffner maintained an office in Los Angeles."

"Right."

"And he also has a home near the town of Needles."

"Now you've got it, Boss."

"Bear, you sit tight. I will call you back in a few minutes. Do not leave your room, understand?"

"Gotcha. I wanted to watch the rest of the ballgame anyway."

I buzzed Mabel. "Get me Lucinda Blackstone."

A moment later, Mabel said, "She's on line one."

"Lucinda, my dear. How are you today?"

"I'll be better once Jack is at my side. Do you have any news?"

"Yes. My operative in Los Angeles has turned up two names I want to run by you for more information. Rene Gagnon and Harold Haffner."

I heard her chuckle. "Pinky, I don't know about Harold. He's a classic example of a bean counter. Give him a column of numbers to total up and the man will have an orgasm. Now Rene is another thing. He and I go way back."

Aha! Perhaps this was where I'd find out why the grieving widow knew Gagnon's address. "Tell me about your relationship."

"At one time, Brady and I were a singing duo. We had a gig at the Quebec Summer Music Festival and that's where we met Rene. The son-of-a-bitch persuaded Brady that I was holding him back from the big time. Unfortunately, for me, Rene was correct. He took Brady under his wing, changed his name, gave him a new act, and inside of two years, my husband was making six figures. A few years later, seven, and then eight figures. Last year, Brady was the top grossing tour in the U. S.

with more than a hundred and fifty million in ticket sales."

I said, "This is all very interesting, but I will never convince the local District Attorney that showing Brady how to make a veritable fortune is a viable motive for murder."

"But that's where you are wrong. Brady had a way about him that made him seem vulnerable to those who didn't know him. Rene treated Brady like he just fell off the turnip truck and that's where Rene made his mistake. They signed a long-term contract that gave Rene twenty-five percent of Brady's tour profits, but after five years, Brady could exercise an escape clause. A year into the contract, Brady told me that he was going to exercise the escape clause, dump Rene and run the tour himself."

I said, "Should I presume that the five year period was reached?"

"A month ago."

"So you think it is possible that Rene killed your husband because he was about to lose his contractual tie to Brady?"

"Pinky, all the cops have to do is take a peek at Rene's contract with Kyle Roubidoux. Kyle's contract has the identical escape clause but it cannot be exercised for ten years. I guess I should have told you this before."

It seemed so obvious to me that I wondered why she had not. "Lucinda, to get to the bottom of this, I need to go to Quebec City."

"What will you do there?"

"Confront Rene with the facts you just presented to me. I could also demand to review his contract with Kyle Roubidoux. If, as you claim, the new contract—"

"Pinky, you can trust what I've told you. I think going to Quebec—"

"Lucinda, to complete my part of our agreement, I have to come up with a viable suspect who has a feasible motive to murder your husband—a person that the Carson City District Attorney will swap for your lover, Jack Spurlock. Gagnon was at the concert the night of the murder—that gives him the opportunity. I believe that the loss of a fortune will suffice as a motive. Now, if you will excuse me, I have to go home and pack my overnight case. By the way, would you care to join me?"

"No, why?"

"I thought you could show me around the city, and help me locate Rene's domicile."

She hesitated, "Sorry, I can't help you there."

Lucinda had told me a great deal, but it seemed there was much more that she was holding back. However, as long as she paid my fee as agreed, I would be happy to let her keep her secrets.

"Goodbye, my dear. I'll keep you abreast of my progress."

I buzzed Mabel. "Get me Bear and wire him another two thousand." I heard Mabel gasp. "And before you summon up the courage to ask for an additional sum of money for yourself, my answer is no."

In a moment, Bear came on the line. "Okay, boss, what's up?"

"This is the plan of attack. I will follow up the Rene Gagnon lead. You will pursue the Harold Haffner angle. Now, before I hang up, I need to make one point perfectly clear. I am not authorizing you, under any circumstances, to use illegal methods. Bear, I cannot allow your actions to jeopardize my ethical standards. Do you understand me?"

"Boss, are you telling me that you don't want to know if I have to break-and-enter like we did—"

"STOP! Do not utter another word. We need to investigate Mr. Haffner's business, and his home life, and learn if he has a connection to your Betty-the-blonde. What I am trying to tell you is that I do not want to be privy to any details concerning your plans, or how you accomplish your task. Do I make myself clear?"

"I think so. But one thing bugs me. Will any of the evidence I might pick up on my way . . . will it be . . . I think you called it inaccessible."

"The word is inadmissible my good man. My boy, don't overtax your little brain. Your mission is to nail Harold Haffner, or the blonde, assuming you can come up with a connection. Understanding the law concerning evidence and selling what I have discovered to Willow is my assignment."

"Right. By the way, if I'm going to stay in southern California much longer, I'll need more expense money."

"Bear, you are like a brother to me, and you know that I take care of my family in spite of personal sacrifice. I believe that when you check with the motel management they will be holding the funds you require."

FOURTEEN

Pinky—Carson City

Mabel spoke to me in her most business-like voice, a tone she used only when she was truly upset with me. "Pinky, you are booked on a red-eye flight to Quebec City that leaves Reno tonight at nine-thirty. I made a reservation at a small hotel called The Maison Amicale inside the walls of the old city. I know you requested the Château Fontenac, but it was completely booked due to the Festival D' Été De Québec."

Ever since her minor uprising, Mabel had lost some of her motherly charm. I could live with that, but sweetness and light seemed to be her singular endearing trait, so I attempted to loosen her up. "Excuse me, but my French is a touch rusty."

"The literal translation is: Festival Of Summer Of Quebec. I checked the web site and you are arriving in the middle of a ten-day musical extravaganza."

"How lucky for me. If all the accommodations are filled, why is there a room available at the Maison Amicale?"

"The proprietor, a friendly woman named Mrs. Thénardier, told me that my phone call had come in no more than ten seconds after an unexpected cancellation."

I weighed the possibility that Mrs. Thénardier was pulling the wool over Mabel's gray hair. More than likely, The Maison Amicale was a dump consisting of four walls that surrounded a few dark and dingy rooms. The proprietress would turn out to be a woman in her sixties with two missing teeth and a hunchback. The morning repast would consist of a stale croissant, watery grape jelly, and black coffee strong enough to strip the spar varnish off an old sailing ship.

My mood dipped past the point of trying to cheer Mabel up. "What makes you think Mrs. Thénardier was telling you the truth?"

"Pinky, after all these years, I don't see how you can—"

"Mabel, I do not understand how a city the size of—"

"Pinky, you are pushing me to the edge of anger. Unless you are willing to sleep on a cot in the YMCA, The Maison Amicale was the best available lodging! Now, please let me continue. I did not rent you a car at the airport. According to Mrs. Thénardier, parking inside the walls is impossible. She recommended you take a cab from the airport to The Maison Amicale. She will organize all your transportation needs after your arrival."

At this point, I could see that my hopes were dashed for a sophisticated, leisurely vacation in eastern Canada. However, like it or not, if I was going to satisfy Lucinda's need for a second suspect, I would simply have to endure a few nights in Quebec City.

"Fine. Now, according to my schedule, I have a —"

"Pinky, please wait for me to finish. I have not completed your trip information. As instructed, I informed the court clerk you have the flu so all of your pending court appearances have been pushed out four days."

"What if I don't return in time?"

Mabel let out one of her if-it-wasn't-for-me-this office-would-collapse sighs. "Then I'll have to tell the court clerk another bold-faced lie. Of course, that would not be my personal best. Three years ago, if my memory serves me well, I had to beg the clerk to—"

"Enough! Do you have any good news?"

"Yes. Lucinda is holding on line two."

Mabel had been a perfect employee. She did everything required for a successful law practice, and more. But lately, there had been days, and those days were becoming more frequent, when the woman seemed to spend more of her time testing my patience.

I punched the button for line two. "Lucinda, talking to you twice has made my day. What can I do for you?"

"Pinky, I haven't been totally honest with you."

Would wonders never cease?

"No problem, my dear. Confession is good for the soul."

She chuckled. "I fear my soul is long past saving. During your trip to Quebec City you'll discover that I know a lot more about Rene Gagnon than I should."

I glanced at my daily printout, an hour-by-hour schedule of my time that Mabel places on my desk each morning. I noted that I was required in court in fifteen minutes. I said, "My dear, I fear that I am due in court, and then, as you well know, I leave for Quebec City from the Reno Airport."

"How about meeting me at my hotel suite before your flight? I'll have the hotel fix you up a snack. Too much of that airplane food will kill a man."

"Perfect. I'll see you at eight."

Now I was positive that Lucinda was concealing some valuable information from me, but that knowledge did little to prepare me for the moment when the desk clerk at Lucinda's hotel informed me that she had checked out.

FIFTEEN

Pinky—Reno/Sparks

A touch shaken, I searched out an old client, Porfirio Garza. Porfirio was the Captain of the bellhop crew and if anyone could tell me what happened to Lucinda, he could.

Porfirio sat behind a desk in a tiny office one flight below the lobby. He gestured for me to sit down, but the only chair looked as if it had done duty during the revolutionary war. I passed on his offer.

"Pinky, long time no see. What do you need?"

Porfirio was like most men, but most men do not catch their wives making love with another male, nor do they shoot six bullets into the man's naked body. However, throughout the world, juries generally take the side of the cuckolded husband, and that's why my old client now sat behind his desk instead of inside the walls of the Nevada State Penitentiary.

I said, "One of your guests, Lucinda Blackstone, checked out sometime today. I need the answer to a few questions. Did your concierge make an airplane reservation for her? And did she make any long distant calls today?"

"And you'd also like to know where to, and who to, right?"

"That is correct."

"Go back upstairs to the bar located left of the front desk. I'll meet you there in ten minutes and you can buy me a gin and tonic."

Before I had finished my drink, Porfirio slipped onto the stool to my right.

I said, "Bartender, a gin and tonic for my friend and a second for me."

We touched glasses and Porfirio said, "Are we talking about the broad who was married to that Brady dude that bought the farm a week ago?"

I nodded.

"Okay. She booked a flight to Quebec City via Los Angeles. To me that seems like the long way to go, but maybe she wanted to stop by Hollywood to get an autograph." He took a sip of his drink, chuckled at his joke, and continued, "Before she left, she made a phone call at 2:18 pm to somewhere in Canada. She talked for twenty-three minutes. Fifteen minutes later one of my boys picked up her luggage and put her into a car to the airport."

"Did you come up with that Canadian phone number?"

Porfirio glanced around and then opened his hand. Inside his palm was a note with a string of numbers. "I was sure you'd want it, but if anyone asks, you don't remember where you got it from. Hey, after the great job you did for me with the law, it's the least I can do."

He picked up his bar napkin, folded it around the slip of paper and pushed the treasure toward me.

"Good luck, counselor."

It turned out that there were no direct flights between Reno and Quebec City. During the long night of stops and plane changes, I attempted to sleep, ignored the movie, and tried to determine what Lucinda's sudden disappearance meant. When I had talked with her, she seemed ready to turn over some vital information, but now she was gone, and all I had was the Canadian telephone number she had called before she vanished.

Eventually my plane landed outside Quebec City. Judging by the airport signs, and listening to the conversations going on around me, French was the primary language spoken here. However, I found a cabbie that understood enough English to take me to my destination.

After a short drive through the streets of a vibrant and bustling city, my taxi passed through an ancient gate and we entered the old walled community of Quebec City. The cab slowly plied the narrow roads and stopped in front of a quaint, three-story building. Over the entrance hung a hand-carved sign proclaiming, 'Maison Amicale'. To my relief, the establishment looked clean and prosperous. The windows on either side of the dark blue front door held flower boxes filled with bright orange marigolds. Could it be possible that Mabel had been told the truth—that Mrs. Thénardier had truly received a cancellation seconds before Mabel called?

I picked up my bag and entered the building with high hopes.

The moment I walked through the door, a female voice called, "Ah, Monsieur Delmont. It is good to have you here. Now come closer. I will take care of the business so we can sit down, have a glass of wine, and get to know each other, no?"

As my eyes got used to the muted light, I was pleased to note that the real Mrs. Thénardier had all her teeth and floated somewhere between thirty-five and fifty. It was hard to be sure because most females color their hair, and many have done the occasional nip and tuck around the jaw-line. I wasn't positive if she had used any of those procedures, but regardless, the final results pleased my eye.

I held out my hand. "Mrs. Thénardier, it is a pleasure to meet you."

"Ah. I am pleased to discover that you are a gentleman who is both good looking and well dressed. Mr. Delmont, that is a rare combination today. My late husband, Claude, was a gentleman, but he was not as handsome a man as you. Claude was . . . shall we say he was my husband, and lover for ten years. Now he's gone, and I miss the closeness of him."

"I am sure you do, Mrs. Thénardier."

"Monsieur Delmont, please call me Danielle."

"I will if you call me Pinky."

Her smile faded a touch. "Pinky? That name seems so childish for a man of your bearing."

"My full name is J. Pincus Delmont if that makes you more comfortable."

Her gaze quickly scanned every inch of me and I was pleased that her eyes lit up. "Monsieur Delmont, I must say that you do not look like a child to me. Tell me, are you here for the music festival?"

"No, I am an attorney, and I am here to clear up some legal matters."

"An attorney. My Claude was an engineer. In my experience professional men are so exciter. . . how do you say it in English, so exciting. Do you speak French?"

"No."

"Too bad, but I'm sure you'll get by with my assistance. I can make phone calls and set up appointments, whatever you need."

"I do not believe that will be necessary." Then I remembered the telephone number Lucinda had called from her hotel room. I pulled the slip of paper from my pocket and handed it to her. "Come to think of it, there is something you can help me with. I have a Canadian telephone number. I am curious if it is a Quebec City telephone number."

She glanced at it and nodded. "Yes. I have the same prefix. It is the number for all phones inside the old city walls. Do you want me to make the call for you?"

"No, thank you. At the moment I believe a short nap is called for."

She placed her hand on my shoulder, not in a suggestive way, but in my exhausted state, I felt a small rush of heat. I struggled to remain calm, but it was possible that my cheeks flushed.

Her eyes informed me that she had picked up my flash of ardor. "Nonsense. I will make the call because the person answering the phone will speak French."

"That is a wonderful idea, but before you do that, could you show me to my room?"

"But of course. How forgetful. Follow me."

We walked past a stairway and down a wood paneled hall. On the left was a door with a brass plaque that said, Degas. At the end of the hall there was another door, but that one did not have a plaque.

Danielle unlocked the first door. "Pinky, I have placed you into the Degas room. I feel the art of Degas radiates energy, not just the ballet dancers, because he captured the erotic essence of all women. I sense there is a touch of Degas in you." She paused and smiled. "The door you see at the end of the hall opens into my personal quarters. During your stay, if you have a need, any need at all, please feel free to knock on my door at any hour."

I was drained from the long flight and had a lot of work to finish over the next few days, but Danielle's thinly veiled invitation had definitely caught my attention.

I entered my room and closed the door behind me. The décor was captivating. It had a large antique bed and a matching desk and dresser. The Degas prints fit perfectly, and upon closer examination, I had to agree with Danielle that there was a high level of energy in the paintings. I set my suitcase down, but before I could open it, heard a light knock. I opened the door and looked into the pleasant face of Danielle Thénardier.

She smiled. "The telephone number belongs to a gentleman named Rene Gagnon. His recording device told me he was out but he could be found at The Place Bistro across the street from the Place Metro music venue. During the festival there are five music venues in the city where musicians perform from noon to midnight every day of the week."

"Sounds interesting. Are we far from there?"

"No. At present we are less than a kilometer from Porte St. Jean. Did that information help you?"

"And what does Porte St. Jean mean?"

"Ah! Porte St. Jean is one of the five gates leading into the walled city."

I smiled. "Thank you, Danielle. You have done a marvelous job decorating my room, and after a short nap, perhaps you can give me directions to Porte St. Jean?"

"Pinky, I will do better than that. We will walk there together."

SIXTEEN

Bear—Los Angeles

"So what did your lord and master tell you to do?"

"Come on, Flo, I'm not Pinky's slave. He pays me damn good money."

Flo rolled her eyes and snorted. "So what are you being paid good money to do?"

"All we've got to do is come up with the goods to prove Harold Haffner killed Brady Blackstone and turn him over to Willow."

"What's that got to do with Betty-the-blonde? How does she figure in this?"

"I don't know, but Pinky told me that I can include her with Harold Haffner if I want to."

"Bear, I don't like this. What if they didn't do it?"

"Babe, that's Willow's problem, not ours."

"Okay," Flo sighed. "But before we do that, I need to get out of my bathing suit, and then we have to stop by my house."

Flo went into the bathroom to change and I knew what that meant. Any time she took her clothes off in another room meant she was still a little pissed off at me. I grabbed the TV remote and turned on the Red Sox game. It was over. Boston won and I'd missed it. I surfed past Oprah to a show with a good-looking broad who was lying on a bed crying into a pillow. Then a guy walked close to the bed, sat down next to the broad and started to stroke her hair. I jumped when Flo tapped me on my shoulder.

"I need to call my real estate guy first."

"Whatever."

Flo dialed a number and said, "Harry, we're heading to my place. We'll be there in about thirty minutes."

She said, "Let's go."

I wanted to stick around to find out what the guy was going to say next to the broad, but I could tell that Flo was still a little pissed off. When she got that way, I knew it was time to turn the TV off.

With Flo barking directions, we pulled up in front of her place inside of twenty minutes. I glanced across the street at the house I had broken into last year. Over the last twelve months, the neighborhood had slipped further downhill. Flo's house looked like it had been redone in the last five years, but all the other places had missed a paintbrush for at least ten years. I didn't know what Flo hoped to get for this dump, but in this neighborhood it wouldn't be much.

Before we got out of my truck, a black Mercedes pulled up. A guy about fifty jumped out. He had a crew cut and had spent a lot of hours pumping iron. The dude's pecks damn near popped the buttons off his white shirt.

He grabbed Flo and gave her a big squeeze. "Flo, long time no see. Your tan looks perfect."

"Thanks, Harry. There's a lot of sunshine in Carson City."

I slammed my truck door real hard.

Flo batted her eyes at the dude like he was a big-time movie star or something. "The name of the guy that just got out of the truck is Bear. We're in LA investigating a murder, and—"

I interrupted, "Flo, I don't think we should be talking about why we're here with every Tom, Dick, and you know who. Our investigative shit is confidential."

"Come on, Bear. I don't see what harm could come—"

I flashed her my nastiest clam-up stare. "I thought you wanted to talk over listing your house with this dork, right?"

Flo rolled her eyes. "Right. Harry, let's go inside."

The muscle-bound dude wandered around the house measuring the rooms and saying, "Oh, this is a nice kitchen . . . I like the picture window . . . This is a really nice place," but I think he was saying all that crap for me because I would have bet a hundred bucks that this wasn't the first time he'd scoped the place out, especially Flo's bedroom.

Fake tour over, he handed Flo a stack of papers.

She sat down and signed her name a bunch of times.

Harry said, "I think that does it. Of course, you realize that the market is very slow, so don't expect anything to happen immediately."

Flo said, "I understand. Will I need to come back to LA when we get a sale?"

"No, I can take care of everything. Okay, I have to head back to my office but I thought we could go out to dinner later and include Mr. Bear of course to celebrate listing your home."

I growled, "Thanks, but I've already made a dinner reservation. Once you figure out how to sell this dump, just send Flo the check care of my place in Carson City."

Fifteen minutes later we were heading west on Wilshire Boulevard to the address of Harold Haffner's office.

Flo said, "Did you really make dinner reservations?"

"Nope."

"You might have acted in a more civil manner toward Harry."

I knew that, but now that bastard knew I was the new captain of Flo's ship.

She said, "And what are we doing that's so confidential that I can't tell an old friend?"

"Flo, we're looking for 8577 Wilshire. Give me a shout when you spot that address."

"Damn it, Bear. You can be so . . . slow down, we just passed 8555. There it is, turn into the next driveway."

I pulled in and parked under a big tree covered with pretty purple flowers. From the truck cab, I saw the entrance to a four-story building where, according to a sign, a pot full of doctors, dentists, lawyers and CPA's had office space. We sat for a minute and watched two men enter.

"Okay, Bear, we're here. Now what do you plan on doing?"

Damn, I wish she would clam-up for a few minutes. "I'm watching."

"Watching for what?"

"Everything and anything."

"And how long do you plan on watching whatever it is you are watching?"

"I don't know."

Flo shook her head. "Bear, there are times when I wonder why I stay with you." She sat back, pulled out the stack of paperwork she had signed at her place and started to read.

I watched the entrance while an hour passed.

Flo said, "I have to pee."

"Good. Let's go in."

"Jesus, were we waiting all this time for me to say I had to pee?"

"Nope."

We got out and walked into the building. There was a lobby with fancy, dark marble floors, two elevators, and a sign that told me the floor where Harold Haffner's offices were located. His place was suite 330. I pushed the elevator button.

Flo said, "Bear, I need to use the bathroom."

"I know that. I'll bet there's a perfect one located on the third floor."

"But I can see a door marked Ladies at the far end of the lobby."

"I know that, but I heard the one on the third floor is even better."

"If I pee in my pants . . . "

The elevator door opened. A woman got out and we got in. I pushed three and in a few seconds the door opened to a large hallway. Directly across from the elevator were men's and women's bathrooms. Flo ran across the hall while I glanced left and right.

I turned left, got lucky, and found Haffner's office on the first try. Down the hall there were four offices tucked behind glass walls, and Harold's was the smallest of the bunch. Gold letters on the glass door said, Harold Haffner, Business Services.

Behind the glass sat an old broad at a receptionist's desk. She didn't look very busy. I watched her knit a light blue sweater while Flo answered her call of nature, and during that time, Harold's phone never rang, and the broad never looked up from needles and yarn.

Flo walked up behind me and said, "So now what?"

I glanced at my watch. "It's almost five. Let's go back to the truck."

"Good, I'm getting hungry."

"We'll do that later. I need to nose around a little more."

After we got in my truck, Flo didn't say anything, but I could tell that she wasn't happy. I watched the entrance to the building.

"I told you I'm starving." Flo whined. "How much longer are we going to sit in this damned parking lot?"

"I don't know. Here's a half a buck. Go buy yourself a paper. I've heard the LA Times is a good one."

Flo sat back, folded her arms across her boobs and pasted on her classic pout.

A few minutes after five the building started to empty out. At ten after, the knitter of ther blue sweater walked out the door. I said, "You sit tight. I'll be back in a couple of minutes."

"Whatever."

I had to wait while the elevators dumped their loads, and I hit the third floor around twenty after five. I walked the hall from end to end. All the offices, including Haffner's, looked empty. I went back to Haffner's and pushed on the door. It was locked.

I returned to the truck.

Flo said, "Now can we eat?"

"Not yet." I looked at my watch. "My guess is his shift won't start until six."

"Stop talking in riddles. Whose shift? Why can't we go eat something?"

109

During an investigation there were times when I really needed Flo, and this was one of those times—otherwise I would have left her by the pool. "Look, Babe, we've got to come up with some incarcerating evidence on Haffner, right?"

She nodded. "I think you meant to say incriminating, but go on."

"Okay. Each one of us has a job here. We need to get inside his office. My job is to get us in. Once we're inside, you can do your thing with his computer system. That's why we have to wait until the first shift of watchmen comes on duty. I have to see what they do and how they do it. Understand?"

"I don't know. This whole operation sounds highly illegal to me."

"But we're not stealing anything. All we need to do is figure out if this guy is hiding something in his office we could use to make him look guilty of Brady's murder."

Flo glared at me. "Bear, that still doesn't sound legal."

"Babe, it's not our job to decide if the guy really did the murder. All we have to do is come up with something that makes him look guilty."

"But what if Haffner is put on trial for Brady's murder? And what if Willow convicts him? And he gets the needle? My God, what if he didn't do it? I couldn't live with—"

"Got to go now. There's the watchman."

I jumped out of my truck and watched a man who was almost as round as he was tall get out of his car and waddle into the building.

I counted to twenty and followed him. When I walked through the main door I heard him say, "Hey, fellow. These offices are closed for the night."

"Damn, I need to talk with my business advisor on the third floor. The IRS is going to throw the book at me and—"

"Sorry, but you'll have to come back tomorrow."

"Shit! Say, is there any chance your guard service is hiring? With my tax problems, I'll have to work at least two jobs to make ends meet."

"I don't know. Give them a call. Their number is in the book."

I said, "Looks like you've got a cool job here. Do you have to walk around all night, or do you just sit here?"

"Oh, I'll move around, but my instructions tie me to the lobby until the FedEx man makes his last delivery at eight."

"Worked here long?"

"Nope. Tonight's my third night. I'm covering for the regular guy who's got a couple of weeks off."

"Wow. You get a paid vacation too?"

"Yup. One week after the first year and two weeks after three years."

"Like I said before, you guys got a cool job." I turned to leave, stopped at the main entrance door, and waved. "Thanks for everything."

Without looking up, the guard said, "No problem."

I returned to the truck and climbed in.

Flo said, "It's about time. I saw a pizza place about a block away. Can we eat there? I'm starving."

"Nope. Tonight we're going to have a steak. But tomorrow we'll scarf down a fresh, hot pizza delivered by my favorite female."

"Huh? I don't understand."

"Don't worry Babe, you will."

SEVENTEEN

Bear—Los Angeles

The following day turned out to be warm and sunny all mixed together with LA's usual crappy air. We woke up late, fooled around for a while, and then ate a big breakfast. Flo spent the early afternoon by the pool while I watched my Red Sox beat the crap out of the damn Yankee's by the lopsided score of ten to three.

Around four forty-five, we pulled into the lot at 8577, and parked under the same tree with the pretty flowers.
I said, "Do you think this kind of tree would grow in Carson City?"

"A Jacaranda? I hope not. That kind of tree makes a big mess. We used to have one in front of my house and I had a man take it out because of the flowers that fall all over the ground, followed by the green seedpods. Then, a few months later, the—"

"I think the flowers are pretty."

"I'll give you that, but not pretty enough for the mess they make. Now stop with all the tree talk and tell me why we are parked here again."

"Okay. The night guard is new and he couldn't pick Haffner out of a line up if he was the only human with a bunch of penguins. I'm going in and talk with the gal behind the desk in Haffner's office. I'll come up with something that lets me put a strip of tape over the door latch, so when she goes home, I'll be able to get back into the office. The guard knows my face, but he doesn't know yours, so at six you're going to make a pizza delivery to your boss, Mr. Haffner, who's in his office working late. Got it so far?"

"I think so."

"Now, if the guard calls Haffner to check out your story, I'll be there to answer the phone. Once we're in Haffner's office, we can eat the pizza while you check out Haffner's computer system. Babe, with any luck, we'll come up with the evidence that will spring Jack Spurlock from the slam. We can go back home and you can work on your tan until winter comes."

"And all I have to do is buy a pizza and then tell a little fib to the guard?"

"Yup. And you can tell him there might be a piece of pizza left over for him. Find out where the guard's break room is and offer to meet him there. That will give me the chance to get out of the building without being seen."

"Okay, I guess that doesn't sound too dishonest."

"Now, like they say in those cool movies—we need to synchronize our watches."

Flo frowned. "But I didn't bring a watch."

Shit. I hadn't thought about that! "Here, take mine. At five-thirty, drive to the pizza parlor and buy a large sausage and olive with anchovies. By the time you get back, I'll be inside of Haffner's office."

"But I don't like anchovies."

Damn! "Okay, tell them to put anchovies on my half."

"I can live with that. Just make sure none of those little fish swim onto my half. I hate those salty little things."

As I entered the building, I checked the clock on the wall in the lobby. It showed ten minutes to five. When I walked into Haffner's office, the broad behind the desk jumped, like people didn't do that very often.

She was in her mid-sixties, seventies, or more. Her hair, a weird rusty color, was pulled straight back, like she hoped the harder she pulled, the less wrinkles would show on her face.

"May I help you?" she said with a smile that made me think she had a bad gas pain in her gut.

I said, "Is Mr. Haffner in?"

"Do you have an appointment?"

"Nope."

"I'm sorry, but Mr. Haffner's contemplating retirement, and he's not taking any new clients."

"But what am I going to do? I need help with my business and this Haffner dude was recommended to me"

"I'm sorry, Mr. . . .?"

"Delmont."

"What exactly is your business problem?"

"Uh . . . I'm starting a new business and need some cool advice."

"Check the Yellow Pages under Business Consultants."

"Thanks"

I turned, but before I started for the door, I reached into my jacket, grabbed my cell phone, and pushed the call button. By the time I reached the door, the rusty-haired broad's phone rang.

When she ducked her head to grab the phone, I made my move and slapped a piece of duct tape across the door latch. Then I hit the end-call button.

"Nobody there." She slammed the phone down, checked the clock, and stuffed her knitting into a bag.

I said, "Ma'am, if you're ready to leave, I'd be pleased to escort you to the elevator."

"Why, Mr. Delmont, that would be most kind of you."

I stood and held the door open for her while she set the lock. After she walked through I followed and closed the door. Then, blocking her direct line of sight, I jammed my toe against the door, and tried to open it. The door didn't budge.

I said, "Can't be too careful."

"You are so correct, Mr. Delmont. You'd never know what madness lurks around the dark corners of this city. And the rabble that congregates in the parking lot during the weekends caused me much grief a few years ago when Mr. Haffner required me to work overtime."

"I can only imagine." I hustled her butt toward the elevator and pushed the down button.

"Mr. Delmont, when I was a little girl my mother informed me that one day I would meet a man like you—a gentleman caller—a man who would hold the door for a lady—a gentleman who would summon the elevator."

"Huh."

"I know it is too late to tell my mother, God rest her soul, but she was correct. I think I have found that man. Will you—"

The elevator door opened and I shoved the broad with the rusty, pulled-back hair inside. "Excuse me Ma'am, but I have an appointment to see a man about a horse."

I waved and waited for the damn door to slide shut.

She waved back.

I kept flapping my arm and the broad started to push her way out, but she didn't make it as the elevator door finally closed.

I ran back to Haffner's office, opened the door, and pulled the tape off the latch.

Before anyone walked past the glass wall separating me from the hall, I ducked into Haffner's inner office.

The room was pretty cool with dark paneled walls and bookcases full of books. There were books about the stock market, books about economics, blue covered books, red covered books. Sitting on a shelf behind a giant desk was a computer terminal.

Along the wall, to the right of the desk, was a door that opened to a toilet and sink.

I sat down in Haffner's soft leather chair and opened the drawers. There were a few files and paperwork, but nothing that I could make into a motive for whacking Blackstone.

Next I checked the trashcan. Empty.

Then I noticed the ash. It looked like someone had burned some paper inside the large ashtray. On the edge of the ashtray lay a burned out match. I tried to lift the ash up and it fell apart.

Did Haffner want to destroy some evidence? Something he wanted to destroy forever?

115

I got up and was tapping the wall panels, trying to find a hidden safe when the phone rang.

"Mr. Haffner?"

"Yes."

"This is Mike in the lobby. I'm the night security man. There is a lady in the lobby who claims to be your secretary. She is carrying a large box. I checked the box and inside was a large sausage and olive pizza with anchovies. Will you give me the okay to send her up?"

"Yes."

A couple of minutes later I let Flo into Haffner's outer office.

I said, "Any trouble?"

Flo shook her head. "He wanted to come with me, to be sure I found my way. I think he's hot after my body, so I reminded him that I worked here and knew where my office was. Then I fed him the line that Mr. Haffner pulled these late-nighters every time the S & P 500 hit a new high."

I didn't know what the hell she was talking about, but every once in a while Flo would pop up with something that would remind me that she was a lot more than a great rack.

We walked into Haffner's inner office. She set the pizza down on Haffner's desk and checked out the digs. "Looks very prosperous! Just the way I'd want my business advisor's office to look."

"That's what I thought before I found the ashes."

"What do you mean?"

"It looks like Haffner burned a piece of paper in the ash tray."

Flo said, "No cigarette butts. Just paper ash?"

"Yup."

"Jesus, maybe this Haffner was really trying to hide something. Let's go to work."

Flo sat down, turned on the computer, and stared at the screen.

I don't like computers because I can't figure out how those damn digit things move around inside that plastic box. Pinky calls it one of my many weaknesses. But Flo understands those digit things. In fact, she knows a lot more about computers than Pinky.

She said, "There are a bunch of files with names."

Oh boy. "Is Brady Blackstone's name on one of them?"

"No, these look like business names."

"Is there one for the Brady Blackstone Tour?"

Flo pushed the button on that mousy thing a couple of times. "No, and that's strange. You told me that Haffner is the tour controller."

"Keep looking, babe. I'm going to grab a piece of pizza."

Flo jumped up. "Not without me, buster. I'm starving."

We sucked up pieces of that pizza like it was the last food on earth. We were down to the last two pieces when Flo screamed, "Don't eat those. I promised the guard some."

Damn. "Right."

Flo checked her hands. "Is there a place where I can wash off this grease?"

I pointed. "On the other side of that door."

While Flo washed up, I pulled out all the desk drawers to check the underside of each drawer. Then I got on all fours and crawled under the desk.

"What the hell are you doing down there?"

"Just nosing around."

Then I spotted a shiny thing under the desk. "Hey, there's something taped up here."

Suddenly, there was a knock on the door. I froze.

She whispered. "Now what do we do?"

I whispered back. "I can't get out! Answer the door, see what happens, but don't let anyone in."

I heard my knees crack against the hard plastic mat covering the rug.

Flo said, "Hello again."

"Just thought I'd better stop by to make sure everything was okay."

"Everything is fine."

I felt a sharp pain in my right shoulder and shifted a little. The desk made a loud creaking noise.

There was a pause and the rent-a-cop said, "What was that?"

Flo said, "What?"

There was a pause. "I don't know. Where's Mr. Haffner?"

"Not that it's any of your beeswax, but he's in the bathroom."

"What's he doing?"

"What everybody does when you sit on the john."

"Oh. My name's Mike. What's yours?"

"Flo."

Sweat dripped off my forehead onto my hands and the plastic mat. I'm a big dude and couldn't remember the last time I spent more than five seconds on my hands and knees. If that damn guard didn't leave soon I was going to lose it.

"Flo, I may look a little old, but I'm only fifty-five. I know I need to lose a few pounds so I bought a treadmill off eBay for only ninety-four bucks. The damn thing was worth at least a hundred and ten. You can get some great deals on eBay, but you have to be careful. Anyway, working these weird hours doesn't give me the opportunity to meet a lot of women —"

"Mike, I'm very flattered, but I'm married."

"No shit! I'm sorry I hit on you, but you weren't wearing a ring, and I thought—"

"I understand. Anything else?"

"No. Got to be on my way."

Thank God. My knees were on fire, my shoulder felt like someone had buried an ice pick in it up to the handle, and my head was spinning so fast that I was about to pass out.

"Mike, hold on. Here's a piece of pizza."

There was a long pause, then the guard said, "Flo, if you ever decide to leave your husband, you can reach me through the We-Never-Sleep-Agency."

"Good bye, Mike."

The second I heard the door close I scooted out from underneath the desk, flopped onto my back and stared at the ceiling. It wasn't just my knees and shoulder; I don't like being trapped in dark, tight places.

Flo said, "Are you okay?"

My breathing was almost back to normal. "Yup."

"Boy, that was close. Show me what you found."

I handed her a key.

Flo checked the key, turning it over and over. "A key with a tag that shows the number 14. That's just what we needed. A key without a lock."

"But look at the label on the key, MASTER."

Flo shook her head and said, "So?"

She turned me on every time she flipped her hair like that but I was still out of it from the desk thing. "All we've got to do is find the matching MASTER Padlock."

"Oh sure, I'm sure there aren't more than a million MASTER Padlocks floating around LA. And don't forget the rest of the world. That would make finding it around one in a billion."

I dropped the key into my pocket. "Hey, I think it's a clue. Why would Haffner tape a key under his desk if it wasn't important?"

"I can't answer that question. I'd better get back on the computer. We can't spend the night here." She fiddled around for a few minutes. "Can you believe that this guy has two solitaire games that I don't have?"

"Come on, Flo. You've got work to do."

"I know that," she snapped, "Have you considered what will happen when Haffner looks for that key?"

Damn, I hadn't thought about that. "I'd better make a copy."

"When?"

"Right now I guess." I grabbed a phone book and found a guy who made keys about two blocks away. I called him and he told me that he'd be open for another thirty minutes. "Babe, I'll need you to run interference so I can get out of this place."

Flo stopped moving the mouse and looked up from the screen. "Run what?"

"You need to lead the way into the downstairs lobby. If the coast is clear, I'll follow. If not, call my cell phone. You don't have to say anything. If I get a ring, I'll know that fat guy is in my way."

Flo frowned, and opened her purse. "I don't know how I get talked into these wild schemes of yours."

"Got my number keyed in?" She nodded. "Once I'm out of the building, head back and finish up the computer crap." This was the next time that guy in the movies would say—synchronize your watches—but Flo had my watch, so that wouldn't work. "Okay, let's go."

I got outside without a hitch and inside of fifteen minutes I had the duplicate in my pocket and was peering around the corner of the front door. The fat guy was propped up in a chair, reading a magazine. I keyed in Flo's cell phone number. When she answered, I said, "Babe, you've got to come downstairs and get this dude out of the lobby."

"And just how do I accomplish that?"

I was afraid that she'd ask me that. "I don't know. You'll think of something."

"Okay, but if he tries to brush any part of his fat, sweaty body against me, I swear I'll deck him."

God help the poor bastard if he accidentally tripped. I waited and in a couple of minutes the elevator door opened. I watched Flo walk into the lobby. She was smiling, and carrying the pizza box in front of her. Now I was glad that Flo hadn't let me eat that last piece. The dude dropped his magazine and jumped off his chair, well he jumped as good as he could, and the two walked through a door behind the chair. I ran through the lobby, into an elevator, and was under the desk, on my hands and knees, taping the original key back to the wood when Flo walked into Haffner's office.

She said, "Are we done yet? I'm tired, and the Sopranos are on HBO in forty-five minutes."

120

I backed out of the wooden tunnel and stood up. "I'm finished. How about you?"

"Don't push me. I'll be ready as soon as I download those two solitaire games."

EIGHTEEN

Pinky—Quebec City

A gentle knocking sound worked its way through my fog of sleep followed by Danielle's muffled voice. "Wake up, Monsieur Pinky."

I opened my eyes, rolled off the bed and stood for a moment on wobbly legs. I'm a man who prides himself on his physical condition. I work out. I don't drink more than I should, except on that rare, celebratory occasion. However, as I have aged, I have noticed that it takes me longer and longer to recover from protracted airline flights. I made a mental note to use Bear on future investigations if the flight time surpasses three hours.

"I am awake, Danielle. Give me a few minutes to freshen up and I'll meet you in the lobby."

I heard a low chuckle from the other side of the door. "In my opinion, the man I talked with earlier was more than fresh, but as you requested, I will wait for you at my desk."

A splash of cold water, a comb through my hair, a clean shirt, and I stood by Danielle's side in no less than three minutes.

She smiled. "Pinky, you look marvelous. Are you ready?"

I gazed at my hostess. During my short rest, an amazing transformation had taken place. She had changed into a fashionable skirt and sweater combination. Her pretty face looked a good ten years younger. I kissed her hand and said, "My destiny is in your hands. Lead the way."

She opened the door and we stepped through. I had not reached the sidewalk when a man crashed into both of us. Somehow Danielle regained her balance, but I hit the cobblestone street, so to speak.

"What the hell . . . "

Danielle and the man both helped me to my feet. Danielle said, "Pinky, I am so sorry, but that was my fault. During the festival there are street performers everywhere and I forgot about the mime troupe working outside my hotel's entrance."

I concentrated on my attacker and he did wear the required mime outfit, black pants, striped shirt, and a black bowler hat with a red carnation. The mime pulled out a small broom and pretended to brush me off. That was when I noticed the laughter from the crowd who had been watching the mime's every move.

The mime removed his hat, and with a large flourish, made a bowing gesture to me, and then to the audience.

I assumed that since he was a mime, that bow was the closest thing to an apology I was going to receive.

I flexed my fingers and shifted my shoulders. "I do not seem to have any broken bones. Let us move on."

Danielle said, "How gracious of you, Pinky. I was concerned that as a lawyer, you might be more of a litigious type. Let's walk around the corner and I'll buy you a glass of wine."

For the first time, I looked down the street and saw a dozen sidewalk cafes. "Sounds like a wonderful idea. What about that one across the street?" I pointed at a place that had a dozen tables under a blue awning. A low fence separated the sidewalk from the tables. Hanging on the fence were boxes brimming with bright flowers. Most of the tables were filled with people laughing, eating and drinking.

"Do you really mean that one?" she asked.

"Yes, it looks very inviting to me."

She snorted, "Trust me, it is a tourist trap." She grabbed my arm and after walking about thirty steps she steered me down a few stairs. "No, we will go in here."

There were no sidewalk tables, no flowers, just a single, dark room. While my eyes adjusted from the bright outside, Danielle pushed me toward an empty table. A large man wearing an apron rushed up and gave Danielle a quick kiss on both cheeks. "Bonjour, Danielle."

"Bonjour, Anthony. I would like you to meet Mr. Delmont. He is from America and I told him that you have the freshest baguettes, the finest cheese, and the top vin de maison in Quebec, if not the whole world."

"Merci. Un litre?"

"No, un demi s'il vous plaît."

"Merci."

In a flash Anthony delivered two glasses and a half-liter carafe that was nearly overflowing with red wine.

She said, "I'm sorry, Pinky. I should have asked if you like wine."

"Danielle, I pride myself on owning the best wine cellar in Nevada. I have the finest wines from California, France, and Italy. If a wine is worth drinking, I have a case or two in my cellar. However, based on past experience, I tend to steer away from the house wines, as they are generally inferior to bottled wines."

She poured two glasses. "I think you are in for a shock."

We both took sips—her's was generous—mine was very timorous.

She smacked her lips. "This is good, no?"

My God, this woman knew her wine. "Danielle, this is unbelievable. My guess is a blend of cabernet and merlot, with just a hint of cab franc. Where does the proprietor get it?"

"His brother owns a small vineyard and winery in Bordeaux. The brother makes the wine, selling most of it through his chateau in Bordeaux. The rest he puts into barrels and ships the lot to this restaurant."

A basket filled with bread and bowl of soft white cheese was delivered. We each took a piece and spread on some of the cheese. The combination was so great that I nearly inhaled my morsel. I lifted the breadbasket and offered Danielle more. She waved her hand and said, "Go ahead, I'm not that hungry."

I am ashamed to admit that I ate all but two pieces of the bread. After our plates were empty, we sipped the rest of the wine. When I had drained the last drop from my glass, I said, "We must come here again. The bread and cheese were prefect and the house wine was fabulous."

"I promise we'll come back. Now we must find Mr. Gagnon at the Place Metro."

I picked up the check. The bread, cheese and half-liter came to $7.50, and that was Canadian! That wine alone, in a decent New York restaurant, would have run at least seventy-five dollars for a bottle. I slipped $10 Canadian under the check and we headed toward the exit. As I pushed the door open, Danielle chuckled, "Watch out for the street performers."

The afternoon sun was warm. The sky was a brilliant blue. The narrow streets were curb to curb with people, and performers, and everyone seemed to be in a festive mood. Quebec City was like walking the back streets of Paris with a county fair thrown in for good measure.

Before we reached Porte St. Jean, we stopped along the way to watch a dog show, two jugglers, a saxophone band consisting of a dozen instruments, and a second mime troupe.

A half a block from the Porte, I heard the faint sounds of folk music coming from the other side of the gray city wall. Once we cleared the Porte, music filled the air. I stopped and took in the scene. On my left was a large stage that backed up to the city wall. In front of the stage moved a mass of people who were dancing and clapping in time with a female performer who was singing something in French.

Danielle said, "Pinky, do you recognize the song?"

"No, but it is a catchy tune."

"It is a popular folk song from Cape Breton."

My expression must have looked puzzled because she went on.

"At one time, Cape Breton was settled by the French and they called their land Acadia. When Great Britain defeated the French, the British renamed the area Nova Scotia. The song is about Le Grand Dérangement. In 1755 the British forcibly moved most of the Acadians from Nova Scotia. Today, what they did we would call ethnic cleansing."

"Where did the Acadian's go?"

"To British prisons, Europe, and a state in your country called Louisiana where the Acadian's became know as Cajuns."

I glanced at the audience and many of the older ones looked to be on the verge of tears.

"But more than two hundred years have passed and yet the words of the song still moves the people?"

"Yes."

I detected a catch in Danielle' s voice, as if she were also moved.

She took my hand in hers. "That was a bad time to be French."

The singer finished the song. The crowd clapped wildly.

I was less than comfortable with Danielle's uncalled for invasion of my personal space, so I took the opportunity to pull my hand away to join in the applause. The performers on stage started to pack up their instruments, and the audience began to disperse.

I said, "This looks like an opportune moment to change the subject. Where is the Place Metro Bistro?"

A big smile replaced Danielle's faraway expression. "Directly behind us. I hope you know what Monsieur Gagnon looks like because—"

I turned and heard Lucinda Blackstone's voice cut through the ambient din that filled the air. "My God, it's Pinky Delmont! Shit, did I forget to tell you that I was leaving Nevada?"

I glanced toward the sidewalk tables and spotted Lucinda sitting with a man. On their table sat a carafe of red wine and two glasses. The man held a pen in his hand and he was fiddling with a tape recorder.

As we approached, Lucinda nodded toward her companion. "Pinky, have you met Rene Gagnon?"

"No, I have not had the pleasure."

Gagnon set down his pen and sighed, as if the burden of common courtesy ranked low on his list of important things to do at the moment. He dipped his head slightly, barely made eye contact, and said, "Monsieur Delmont."

Two can play at that game. Without offering my hand, I responded in kind and said, "Mister Gagnon."

Lucinda said, "And is this your latest paramour?"

I gritted my teeth. Lucinda had never shown much class, but today I felt she had reached a new low. "I would like to introduce you both to Danielle Thénardier. She has agreed to work as my interpreter during my stay in Quebec City."

Lucinda looked Danielle up and down. "How convenient for you both."

I ignored her insinuation and pressed forward. "Lucinda, what is going on?"

She sat back, poured some wine into her glass, and said, "After you left my hotel room I drove to the Carson City jail." She set the carafe down. "I felt the need to talk—"

I interrupted. "Excuse me, Lucinda." I did not like being played the fool, and it was obvious to everyone that Lucinda was not going to extend common courtesy toward Danielle and myself by offering wine or a seat at her table. I motioned to a waiter.

He jumped to attention.

Danielle looked at me.

I nodded.

She said to the waiter, "Une bouteille de votre vin rouge plus fin."

I pulled two chairs from an adjoining table, one for Danielle, and after she sat down, I did the same. "I apologize for the interruption, Lucinda. Please conclude your trivial story."

"You're a little prick, Pinky."

"Everyone is entitled to their opinion, but please remember that your size evaluation is not based on fact." I shifted my attention toward Rene Gagnon. "Mister Gagnon, are you enjoying the music?"

He looked at me and frowned. "I am not here to enjoy anything, Monsieur Delmont. I am working—to discover new talent."

I said, "Is this where you first discovered Brady Blackstone?"

"Yes, and last year, Kyle Roubidoux. Now, if you'll excuse me, I have work to do."

The waiter appeared and opened our bottle of wine. He poured some into a glass for Danielle and myself, and then glanced at me to ask if he should pour some of my wine into Rene's empty glass. I shook my head. He set the bottle down and left.

I said, "Excuse me, Lucinda, are you ever going to complete your story?"

She said, "First, before I forget, you're fired."

I took a sip of my wine. It was a very nice Bordeaux, not as good as the house wine I had sipped earlier, but I was positive that my wine was better than the swill that Lucinda and Rene were drinking. "Lucinda, you have the right to fire me at any time. However, if you think dismissing me will allow you to back out of our agreement, you are grievously mistaken. We have a verbal contract that you will pay me one million, nine hundred thousand dollars once I turn over a viable suspect to the Carson City District Attorney—someone who would replace your lover, Jack Spurlock, who is presently confined in the Carson City jail awaiting trial for first-degree murder."

"I know all that, but a verbal contract is just your word against mine."

I took a sip of wine. "Who convinced you to change your mind?"

"Jack Spurlock, for one. When we last talked I realized that I didn't love him anymore."

"Poor Jack. Do you still think he is innocent?"

"I don't care. Didn't you hear what I just told you? I don't love him anymore."

As an attorney, I try to remain above the emotional ups and downs exhibited by my clients. That said, I could not recall ever having been involved with a more fickle female. "And my dear Lucinda, our contract is not just a case of your word against mine. There are those occasions when I take precautions for circumstances such as this." I reached into my pocket and pulled out a digital recorder. "Would you care to listen?"

Both Danielle and Gagnon leaned closer.

We all heard Lucinda's voice say, *"Pinky, are you a gambling man?"*

"Occasionally, but I limit my madness to a few rolls of the dice at a local casino in Carson City. Why?"

"I'll make you an offer. You get Jack released from jail inside of two weeks and I'll double your five hundred thousand retainer to a cool million."

"And what happens if I fail?"

"It's a simple double or nothing bet."

"I am afraid that my expenses, and my common sense, will not allow me to accept your bet. However, I am willing to make you a counter offer. Tear up your check, and make me a new one for one hundred thousand dollars. That money is not refundable. When I come up with a viable suspect, a man or woman that the District Attorney agrees murdered Brady Blackstone you will owe me two million dollars."

"Pinky, you have balls. Perhaps my sources had underrated you, but no matter, I accept. I will give you a check for one hundred thousand dollars today, and a million, nine hundred thousand dollars once you get Jack out of jail."

Lucinda tried to grab the recorder, but I had anticipated her move.

"Pinky, that recording won't hold up in court."

"Perhaps, but I do believe the legal case has gone above a he said, she said situation. Now, if you will excuse me, I have some important work to complete. Mister Gagnon, I flew thousands of miles to talk with you concerning your business relationship with Brady Blackstone."

He checked a printed listing that had been lying next to his legal pad. "You are fortunate. I'm not interested in the next act. What do you want to know?"

I picked up my bottle of wine, ignored Lucinda and filled Rene's glass. "Let us start at the beginning, back to the first time you saw Brady perform."

"I was sitting at this very bistro, many years ago."

Lucinda said, "Don't forget, I was there too."

Rene sighed. "Yes, Lucinda, you were part of his act. A couple of raw kids from PEI."

I said, "Excuse me, PEI?"

"Prince Edward Island. Most of the people there either grow potatoes or catch lobster, but nearly every man, woman and child on the island sings, or plays an instrument. Brady, come to think of it, that wasn't his name back then. No, his name was Tommy Cassidy. Tommy was a good singer, weak with the guitar, but there was something different about Tommy. The moment he walked on stage, the eyes of each female at the venue followed his sensual moves. It was as if he was having a sexual experience with every woman in the audience."

Lucinda whined, "I keep reminding you, I was on stage with him. What about me?" She grabbed the carafe and emptied the dregs into her glass.

Rene ignored Lucinda and said. "After Tommy's set was over, I cornered him and asked him if he had a manager."

Lucinda said, "We didn't."

Rene turned toward Lucinda. His gaze measured her for a moment, as if he was looking at a fly struggling to escape his web, and he was a spider trying to decide if he was hungry for dinner. "Yes, Lucinda, at one time you were a part of Tommy Cassidy's act, but that day is long gone, and all the money in the world will never change the fact that you lacked enough talent to make it big. Now, Mr. Delmont, as I was saying, the moment Tommy told me he was without management, I signed him to a contract and took him under my wing."

I said, "And taking him under your wing included changing his name from Tommy Cassidy to Brady Blackstone?"

Rene chuckled. "Changing his name was the easy part. I hired coaches who taught him how to sing correctly—how to play the guitar—how to move around the stage. The only thing I didn't have to coach him on was how to play up to the females in the audience. What I accomplished with Tommy, excuse me, Brady, was a major transformation, not unlike Shaw's Pygmalion. I took a boy out of the kay-lee circuit in PEI, and created a world-class musical icon who earned millions."

I said, "What is the kay-lee circuit?"

"Kay-lee is a Celtic word spelled Ceilidh. In Gaelic, Ceilidh means to visit, so a kay-lee began as an informal gathering in people's homes. Today, on PEI, there's at least one kay-lee show every night of the week, somewhere on the island, where musicians perform for their friends and the tourist trade."

I said, "So singing Celtic music with his family was the training ground that spawned Brady Blackstone?"

"Oui, Monsieur Delmont." Rene glanced at his watch. "Now, according to my schedule, I have but a few minutes before I must concentrate on the next act."

"I have only a few questions left. I understand you had a contract with Brady Blackstone that gave you a very generous twenty-five percent of the tour profits."

Rene glanced at Lucinda and scowled, "I'm sorry, but the details of my contract with Brady are confidential."

"Was your contract open-ended, or was it for a specific period of time?"

Rene sat back, as if he was trying to decide if that section of his contract was open for discussion. "It was open-ended."

I leaned closer. "Was there an escape clause? A way for either of you to terminate the contract?"

"But of course. As an attorney, I'm sure that you're aware that's a standard clause in contracts of this type. Either party could terminate the agreement upon six months notice. Why do you ask?"

"Mister Gagnon, it is my understanding that the six month termination clause would not take effect until the contract had been valid for five years."

Gagnon slammed his fist on the table and glared at Lucinda. "Yes, there was a five year period." He sighed. "I had the right to protect my financial investment. Along with thousands of dollars, I gave years of my life shaping Brady Blackstone into an American icon."

"Two more questions. Did Brady give you six months notice that he wanted to terminate his contract?"

Rene's expression changed from anger to puzzlement. "Are you implying that due to a potential termination of my contract with Brady that I had a hand in his death?"

I said, "Mister Gagnon, we are talking about a financial loss to you of millions in future earnings. People have been known to kill for less."

"Monsieur Delmont, I did not kill Brady."

It was time to turn the screws tighter to see if Gagnon would crack. "My final question. Does your new contract with Kyle Roubidoux include a five year termination clause or did you extended that span to ten years?"

Rene Gagnon gestured toward Lucinda. "I believe you need to direct that question to the new owner of Roubidoux's contract."

I had to admit his revelation caught me off-guard. "But why would you sell Kyle's contract?"

"I have no doubt that Kyle will make a lot of money, but I've worked with the best, and I don't feel like lowering my standards." Then Gagnon stood, picked up his tape recorder and legal pad. "Now if you'll excuse me, I have important work to do. And Monsieur Delmont, I'm sorry that you had to fly all this way to discover that I didn't kill Brady, but I hope you succeed in finding the culprit because, for all his faults, Brady was a performing genius, and trust me, stars of that magnitude are not easy to find."

As Gagnon disappeared into the crowd, Danielle patted my hand. "Pinky, I thought you were magnificent."

Lucinda grabbed my bottle of wine and poured some into her glass. "Magnificent my ass! Pinky's nothing but smoke and mirrors."

Danielle looked at me.

I nodded, "I fear that Lucinda is correct. I took a wild guess on the language in Kyle's contract."

Lucinda swirled her wine. "Not surprising because I'm the only person, outside of Kyle, who possesses a copy of that document."

I said, "Danielle, there are times when my job is similar to playing poker. Once your hand is dealt, and your cards are worthless, you have two choices—throw in your hand, or see if you can win the pot with a bluff. In this case I tried a bluff."

Lucinda laughed. "And Gagnon didn't fall for it."

I ignored her remark and said, "Danielle, I need you to order me another bottle of wine and then leave. Lucinda and I are about to have a private discussion and my needs for a translator have ended."

The perky corners of Danielle's mouth plunged at my abrupt dismissal. "But I thought that we'd—"

I had a feeling that she had read more into our relationship than business. "As I requested, order me a second bottle of wine and return to the hotel."

Danielle pulled out a white hanky and dabbed at her eyes. Then she jumped up, walked to the waiter, said something in his ear, and quickly faded into the crowd.

Lucinda drained her glass. "You could have handled that situation a little more diplomatically."

"You should know me well enough by now to realize that diplomacy is not my style."

"True. So if Rene didn't do it, you're down to Haffner and little old moi."

After I paid the waiter for the wine, I looked into Lucinda's eyes. They had a depleted, worn look, as if she had been awake for twenty-four hours. Her hair bordered on unkempt. It was obvious to me that Lucinda's triumphant return to Quebec City had been less than successful. I filled her glass and said, "We both know you didn't kill your husband. Now sit back, enjoy the music and the wine, and explain to me what possessed you to buy Kyle's contract."

Suddenly tears filled Lucinda's eyes. "I don't know and now that I think about it, the deal was too easy. Rene told me that Kyle had a great future, but then he just told you that Kyle would never be another Brady Blackstone."

"But in your gut you knew that, so why did you buy the contract?"

She downed her wine and set the glass down. "I guess that I'm not ready to give up the fast life I've lead for the last ten years."

My God, she's betting that Kyle will replace Brady! I considered telling her that she was wasting her time and money. However, that would be undiplomatic of me, and I knew how she felt about diplomacy. I backed away and flashed her my winning smile. "My dear, I am sure that your belief in Kyle's musical career will turn into a financially sound investment."

"Thanks." She lifted her glass. "And thanks for the wine. Your bottle is much better than that crap Rene bought." She reached across the table and rubbed the back of my hand. "You know, Pinky, once you get control of that ugly-lawyer side of you, you're not such a bad guy."

NINETEEN

Bear—Los Angeles, California

"How many times do I have to tell you?" Flo punched my arm. "In California it's against the law to talk on a cell phone while you drive a car."

"Look, it's hard enough to drive around this crazy place and hitting me doesn't make it any easier. I've got to call Mabel to get more money."

"You could hand me the phone and I could tell her."

"I don't think that would fly. I work for Pinky. Mabel needs to hear it from me or—"

I heard Mabel's voice come on my cell phone. "Law office of Pinky Delmont. How may I assist you?"

"Mabel, we just left LA and are on our way to Needles. That means I'm going to need another three thousand."

"Bear, I understand that I'm not in a position to criticize, but you have received enough expense money for five trips."

I never was very good at getting tough with women and the gray-haired ones were even harder.

Flo said, "Well, what was her answer?"

I looked at Flo and said, "Hold it down. I'm talking with Mabel."

"I know that. I asked you what did she say after you told you needed three thousand more?"

Driving down Highway 10 at seventy with cars and trucks all around and two females biting your butt was not how I had planned to spend my afternoon. "Flo, shut up. I have to finish with Mabel."

"Don't tell me to shut up!"

"Okay. Be quiet."

"Whatever."

"Bear!" Mabel's voice shot through the cell phone. "I am still waiting for your explanation concerning your excessive expenses."

"Damn it, I'm driving down the highway and making an illegal cell phone call. Don't give me any more crap. Wire my money to The Golden Sun Motel, or we're heading back to Carson City without the name of a suspect, and Pinky will know the reason why."

"I take that to mean you are going to ignore my demand for an explanation?"

"I don't have to explain anything to you."

"I'll have to call Pinky to get his approval first."

Damn she was a pain-in-the-ass broad. "Why didn't you say that five minutes ago?" I punched the off-button on the cell phone and felt like throwing the damned thing out the window.

"So what was her answer?"

"She'll call me back after she talks to Pinky."

"I suppose that's better than nothing."

Flo looked up from the road map. "The traffic sure thins out once you get clear of LA. Do you want to stay on the freeways?"

"Yup. I guess. Why?"

"The map shows a couple of shortcuts, but God knows the condition of the roads. If we stay on the freeways, you'll see a sign about ten miles from here. Follow that road and we'll get off Interstate 10 and onto Interstate 15."

"Got it."

Flo folded the map and said, "We got real lucky at Haffner's office. If I hadn't downloaded those games, I would never have discovered those files Haffner had hidden in the solitaire game folder. That little bit of skullduggery makes me think our bean counter had something to hide."

"But you found them, Babe, just like I thought you would."

"There they were just as big as life. Two files titled Blackstone Tour and Blackstone Tour A."

A big rig started to crowd me out of my lane so I laid on my horn. The bastard steering the tractor must of reached across the cab to give me the finger. I hit the gas pedal, pulled along side, and rolled my window down.

Flo said, "Why are we going so fast?"

I raised my left arm and gave him the same salute. "Just sending that dude a message."

She said, "You're both acting like a couple of spoiled brats driving their kiddy cars down a strip of concrete at eighty miles an hour trying to give each other the finger. By the way, I don't think the driver can see your arm much less your upraised finger. When are you going to grow—"

The trucker blasted his horn three times and drowned out the rest of Flo's bullshit.

"Hey, he cut me off. A professional driver should know better."

I floored the pedal and in a couple of minutes the truck was out of my rear view mirror. "You were telling me about those file things you found on the computer."

"I don't know why I bother."

"Come on, Babe, I have to know what's going on with this Haffner dude."

"Okay. There were two files. The first one looked like a regular spread sheet concerning the tour. You know, expenses for food, motels, that kind of stuff. But the one with the appendage A—"

"I thought an appendage was one of those things next to your stomach they operated on before it popped. I heard you could die if it—"

"That's an appendix. They rush you to the hospital to remove your appendix before it bursts."

"Oh."

"Anyway, in the file with appendage A there was a second spreadsheet, but on this one, all of the costs were a lot lower. For example, the first one averaged $3500 per day for the crew's meals. The A file showed an average of $1650 per day. That alone totals up to $55,500 for one month."

"I still don't get it."

"Okay. Lets say I'm Haffner, and assuming I could work out the details, I'd bill the tour $105,000 in the month of June for meals, but the actual cost only came to $49,500. I would pocket a cool, tax free profit of $55,500 that month."

"Wow! Could he do that with more than the food?"

"I don't think so. It looked like there were only so many discretionary expenses."

"Huh?"

"There are certain items, like salaries and diesel fuel for the big rigs and the busses that are set in stone. You can't screw around with those, but the food and coffee expenses are flexible."

"Hey, during the interviews in Oakland, one of those guys told me that the food used to be great, but lately it had turned to crap."

"See there? That's what I'm talking about. Haffner could show the higher cost on the books, but serve lesser quality food, and pocket the difference."

"Sounds like a good scam but I'll bet he never figured he'd run up against a computer wiz like you."

"Thanks, but what's more important to me now is that I have to pee. Find a place to stop with clean restrooms and make it quick."

I pulled into the first big gas station. Flo jumped out and disappeared into the building with lots of johns and a store that sells big packs of beef jerky, and hot pepper Cheetos.

I leaned forward to change the radio station when I heard a big rig horn give three blasts.

I glanced to my left and there was the same guy who damn near cut me off, and gave me the finger.

He rolled down his window and yelled, "Stay right where you are." He opened the door and jumped onto the asphalt. "Nobody flips me the bone and gets away with it."

I opened my door and stepped out. We were about twenty feet apart. The trucker's eyes got as big as a couple of frying pans. The poor bastard was all hat and no cattle. He was about five-three and weighed maybe a hundred and fifty if he carried a couple of ten-pound lead weights in each pocket.

Looking like a fish flopping on dry land, his mouth grabbed big bites of air. "Sorry, fella. Must have screwed up. The guy that flipped me off was driving a pickup like yours, but the truck was painted a different shade of blue."

The little dude scrambled up the steps into his rig. He fired up the diesel and was back on the highway quicker than Flo could drain a glass of red wine.

"What was that all about?" Flo's voice cut through the air, thick with diesel smoke. "I leave you alone for a minute and you end up in some kind of trouble."

"Come on Flo, cut me a little slack. You burn my ass if I hit 'em, and you burn my ass when I let 'em get away."

TWENTY

Pinky—Quebec City, Canada

Lucinda ceased tickling the back of my hand, and with a calculated move, let her hand drop to my thigh. "Pinky, I know a great place for lunch and after that we could go to my place for ah . . . we could call it an afternoon nightcap."

As she spoke, weariness faded from her eyes. The intimacy of her hand reminded me that a liaison with Lucinda Blackstone had been on my to-do list since we had first met. But at present, I saw no reason to reveal that particular gem of knowledge. "I think not. You see I have a personal commitment back home."

"Don't give me that. Come on, Pinky, God knows neither of us are angels."

"That is true. However, regardless of what you think of my personal—"

My cell phone rang. That was odd because Mabel was the only one that had my number, and I had given her specific instructions not to call me under any circumstances.

I turned. "Please excuse me," and moved to a chair a few feet away from the table.

Across thousands of miles, Mabel's shrill voice pounded at me. "Pinky, that Bear creature called again. He's on his way to Needles and claims he requires another three thousand for expenses."

With Rene and Lucinda out of the picture, my quest for the two million had come down to Bear's pursuit of Harold Haffner. Not a perfect solution to my dilemma, but one that I could live with. However, allowing Mabel to interrupt me against my explicit orders was not an act that I could allow to continue unabated.

140

"Mabel, what possessed you to contradict my explicit command?"

She paused. "I'm sorry I was so abrupt, but I think Bear comes up with these outlandish demands to deliberately upset me."

"Mabel, one of the differences between us is that I classify every word Bear utters as outlandish, and as such, gibberish to be ignored. That said, I am surprised that you continue to let him verbally manipulate you." Lucinda moved to my side, sat down, and her fingertips again started to tickle my thigh. "Now, you have interrupted me in the middle of a delicate negotiation. Why have you called me?"

"I told you, Bear claims he needs three thousand more for expenses. He wants the money wired to The Golden Sun Motel in Needles. Frankly, other than buying more booze and keeping that brazen woman he consorts with, I don't see how he could have spent all the money we've already sent him."

"Mabel—"

"So, in your absence, I made a managerial decision and informed Bear that we wouldn't send him a penny more. I'm sure you recall that I warned you a few days ago that he was taking advantage of you and—"

Mabel's rant was becoming repetitious and her attitude was beginning to get under my skin. I am a patient man, but I do have my limits. I brushed Lucinda's hand away, and said, "Mabel, we have covered this ground before. Immediately wire him the money he requested."

"Pinky, I'm sorry, but I cannot allow you to make that kind of mistake."

I sat straight up. The music, the crowds, even the image of Lucinda's luscious body faded from my consciousness. Did I just hear my employee tell me what she would and would not allow me to do? "Mabel, I understand your concerns, but if you continue to exceed the limits of your position, then as your employer, I am

141

required by Nevada law to inform you that you are skating on thin ice."

"I'm pleased to hear that you get it now. I won't wire Bear what he asked for."

"Mabel, stop babbling on and listen to me very carefully. You will wire Bear the money he requested and you will accomplish that task immediately."

"But he's stealing from you, and—"

"SEND HIM THE MONEY!"

"But—"

I heard Lucinda's chair scrape against the sidewalk. I turned and she was staring at me, and obviously hanging on every word. I could not back down now even if I wanted to.

"Mabel, you have two choices. Send Bear the money he requested or you will seek other employment!"

I heard Mabel suck in air. There was a pause of a few seconds and then she blurted, "You can't fire me, I quit!"

"Then I say good riddance! Mabel, once you clean out your desk, do not forget to take your picture of that ugly feline."

"But I thought you liked Puffy!"

"My dear, just another of your miscalculations. Tomorrow, a messenger will deliver your final check, including all unused vacation and sick pay, to your domicile. Finally, I am sure you would like a letter of recommendation indicating that your tenure with me was acceptable, but alas, that would place me at the same level as your naïveté."

I hit the end-call button on my cell. "As I was saying, Lucinda, regardless of what you think of my personal attributes, I have an ethical benchmark to adhere to when I deal with clients."

"Pinky, what was that all about over the phone?"

"I just fired my secretary. The problem had been brewing for some time, and today, the pot boiled over, so to speak."

"How long had she worked for you?"

I sat back and took a sip of wine. "Five, no, seven years. Now as you were—"

"And you fired her," Lucinda snapped her fingers, "Just that easily?"

"Yes. Now let us return this conversation back to us. If I recall, you had suggested an afternoon encounter at your place."

Lucinda stood up. "I don't think so."

"Sit down, act like an adult and have some more wine."

"I used to think Brady was a cold bastard. Hell, my deceased husband couldn't hold a candle to you. I know we have a deal to find the person that killed my husband, but I've become bored with you and your nasty ways. I'll give you two weeks, no make that one week to find that person."

I jumped up, ready to protest, but before I could say anything, Lucinda said, "I know that's a breech of my verbal contract, but I don't give a damn. Find me another suspect in seven days or my two million dollar offer is off the table. Pinky, I know you can take me to court. I know you can litigate me until the cows come home. But as you also know, I'm a very wealthy woman and I'm betting you'll run out of years before I run out of money. Now, I'm going to leave. Don't try to stop me, and except to give me the name, don't ever attempt to contact me again."

She spun around and I watched Lucinda push her way through the crowd until she disappeared. An afternoon with her would have been fun, but now any thoughts of recreation must take a backseat to the new deadline. Positive that Mabel's threat was hollow I pulled out my cell phone and punched in my office number.

Two rings.

By this time she had usually picked up the phone.

Four rings.

Was it possible that Mabel had misinterpreted my tone?

Six rings.

Well, two can play that game. I ended the call and scrolled through my number list. Finding the desired one, I hit the call button.

"Rapid Replacement Agency. This is Louis Loomer."

"Louis, this is Pinky Delmont."

"Mr. Delmont, it's been awhile. What can I do for you?"

"I need a legal secretary replacement."

"Will that be a temporary, or a permanent position?"

"Considering that I just called my office and no one answered, I would guess a permanent position."

"You're in luck. I just completed an interview with a young woman who would fit your rigid requirements perfectly."

"Louis, I am in a bit of a predicament. At the present, I am calling you from Quebec City in Canada. My secretary just quit and has abandoned my office. As you can see, my situation is not grave, but tenuous. If you have a qualified replacement, someone in which you have the utmost confidence, then send her to my office at once and have her call me on my cell number."

"Mr. Delmont, my candidate will call you in less than fifteen minutes."

"Thank you, Louis. When I return I will contact you to discuss your fee which will include a large bonus for your immediate assistance."

"Thank you, Mr. Delmont."

I sat back, sipped my wine, and enjoyed the music. About the time I was going to check my watch to see if a quarter-hour had passed, my cell phone rang.

"Mr. Delmont?"

"Yes. To whom am I speaking?"

"Jung Lu."

"Is that Chinese?"

"Yes. Will my ethnicity be a problem?"

"No! Of course not. Your name momentarily caught me off guard. Have you arrived at my office?"

"Yes."

"Was anyone there?"

144

"No."

"Good. What should I call you, Jung or Lu?"

"Call me Lu, spelled L-u."

"Fine. From now on you will address me as Pinky. Now pull open the top desk drawer on the secretary's desk."

"Done."

"There should be a key inside."

"There is a key and a can of Lemon Pledge."

"Good. That key fits the front door. I will expect you to lock that door at five, re-open my office tomorrow at nine, and wait for me. Are you with me so far?"

"Yes, I am."

"Lu, at the moment, I am in eastern Canada. I have completed my business here and will leave as soon as possible and I am about to make you a proposal."

"Go ahead. I'm listening."

I liked Lu's ability to make a quick decision. "I will arrive at my office tomorrow afternoon before five. If for any reason I will arrive later than five, I will call and let you know."

"Fine. Is that all?"

"No. We have not discussed your compensation. I will pay you the handsome sum of one thousand dollars to lock up today and cover my office until I arrive tomorrow."

"Pinky, that's most generous. I am to answer the phones and take messages, correct?"

"Lu, there is one final item. Go into my office and get me the phone number for the manager of the Silver State Bank off my Roll-a-Dex."

A moment later she rattled off the number. "Is there anything else I can do?"

"No, that is all I require at the moment. We will meet in person tomorrow."

"Not so fast. Before I accept your proposal, we need to discuss what happens to me after you return."

What ever became of the subservient female? "Lu, I was in such a rush to solve the immediate problem that I had not allowed myself to peer into the future. What exactly did you have in mind my dear?"

"A full-time position that starts at sixty thousand per year with automatic raises of seven percent for the first five years. One-week sick pay. Three weeks vacation after two years. Full medical coverage and a 401K program."

I paused. Without question, the modern day woman knew her worth and then some. "That all sounds fine to me. We can go over the details after I return."

"Fine. I accept your proposal and the full-time job offer. I'm looking forward to meeting you soon."

I sat back and downed the last of the wine. Then I keyed in the bank manager's number.

"Tim Autry."

"Tim, this is Pinky Delmont. I find myself in a rather unusual situation that requires your immediate attention."

"Of course, Pinky. When I think of all the times you have—"

"Tim, I need you to facilitate a wire transfer of three thousand dollars from my regular checking account to Bear Zabarte, care of the Golden Sun Motel, Needles, California."

"Consider it done."

"Also, I just fired Mabel, my secretary. I had granted her the right of entry to my business accounts and—"

"Say no more. From this moment Mabel will not be allowed access to any of your accounts."

"I knew I could count on you, Tim."

I stared at the empty wine glass and keyed in a final number.

"Danielle? I have a radical change in my plans. My work in Quebec City is completed. I need a reservation on the first flight to Reno, Nevada, and a taxi to take me to the airport."

"But, I thought we were going to return to your favorite restaurant for dinner. And before that, the art

146

museum. And Pinky, I cannot allow you to miss the spectacular show at the Bell venue after dinner."

"I am sorry, but my business requires my immediate presence in Carson City."

"Pinky, all work and no play makes for a very dull boy. What happened to your joie de vivre?"

Damn it, why do perfect strangers feel they have the right to challenge my life style? "Danielle, I fear you have overstepped your bounds. The demands on my time have changed. Have a cab waiting for my departure."

I listened to stony silence for a moment, and then Danielle said, "As you requested, Mr. Delmont. I will make your airplane reservation and a cab will be waiting for you at the inn's entrance in ten minutes."

The longer I lived the more I learned that, with the singular exception of my ex-wife, Willow, there seemed to be little room in my life for members of the opposite sex.

The situation concerning Mabel might be considered partially my fault because I allowed a member of my staff to think she was something other than an employee.

Lucinda was the perfect example of why one should never sleep with his source of income.

And Danielle? From our first encounter, she had attempted to push herself at me in a way that was frankly unnerving.

However, I had used the classic surgeon's solution to remove a malignant cancer. Lucinda and Danielle were cut from my life without remorse, but for some reason, a tiny sliver of regret lingered concerning the way I had handled Mabel.

I called my office.

"Law Offices of Pinky Delmont."

"Lu, this is Pinky. Did you say there was a can of Lemon Pledge in the top drawer?"

"Yes. In fact it's sitting in front of me as we speak."

"Fine. I have one additional task for you before you lock up tonight. Polish my desk with the Lemon Pledge before you go home."

"I'll do that. Was that something your past secretary did for you?"

Had Lucinda not been sitting at my side when Mabel challenged my authority I might have acted differently. But Lucinda had been there, and her presence had given me no other choice.

"Yes, she did. I guess . . . I must have become accustomed to the aroma of fresh lemons every morning."

"Any other instructions?"

"Ah . . . no. Good bye, Lu."

When I returned home, I would call Mabel and give her a little pep talk. Perhaps even tell her, that with a touch of contrition on her part, I would consider accepting her back. However, Mabel's return was not my biggest concern. There were millions of dollars at stake, and be it Jung Lu or Mabel, it was time to return home and start cracking the whip.

TWENTY-ONE

Bear—Needles, California

Outside of making Flo happy in bed, I couldn't seem to do a damn thing to keep that woman contented. I busted my ass finding her a nice motel. The joint had a pool with clean water. There was a whole bunch of those fancy couch things and soft blue pads. Jesus, the joint even had a coke machine by the pool.

But did she appreciate all I did for her? Hell no!

While she buzzed around the bathroom setting up her new nest, she cried, "I don't think I'm going to like it in Needles. It's too damn hot!"

I opened the phone book and flipped to the H page.

"Bear, did you see that temperature on that bank sign when we rolled into town?"

H-A-F . . . F-N-E-R . . . Damn! There it was! A phone number and address for Harold Haffner.

"It said a hundred and ten degrees! My God, how hot can a place get before the asphalt on the road starts to melt?"

I wrote down Haffner's address on one of those cool little note pads you find in all the good motels.

"Bear, are you listening to me? Have you heard one word that I said?"

"Yup."

I stuffed the note in my pocket.

"A hundred degrees in the shade is way too hot for a woman with my delicate skin."

"So stay in the room and watch TV."

"But I want to go with you."

Shit! I liked hanging out with Flo—most of the time—especially when she was naked—but I needed to nose around Needles without her ragging at me all the time. I said, "Babe, I have to . . . I'm going to—"

"Damn it, don't beat around the bush—we're adults—if you don't want me to go with you, just say the word!"

"Okay, I need some time to look around with some peace and quiet."

I guess that wasn't the right thing to say 'cause Flo started to pout. Then she made a couple of loud snorts and her nose started to drip. The next thing I knew she was bawling like a three day-old lamb in a late spring snowstorm. I put my arm around her and said, "Hey Babe, I didn't mean I don't want you around. I just thought you'd be more comfortable in the cool motel room than outside in that damn heat. See, I'm going to be sitting in the truck, and it could take hours, and you said it's hotter than hell outside, and I won't have the air on, and—"

"Why didn't you tell me that in the first place? I'll stay in the room, sip a little wine, and catch up on General Hospital."

A couple of minutes later I was tooling down the road alone and looking at an afternoon of peace and quiet.

I pulled up on a quiet street and parked under a palm tree across the road, and a good half a block away from Harold Haffner's house. I sat back and guessed that it had to be the right place 'cause how many Harold Haffner's would be stuck out here in the boonies? The building sat back from the road. The joint was big, but the siding hadn't come close to a paintbrush for at least twenty years.

I jumped out of my truck and the hot air hit me like a surprise punch in the gut. I forgot that I had been sitting in an air-conditioned cab. Jesus, how could anyone live in this hellhole? Sweating like a gravedigger at high noon, I walked up the driveway and headed toward the backyard.

I figured if Harold charged out waving a shotgun I'd just tell him I was there to read his gas meter.

150

Except for a lawn that had to be at least two years dead, and a couple of dried up orange trees, the backyard was empty.

By this time I guessed that nobody was home so I went up the stairs to the front porch. The floorboards creaked louder than me ringing the doorbell. I stood there for a second and the front door flew open. A man with white hair, a couple of days stubble, and squinty eyes, said, "You don't look like one of my daughter's friends," and the old dude started to close the door.

I stuck my big number twelve between the door and the jam. "Excuse me, sir, this is your lucky day."

His wrinkly brow jumped. "Really?"

"Yes, sir. I'm here today concerning the rotten wood that's barely holding up your front porch."

He looked down at the floorboards like he'd never seen them before. About ten seconds went by and he kept staring at the porch floor.

I jumped up and down a couple of times, and we both heard the wood crack and groan.

The old coot's gaze wandered back to me. "Young fella, you've made your point."

"Thanks."

"Okay, so my front porch is in bad shape. What's that mean to you?"

I said, "Sir, as I told you before, this is your lucky day! My construction company specializes in rebuilding old wood porches. I'll have a crew in your neighborhood next week and all I ask is that you listen to a remodel proposal from my foreman."

The old dude's lips moved but nothing came out for a second, sort of like all the connections between his mouth and his brain weren't working to good. "Have we met before?"

"Yup, about thirty seconds ago."

He pulled back into the house and waved. "Stop by again."

Once the front door lock clicked, I walked down the stairs and climbed into my truck. At least now I knew what Harold Haffner looked like, but beyond that, I didn't know what the hell I was going to do next.

My problem got fixed real quick when I saw a bright red Porsche back out of the Haffner driveway. Sitting behind the wheel was Betty-the-blonde. I ducked down as the sports car passed. We'd only met that one time in Oakland, but I was sure she'd remember me 'cause Flo told me that I affect most broads that way.

I watched the Haffner house for another ten minutes and then went back to the motel.

Flo was sitting with her feet propped on the bed. The temperature was a cool seventy-two. In her left hand she held a glass of red wine, and a big bag of fried pork rinds sat on a table to her right next to the TV remote.

Without taking her eyes off the TV screen she said, "That was quick."

I said, "It was quick 'cause I found Betty-the-blonde."

She sat up and turned the TV off. "You're kidding. Did she see you?"

"Don't think so."

"Come on, Bear, tell me everything, and don't leave out any of the juicy details."

I told her about my meeting Haffner on his front porch, and how I spotted Betty-the-blonde backing out of the driveway. Then I told her the rest of my plan that I figured out on the way back to the motel. "First, I have to get into Haffner's house—to find the lock that goes with the key I got from his office in LA."

"But how will you know when it's safe?"

"That's easy. I'll follow Haffner every time he leaves his house. After a couple of days I'll pick up a pattern —like on Monday's he gets his haircut—Tuesday, he goes to the bank, that sort of thing. Once I figure out his routine, I'll know how much time I have to search through his house and garage."

Flo said, "Your plan won't work because he knows what you look like and he'll know it's you following him."

152

"Jesus, Flo, you're right. I can't let him spot me again because he'll know it's me. Shit, this job is turning out to be a lot tougher than I thought."

Flo took a big slug of her wine. It must have only been her second glass because she was still talking clear. "So how are—"

"Hold it down, damn it, and give me a chance to think."

"That's it! Until you learn to talk with me in a civil way, I'm through with this investigation." Flo topped off her glass with more of that red crap and turned the TV volume up to high.

Shit, I really put my foot in my mouth that time. I said, "I'm sorry, Babe, I get sort of grouchy when I don't know what to do next."

"Humph."

I started to rub Flo's shoulders—then her back—then her waist. She set her glass down.

She said, "I guess the heat is making me a little grouchy too."

I was reaching for the TV remote when the answer hit me. "Hey, I've got the answer. It's simple. You can follow him. It'll be perfect. Haffner's never seen you so he'll never tumble to being followed."

"Hold on. You know that I don't have any of that sort of training, and—"

"Nothing to it, Babe. You'll take my truck, follow the guy, and write down everywhere he goes."

"If I'm going to agree to do this job, and I haven't said I will take on this task, I'll require a different vehicle."

"Why?"

"Did Haffner see your truck?"

"Huh . . . I don't think so."

"Are you positive?"

"Huh . . . no"

"If I'm going to follow him than I will require a second vehicle."

"But—"

"No buts. Think about it."

Damn, she was right again. Unless Haffner's eyes were as bad as the boards on his porch, he probably did see me drive away from his place in my pick-up. "Okay, we'll rent you a car."

"And not one of those tinny, cheap, little compacts. No, I will require a big SUV."

"But Babe, you won't need that much room, and—"

"No more buts, damn it. It's a big SUV, or you follow Haffner and blow your cover."

She had me and she knew it. "Okay, a big SUV."

"And it has to come equipped with a DVD player."

"Jesus, why a DVD player?"

"If Haffner goes into a place for a long time, like if he gets his haircut or something, I'll need to watch a DVD to pass the time."

Shit! "Okay, a big SUV with a DVD player, but that's it. Don't ask for anything else."

"One more thing. For the first week, I'll need seven DVD's, and I get to choose them."

She had me between a rock and a hard spot. "Okay, but don't say another word."

"Fine."

"I TOLD YOU NOT TO SAY—"

"I don't understand what all the fuss is about. An SUV rental would be a legitimate expense so Pinky will pay for it. And what are you going to do while I'm out there trying to survive in that killer heat?"

I didn't have a clue, so I fired off a line of bull. "I plan on spending a couple of days at the County Recorder's office checking to see if Haffner owns more property. Like Pinky said, we're looking for a motive, a good reason why Haffner would murder Brady Blackstone."

Flo nodded, but her eyes told me that she wasn't sure if I was bull-shitting her. She grabbed her glass, downed the rest of her wine, and started to fill it up again. I had to get some food into her or this was going to be a long, lonely night.

I said, "Babe. Let's go get us something to eat and tonight the sky's the limit. What the hell, like you said, Pinky's picking up the tab."

TWENTY-TWO

Bear—Needles, California

The next morning, Flo got her big, fancy SUV, and seven brand new DVD's. After she headed to the Haffner house, I jumped into my pick-up and drove to a nice spot, under the shade of a cottonwood tree, where I could keep an eye on Flo while she followed the old dude, without being seen.

A few minutes after I arrived, I watched an older, white Cadillac back out of Haffner's driveway. Behind the wheel was Betty-the-blonde and next to her sat Haffner. Ten seconds later, Flo's silver SUV pulled out. In the old days, if I had tried to follow someone in a silver anything, I would have stood out like Donald Trump at a rescue mission-dining hall. But today every other female driver on the road was pushing one of those shiny SUV's around, so Flo's cover was perfect.

I followed Flo who was following the Caddy for a few minutes and then I turned around and went back to the motel to watch the Red Sox on TV.

Flo came in around five and said, "First, the old fart doesn't drive. That task was done by a young, perky little blonde that I will assume is your Betty."

"Hey, she's not my Betty."

"Whatever! Betty drove Haffner to the bank, a grocery store, and then the old fart spent over two hours inside a gym while Betty bleached her tresses at the beauty parlor next door. While they were doing their long-term thing I stayed in my big SUV with the motor running and the air on. I watched the movie, Daddy Long Legs. That Fred Astaire wasn't much of a singer, but damn, he sure could dance up a storm. Then I followed the Caddy back to Haffner's house and came back here."

"Great job, Babe."

"Thank you. Now, I'm hungry. Let's eat dinner."

The next day I watched another great Red Sox game. When Flo got back to the motel she told me how Betty and Haffner followed the same pattern, except while Harold spent his two hours in the gym, Betty went to the library, and Flo went on and on about an old chick-flick called, Love Is A Many Splendored Thing.

By the third day, even a blind man could see that Haffner was a man set in his ways, except this day, Betty went to a movie while Flo watched Batman II. The Red Sox had the day off so I stayed inside the air-conditioned motel room, downed a couple of brews, and watch the old Journey To The center Of The Earth on TV.

Before Flo left the motel on the fourth day, I said, "Babe, you're doing great, but today we need to try something different. Once Haffner goes into that gym, I want you to follow him inside. This motel offers all guests a temporary membership to the gym. I picked up your temporary card at the front desk, and according to the dude who runs the motel, all you have to do is give the card to the man sitting behind the desk at the gym."

Flo grabbed the card and flipped it over and over like she was trying to be sure it wouldn't bite her. "And what am I suppose to do after I give the man the card?"

"Shit, I don't know. You're going to find out what Haffner does inside that building every day for a couple of hours."

"But I can't just sit there. I'll have to do exercises."

"So what's wrong with that?"

"Damn it, I don't have the right clothes, that's what's wrong." She glanced at her watch. "But if we leave this very minute, I can hit the mall to buy some proper shoes and a couple of spandex outfits."

Whoa! The thought of Flo wearing spandex gave me goose bumps where guys shouldn't get goose bumps. "No, Babe. No spandex! I let you get the big SUV because big SUV's are a dime a dozen, but every man, woman and child in Needles would be talking about the new babe in town an hour after you walked into that gym wearing

157

spandex. You don't get it. You're supposed to blend in, like the wallpaper, and trust me, that'll never happen with you walking around in spandex. We'll head to the mall, but you'll buy a couple of sweat suit outfits that are at least two sizes too big."

"Okay, no spandex, but I get to pick out the shoes."

"Babe, you're doing great. After tomorrow, you'll only have to follow them one more day."

"What happens then?"

"You'll follow them, just like every other day, but I'll be going through their house five minutes after the Caddy leaves the place."

Flo's eyes lit up. "I get it now. You've got around three hours to look for the lock, and if they decided to come home early, I can warn you on your cell phone."

The next afternoon, I was in the middle of watching my Red Sox pound the crap out the Baltimore Orioles when Flo walked in about an hour early.

She snorted. "I thought you were down at the County Recorder's office, looking up deeds and other important financial things."

"I've been there every day and just got through an hour ago. What did you find out inside the gym?"

Flo pulled out a little pad and checked her notes. I was pretty damn proud of her. She even looked like a real private eye.

"Okay. Today Haffner spent around thirty minutes on a stationary bike. Then he walked for thirty minutes on a treadmill. That takes care of the first hour. Oh, during the first half hour he stared at a TV tuned into CNBC Market Watch. Trust me, watching those talking heads for thirty minutes was as boring as waiting for grass to grow. Then he went back to the bike, set up a plastic thing on the handlebars and read a newspaper for the next thirty minutes. Now here comes the part of your plan that didn't work."

"What do you mean, didn't work?"

"Haffner spent his final thirty minutes in an area for men only."

Shit, I hadn't thought of that.

Flo said, "I checked out the women's area. There was a very nice hot tub and sauna, as if the temperature outside the gym wasn't hot enough. It also had showers and lockers. I told the man at the desk that my husband was considering a membership and asked him if the men's area was as nice as the women's. He told me that the two facilities were identical."

"Hey, you did some good—"

"Hold on. There's one other thing that we didn't plan on, and I think it's important. During the last few days, every morning around ten, while I was waiting for Haffner, I saw a guy walk into the gym."

"So?"

"If I was a betting woman, I'd guess the guy was homeless. Something about his clothes, and the way he looked when he arrived."

Shit, the Sox pitcher just walked in a run. The Orioles were down only three and they had the bases loaded.

"Bear, turn that damned TV off and listen to me. This is important."

I hit the mute button, but kept one eye on the game. The damn Orioles were breathing down Boston's neck and they couldn't afford to lose this game. "I am listening. Okay, so you've fingered some guy who walks into the gym every day and—"

"That's the point, damn it. He's not just some guy. I told you that he looked homeless. So while I watched Haffner pedal and walk, I kept an eye out for the homeless guy and everyday at ten on the nose he walked in. He showed his card to the man at the desk and went straight to the men's area."

"I still don't get it."

"When he went into the men's area, he had a dark five o'clock shadow. His face was all puffy, and his hair was going in ten different directions. He looked like you do when you crawl out of your cave in the morning. But when he came out of the men's area, a half an hour later, he was all sparkly, with clean hair, and no chin whiskers."

"So you found a man who goes to a gym for his morning shower, what's so import—"

"Wake up and smell the coffee, Bear. I can't go in the men's area for obvious reasons. You can't walk into the gym because you're afraid that Haffner will spot you. This homeless guy can tell you what Haffner's doing in the men's area everyday."

TWENTY-THREE

Pinky—Carson City, Nevada

Evening shadows had lengthened by the time I pulled into my reserved parking space outside my office. In Mabel's old parking slot sat a VW bug, circa 1980. It was obvious that Jung Lu didn't spend all her hard earned assets on transportation.

Not sure what to expect, I grabbed my briefcase and entered my building. Tucked behind Mabel's desk was a stunningly beautiful, twenty-something Asian female.

She stood, gave a slight bow and said, "Mr. Delmont."

"Pinky."

"Ah yes, Pinky. Did you have a good flight?"

"Considering the dismal condition of the air transportation industry, about as good as one could expect."

Lu's face was flawless. Her dark jade eyes complimented her coal-black hair and nearly took my breath away.

I stammered, "Do . . . do I have any messages?"

She handed me a stack of pink notes. Lu's figure was astonishing. A slim waist blossomed into impeccably proportioned hips. Her bust filled out her white blouse to perfection. After years of staring at Mabel, a plump, fiftyish-year-old matron, concentrating on legal work was going to take a conscientious effort on my part.

I took the messages and said, "Thank you. I will be in my office. Hold all calls unless they come from Willow or Bear."

Once I sat down behind my desk, I thought, Pinky, get a hold of yourself. You have a youthful beauty sitting outside your office, but can she type? Is she responsible? Is she trustworthy? When Mabel was temporarily missing

161

some time back, the cursory vetting of her replacement damn near cost me my life. A pretty face, regardless of its youth, was not worth my existence.

Lu's voice over the intercom interrupted my reverie. "Willow's on line one."

I picked up the phone. "My love, I truly missed your company in Quebec City. The town was built for lovers. That is why I regret you were not by my si —"

"Who answered your office phone?"

"That was Jung Lu."

"What happened to Mabel?"

"We had a parting of the ways."

"I'm going to make a wild guess, Mabel's replacement is young."

"My dear, I don't like the direction of this conversation."

"Your evasive response informs me that she's under thirty."

"Are you attempting to entrap me?"

"And she must be good looking."

"Willow, I was three thousand miles east when Mabel walked out of my life. I called a local agency and they sent me a temporary to cover my office. I had nothing to do with the selection of the replacement. I took potluck, so to speak. And at the moment, Lu is here on a day-to-day basis. At this juncture, I have not decided if she is a worthy candidate for permanent employment."

Willow paused, and she then said, "I apologize. I jumped to a conclusion without the facts. Now, I'm sure we're both busy so let's cut to the chase. Did you come up with anything in Quebec City that would create some reasonable doubt in my air-tight case against Jack Spurlock?"

"No, I struck out, but Bear has—"

"Stop right there, Pinky Delmont. The last time we spoke you promised me that you had no idea where Bear was located. In case you've forgotten, there's an outstanding warrant in this county because your man assaulted an officer of the law."

162

"Willow, we both know that the altercation between Bear and Ice was nothing more—"

"STOP TALKING AND LISTEN TO ME. You stay in your office and don't move. I'll be there in three minutes and I'll give you the opportunity to talk me out of filing charges against you for obstruction of justice."

The phone went dead. Under normal circumstances, I was positive that my ex-wife would never file charges against me—but I was not sure what she would do the moment she gazed at Lu's unadulterated beauty.

I ran to the outer office and found Lu sitting at Mabel's desk. "Lu, I love what you have done so far. I understand that I am acting impulsively, but you must vacate my office immediately. I will see you here tomorrow at nine and I will explain everything at that time."

Lu jumped up, grabbed her purse, and as she pushed her way through the front door, she said, "I don't understand what's going on, but I love the excitement, so I'll see you in the morning."

TWENTY-FOUR

Bear—Needles, California

It was damn near noon and the back of my neck felt like a piece of fried bacon. I was hunkered down behind a metal culvert. Sweat poured off my forehead like I was parked under a garden hose. All this because Flo thought I needed to talk to some guy who showered and shaved at the gym every day.

Growing up in Elko, searching for stray sheep with my Pop, I got real good at tracking animals without spooking them, but somehow this dude seemed to pick up that I was trailing him because he suddenly ducked into an alley and disappeared into the desert down a dry wash. I followed the wash for a quarter mile and now I was stuck behind an eight-foot metal culvert that took the wash under a county road. I knew that once I moved in front of the culvert, and if he was waiting for me inside, he'd have me. I guessed that would be okay as long as I didn't startle him. Running around the northern Nevada wilderness with Pop had taught me how—

"I know you're out there so put your hands in the air." A man's voice pounded out of the culvert. "I've got you in my sights, and if you twitch an eyebrow, what's left of your head will feed the coyotes for a week."

"Okay, I won't move."

The voice softened. "Why are you following me?"

My arms were getting tired. "Can I lower my hands?"

"Do you think I'm playing some sort of a game here?"

"Nope."

"Then keep your hands up and answer my question."

"Hey, I followed you out here because I want to hire you to do a job."

164

A high cackle bounced off the metal walls. "Me? Do a job? Shit, there're a hundred guys in town that can do that. Cut the bull. I need proof that you're not part of the Cong. Move your face into the light so I can see that you're not a slant-eye."

This guy sounded a little weird, like all his gears weren't coming together the way they should. "Hey, hold the gun on me, hell, go on and shoot me, but I've got to get out of this damn sun before I cook."

"Okay, but there's no guarantee I won't blow your head off if you make a sudden move."

Arms held high, I walked into the culvert, and as my eyes got used to the dim light, I saw that the guy had built a little house out of wood, old chairs, and cardboard. I stood there for a minute. "Do I pass muster?"

"Yeah, I can see you're not Charlie."

The guy was about my height, but skinnier. His face was a lot older than his body, but living under a county road in the desert could do that to a dude. A greasy LA Dodger cap tried to corral a mess of gray hair. The only scary thing, besides the army-issue 45 he held in his right hand, was the color of his eyes. They looked like two, yellow piss holes in the snow and jumped around all the time, like he was afraid that any second, someone or something was going to drop out of the sky.

If he wanted to pull the trigger I was a dead duck. This far out of town no one would hear a thing, so I shrugged my shoulders. "Thanks for letting me come in out of the sun. Now that you see I'm not packing, can I drop my arms?"

"I guess that'll be okay." He seemed to think that was funny because that same high-pitched cackle I had heard before jumped out of his twisted mouth. "You're right, the heat's bad out there, but nothing like it was in Nam once you added that damn humidity. How 'bout a beer?"

I lowered my arms. "Thanks. That sounds great."

The guy set his pistol down on a white plastic table and opened a cooler. I was pretty sure I could have jumped

165

him and grabbed the gun, but he'd calmed down, and whatever was bugging him seemed to have passed.

Beer in hand, he dropped onto a beat-up couch while I tested the leg strength of an old folding chair. After we knocked off our second brew, I said, "Nice little place you got here."

He looked around and smiled. "I think so. Cool enough in the summer and warm enough in the winter."

I said, "Speaking of winter, have you ever had a problem when it rains?"

"You mean it could be risky living in a dry wash under the road?"

"Yup. I grew up in northern Nevada and we'd get flash floods that would wipe out a place like this."

"Look around. What am I going to lose? A couple of sticks of wood? A worn out couch? A few years ago, during a big rain storm, I heard a loud noise—like there was an eighteen wheeler coming down the wash—I grabbed my sleeping bag, the beer, and got out just before the shit hit the fan." He pointed to a line of mud on the metal wall about two feet above his cooler. "See here, this is how high the water got. Shit, if I survived two years of hell in Nam, a little water isn't going to scare me. Now, let's get down to the important shit. Why are you following me?"

I glanced at the gun. He followed my eyes, picked it up and tucked the weapon under his sleeping bag. Then he popped open two more beers.

I said, "I'm a private detective and I've been following a local dude who goes to the gym every day."

His piss-yellow eyes lit up. "Was that sexy new babe who showed up at the gym a couple of days ago part of your team?"

I nodded.

He reached toward my beer and touched my bottle. "In case you haven't noticed, she's a hot ticket. So what about the dude?"

"Every day he goes into the men's area and my female operative can't follow him. Then she noticed you come to the gym every day about the same time and head to the men's area. I thought you'd want to pick up a hundred to be my eyes and ears."

"Are you telling me that I go to the gym every day? I must be getting old. In Nam, if I fell into a pattern like that, Charlie would have cut off my balls and fed them to me for lunch."

I said, "Did you really think I was part of the Viet Cong?"

"I know it's a stretch, but you can never be too careful."

"Right." I drained the last dregs of my beer. "Now, what about my offer. Do you want the job?"

"How much did you say?"

"A hundred."

"I know you don't give a shit about an old Nam vet, but I live on a disability check from the army. It's a monthly check I get that reminds me that I spent a couple of years murdering innocent women and children for no good reason."

He was right, I didn't give a shit about his being a Nam vet, but I'd learned from Pinky that sometimes I had to pretend that I cared. "Sorry to hear that."

"Hell, you don't know the worst part. My disability check doesn't give me enough to live in a house or a motel like a normal person. I have to get by in a shit hole under a county road for Christ sake. But my check gives me enough to buy beer, and pay the thirty-five a month for my gym membership so I can shower and shit every day."

I said, "I tell you what, I'll make that two hundred." He smiled and his piss-holes-in-the-snow eyes changed into a more-green-than-yellow color. "I thought you'd come around. But we need to get one thing straight. I don't kill dudes for two hundred. That'll cost you at least five hundred."

"Hey, I don't want him dead. All I need to find out is what he does when he goes into the men's area."

"Probably takes a shower and a shit. That's what I do."

"Good. I'm counting on you to tell me everything he does after those two things."

"Hey, what's your name?"

"Bear Zabarte. What's yours?"

"You really don't want to know."

"Okay. Mind if I call you Gym Guy?"

"That'll be fine with me."

"Okay, Gym Guy, we've got a deal."

"Bear, how 'bout we seal the deal with another brew?"

"Sounds good to me."

"Okay, meet me here tomorrow at noon. Don't forget to bring the two hundred, in cash, and I won't take any bill larger than a twenty."

TWENTY-FIVE

Pinky—Carson City, Nevada

During the first hour of our joyous reunion, Willow berated me concerning my ethics, or as she put it, my lack of same. Then she reminded me about my failings as a husband. The fact that we were not married anymore, and that we had not been married for years, did not slow her down. Finally, after two and a half hours, her anger spent, she finally accepted my invitation to dine out at Carson City's finest restaurant. After dinner we . . . I apologize, but my gentleman's code brings down a curtain of silence concerning the remainder of our evening.

The following morning, to use a pugilistic analogy, Willow and I returned to our respective corners to await the sound of the bell for the next round.

With a satisfied smile on my face, I walked into my office and Lu was sitting at Mabel's . . . no, the ownership of that desk had changed hands, so Lu was sitting at Lu's desk.

"Pinky, the court clerk called to be sure you had returned from Canada. He told me that you have three arraignments and—"

"Lu, yesterday I told you I would only accept calls from two people named Willow or Bear. It is time that I inform you that Willow is the Deputy District Attorney for the county, and she also happens to be my ex-wife."

An inscrutable smile formed on her lips. "That's an unusual combination, but I'm sure you both have figured out a solution that meets your respective requirements."

Lu's well-crafted conclusion indicated to me that this young woman was wise beyond her years. I said, "We have reached a near perfect resolution. Now the other name I mentioned—"

"Bear?"

"Correct. Bear Zabarte is my full time field operative. The last time we communicated he was in Needles, California. You need to know that Bear is a capable investigator, but he is totally unreliable as an employee. He should never be trusted concerning his expense account, or his—"

The phone rang. Lu picked it up. "Law office of Pinky Delmont. Yes, he's here. Just a moment please."

She turned to me and said, "It's Bear."

I took the phone out of her hand. "Bear, we have a problem."

"Boss, I'm glad you're back. How was your vacation in Canada?"

Bear's voice was clear, another example that Mr. Bell's telephonic invention had achieved near perfection. "I was not on vacation. Now on to our problem and do not interrupt me."

"Right, I'll sit here and listen."

"I told you to not interrupt me."

"Right."

"Damn it, stop saying right."

"Okay."

I paused a moment to give my blood pressure the opportunity to ebb a few notches, and continued. "Willow reminded me last night that you remain a fugitive of justice. Remember that little altercation with Ice Conner?"

I could hear Bear's hot breath pulsate against the transmitter of the phone. "Bear, answer me."

"But you told me to clam up."

"Damn it, when I ask you a question I expect you to answer me."

"Right."

Again I waited in vain for his response. "Bear, answer my question."

"Okay! I know that dirty cop lied to the judge and I can't come back home until you can find a way to kill the

170

warrant, or I figure out a way to wring the bastard's neck."

I said, "Now that we are on the same page, last night I informed Willow that I did not know your whereabouts, nor had I spoken to you for some time."

"That's okay, boss. We all have to fudge a little once in a while."

"Stop interrupting me. Now, I have a way around our communication dilemma. From this point on, you will make all future reports using email to Lu."

"Lou who?"

"Lu. She took over for Mabel."

"I was going to ask you who answered the phone. Boss, you can tell me, is she young and good looking?"

"Bear, get your mind out of the gutter. At the conclusion of this phone call, I will not converse with you again because of my promise to Willow. From this point on you will send a daily email to Lu. Your email will include all activities pertinent to your investigation. If, on an occasional basis, I happen to walk by Lu's desk, look down and see the email, I do not see how that innocent act could be interpreted as breaking my pledge to the deputy district attorney. Any questions?"

"Why did Mabel leave?"

"Damn it, I meant questions concerning our pending method of communication."

"Nope, but don't forget, Flo will have to write my emails because I don't understand those digit things that run around inside that computer box."

"Bear, I do not care who composes your emails, and that includes the wicked witch, or the Spelling Bee Champion of Needles. Now for the second problem. We have but six days to turn the suspect over to Willow."

"What happens in six days?"

I could not let Bear know what I stood to lose. "We have spent enough time on this project. I have other clients who need my attention."

I listened to Bear gnash his teeth for a moment, as if mimicking the gears grinding in his marginally adequate

171

gray matter. "Boss, it's not that I don't believe you, but it sounds like you have been given a deadline, and if you don't make the deadline, you'll lose something big. We both know that you only work for money, so I'm guessing you'll lose a shit-pot full of dough if I don't come up with a name."

"Bear, we have to trust each other. What sort of a relationship would we have if—"

Bear growled, "Boss, when I get the name, and I'll get it, it's going to cost you five big ones as a bonus."

There have been times when working with Bear was frustrating, but throwing him a five thousand dollar bonus so I could collect two million sounded like a deal. However, Bear must not be allowed to perceive that I gave in too easily, nor that he was all I had left in this investigation. "Bear, I pay you more than a decent salary to conduct this sort of investigation."

"Boss, it's a simple deal. No bonus, no name."

"All right, all right, I will agree to your request. Of course, your demands for a quick reward will not come without some risk. If you fail to give me a name in six days or less, you are fired."

"Fired! You can't fire me."

"My good man, I can replace you as easily as I replaced Mabel with Lu."

For some time I listened to my ursine friend's heavy breathing. Then he said, "Right. If I don't come up with a name, I'm back to tending bar."

"Now that we are on the same page, I have a few minutes before I am due in court. Just enough time for you to bring me up to date concerning your most recent activities."

TWENTY-SIX

Bear—Needles, California

The next day, around ten minutes to twelve, I walked toward the culvert. Just before I reached the dark opening, I heard a voice say, "Stop where you are. Raise your hands to the sky and don't move another step or I'll blow your brains to kingdom come."

"Hey, Gym Guy, don't shoot. It's me, Bear Zabarte."

"How do I know it's you?"

Shit, dealing with a whacked-out low-life was a lot harder than dealing with a regular low-life. "I'm doing exactly what you told me to do—meet you here at noon."

"Don't give me that crap. It's ten, no, eight minutes to twelve. Move closer and keep your hands up."

I took a step forward and stopped. I was fed up with him ordering me around and threatening to shoot me. I would have turned and gone back to the motel, except the crazy bastard might pump a bullet through the back of my skull for the two hundred I had in my pocket.

The voice said, "Okay. I can see that you're the same big guy I made the deal with yesterday. You can put your hands down, but in the future don't show up so damned early. You can never be too safe. How about a beer?"

"Sounds good." I stepped into the shade, sat down on my rickety folding chair, downed about half the beer in one slug, and said, "What did you find out?"

He cackled. "If I had known who it was you wanted me to check on I would have turned you down. But a deal's a deal. Give me the two hundred first and then I'll tell you what I found."

I reached into my jeans pocket and pulled out a wad of bills. I had left the rest of my money along with my

173

credit cards in the motel room. As the Gym Guy said, you can't be too careful. "As requested, ten Jacksons."

His piss-hole eyes glowed as he counted out the stash. "Okay, the dude's name you wanted me to follow was Haffner, right?"

"Right, but you said—"

"Slow down, I'll get to that in a minute. Okay, when I went into the men's area, Haffner was sitting on a bench by his locker. I know that was his locker because there was a piece of black tape with white letters that spelled, H-A-F-F-N-E-R. He was—"

"Did the locker have a lock?"

"Hell yes. We're talking about a locker room in a public gym, not a monastery. Even this desert hell-hole has its share of sticky fingered thieves."

"Did you happen to notice the brand of lock?"

"Now why would I do that? Bear, you ask me a stupid question one more time, the deal's off, and I keep the money. Now, Haffner was sitting by his locker and he was sorting through a bunch of paper work."

"Could you see what the papers were all about?"

"No, but I could see it was official looking junk, the kind of endless government crap I get from the VA."

"Then what happened?"

"I watched him shuffle papers. He'd read the top one, move it to the bottom, read the next one, move it to the bottom, that sort of thing for half an hour. Then he got up, stuffed the papers back into his locker and left me alone in the room. I took a shower, a shit, and came back here to pick up my cash."

"Good job, Gym Guy. Now why didn't you want to do the job?"

"There's something wrong with the old dude. Haffner and I go way back here in Needles. Hell, when I was a kid I used to cut his lawn, but you don't care about that. Haffner was a big mover and shaker around this neck of the woods. I heard he made a pile investing other people's money. I think he was working a big deal, I mean a really big deal and then something changed. I don't know exactly why, but there are some loose screws inside the old dude's head. Hell, for the third day in a row I had to tell him my name."

"What's your name, Gym Guy?"

"You didn't pay me enough for that information."

"Okay, why do you think there's something wrong with Haffner?"

"The way he fumbled through those papers is a good example. He looked at each sheet, but I don't think anything was clicking between his eyes and his brain. In Nam, I had a buddy who fell off a truck when it hit a big bump in the road. From that day on, according to the medic, my buddy lost his short term memory."

"Huh? What do you mean lost his short-term memory?"

"I thought you'd ask me that. Bear, you're a lucky guy. If you hadn't jacked up my payment to two hundred, this conversation would be over. But for that kind of money you get my premium service. I stopped by the library; got online and looked up short-term memory loss. The official medical name is," Gym Guy pulled out a piece of paper. "The medical name is Antegrade Amnesia. I think Old Haffner has the same thing my bud in Nam had. They can remember all kinds of shit from their past, but the poor bastards can't recall what happened to them an hour ago."

"I still don't understand. Give me an example."

"Take me. He sees me every day in the men's locker room and every day he wants to know my name. I tell him and the next day I have to tell him the same thing again. The funny thing is, according to the online source, they really don't have a short memory loss, just a loose wire so they can't transfer their short-term memory into the long-term part of their brain. Pretty cool."

Shit. If he was telling me the truth, Haffner wouldn't remember meeting me on his front porch. If Pinky ever found out that I didn't need to rent the SUV for Flo, or pay two hundred to—

175

"Bear, I've been thinking about that hot chick that works with you. Is there something going on between you two, or is yours strictly a business relationship?"

"Gym Guy, there are a bunch of times when I wished it was only a business deal, but this ain't one of them. Sorry."

"No problem. I think it's important that civilized men have a clear understanding about the most important aspects of life."

I'll be damned. The Gym Guy was asking me if it was okay for him to hit on Flo! I looked around the shithole where the poor bastard lived and decided that if Flo ever saw this dump, and knew that the Gym Guy wanted her to join him, she'd puke all over his cooler full of beer.

I said, "You know, I could go for another brew before I head back into that heat."

"My pleasure." He twisted the tops off two bottles and handed me one of them. "Don't forget, Bear, if you need more information on Haffner, especially for five or ten more Jacksons, I'm your man."

TWENTY-SEVEN

Pinky—Carson City, Nevada

It was nine on the dot when I walked through the front door of my office, ready and eager to slay any of the legal dragons that lurked in the dark environs of Nevada's capital city.

If it was possible, Lu looked brighter and fresher than she had the day before.

She smiled and her perfect teeth glistened in the sunlight. "Good morning, Pinky. I have a few messages for you."

As I shuffled through the pink notes, I found myself sheepishly grinning back. "Good morning, Lu."

My morning euphoria quickly faded as I spotted a message from Judge Anderson regarding George Sterling.

Every attorney needed to have a few pro bono clients. Helping out the indigent looked good for our profession, and God knows that our profession needed all the assistance it could get. But a pro bono client paid nothing for their legal advice, so a plethora of that sort of client could become a financial burden for an attorney busy with paying clients. I viewed my pro bono situation as a simple balance between two needs, the freeloading client's and mine. A few years ago, to solve my pro bono dilemma, I had taken on George Sterling as a client. George was a part-time blackjack dealer and a full-time alcoholic. Within the year, at the conclusion of his third DUI trial, I had agreed to hold his driver's license in my safe. Because I had kept George's gin-soaked soul off the streets of Carson City for the past six months, I felt that my endeavors qualified him as a legitimate pro bono client, regardless of how much time I actually spent with him. Now, this morning, I had received this message from Judge Anderson regarding George Sterling. It was obvious I had to immediately return the judge's call. Finding a pro bono client like George, a man who demanded a modicum of legal advice from me, was like discovering a five-ounce gold nugget on the sidewalk. I had to do whatever the judge required of me to maintain control of my pro bono commitment.

I said, "Lu, pull up George Sterling on the computer."

She tapped a few keys and said, "During the past four months, George Sterling left seven message srequesting that you call him."

I must be slipping. I recalled only five attempts. "And did I return any of his calls?"

"Not according to this data base."

I reviewed the monitor screen. "Now I understand. It looks as if Mabel took it upon herself to act as my gate-keeper—to protect me from the George Sterlings of the world, so to speak."

I had much to accomplish over the next few days or millions of dollars, money that was within a gnat's eyebrow of being deposited into my bank account, would vanish faster than the morning mist. I picked up the phone and dialed Judge Anderson's number. At that moment, a discussion about an alcoholic client was at the bottom of my list, but when a judge wanted an attorney to return his call, no lawyer in his right mind could afford to ignore the request. As I listened to the rings, I forced the aggravation from my voice. "Judge Anderson? Good morning. This is Pinky Delmont returning your call. How are you today?"

"Not good. George Sterling interrupted my lunch yesterday to complain that he has been unable to contact you. Pinky, I'm sure you recall that I treasure my moments of solitude while I consume my Caesar salad topped with strips of broiled chicken breast. Therefore, you must understand why I was appalled when that . . . that creature summoned up the nerve to sit down at my table and beg me to reinstate his driving privileges."

I thought every citizen in northern Nevada knew better than to interrupt Judge Anderson during his lunch. "I understand, Your Honor. I just checked—"

"Pinky, I know that George is your pro bono client. However, if you are too busy with other clients, I can find another attorney to represent Mr. Sterling concerning his DUI record and the possible reinstatement of his driving privileges."

"My dear Judge Anderson, even taking into consideration my heavy case load, please understand that I am never too busy to assist the oppressed and under-represented members of our society who, by reasons beyond their control, are forced to seek free legal advice. I treasure Mr. Sterling as a client and look forward to his occasional need for legal advice."

"That's the problem here. George tells me that you have been avoiding him."

"Your Honor, I just reviewed my records and was shocked to discover that George requested an appointment with me seven times over the past six months. In every case, my secretary, Mabel, took it upon herself to close the gate on George. What I am telling you is that the lack of communication with my client was not my fault, and over-stepping her bounds was the major reason I fired Mabel."

"Frankly, I don't care an iota what one of your employees did or didn't do. Fix this annoyance immediately and make sure Mr. Sterling does not interrupt my midday repast ever again!"

"Your Honor, the moment I conclude our call, I will instruct Lu, who has taken over for Mabel, to set up an immediate appointment with George."

"Sounds to me as if you have everything under control. Pinky, just between us, I'm not sure that allowing Mr. Sterling to sit behind the wheel of a vehicle on the streets of Carson City would be in the best interest of the citizens of our community."

"Sir, on that point, we could not agree more. My plan, with your concurrence of course, would be to keep

George's driver's license securely locked up in my safe. That way, as instructed by you, we will keep a potential killer off the roads of our fair city, and of course, neither of us could be held responsible if George decides to drive illegally."

"When you meet with Mr. Sterling, please make sure he understands that in the future I will hold him in contempt of court and he will spend thirty days in jail, if he attempts to interrupt my lunch again."

"I will do that. Now, I bumped into your lovely wife at the downtown luggage store. Are you two lovebirds planning a trip?"

"Why yes, we are looking forward to a few weeks at the Mani Lani Resort on the big island. I go for the golf and Doris just adores being pampered at the spa. Pinky, I knew I could count on you to solve our little dilemma."

After the judge hung up, I snapped, "Lu, get George Sterling on the phone."

In a moment she handed me the phone. "Good morning, George, how have you been?"

"Pinky, I'm sorry I went to the judge, but I've been sober for eight weeks in a row and I'm ready to drive my car again."

"George, we have known each other for a long time."

"That's true. I can remember when—"

I interrupted. "And during all that time, did I ever do anything to lose your trust?"

"Ah . . . no, but Pinky, I've been trying to—"

I had a small problem in my office by the name of Mabel, and I have removed that problem.

"What's Mabel got to do with—"

"Until I received a call from Judge Anderson I was unaware that you had attempted to contact me. Today, I discovered that you bravely tried to reach out to me but my secretary thwarted your efforts. George, you will be pleased to learn that I have fired Mabel for her perfidious performance. From this day forward, I have instructed my new secretary, Lu, to inform me of your calls, and if I am in my office, to immediately put your call through to me."

"Are you telling me that Mabel's the reason that I—"

"And in the future, if you feel the need to go over my head and talk with Judge Anderson, do not, I repeat, do not interrupt him during his lunch time meal. The judge informed me that if you were to do that again, he would place you in jail on a contempt of court charge. Do I make myself clear?"

"Yes. No matter what happens I won't talk to the judge again. Now about my sobriety. As I said—"

"George, you will have to excuse me. I am boarding a plane for California in thirty minutes. Lu will call you and make an appointment so we can discuss all the positive changes and improvements you have made to your lifestyle. Goodbye."

I cut the connection, handed Lu her phone, and said, "After I leave the office call George back and allot him ten minutes of my valuable time, no more, no less, about three weeks from today. If he complains, remind him that I am involved in an important murder case."

"Right. Are you really flying to California?"

"I fear that is a fact. I have but a few fleeting days left to tie up the loose ends of an important case and depending on my Basque friend to complete the task is turning out to be less than a viable alternative. You had better take this down."

Lu grabbed a pen and a pad of paper. "Ready."

"Find out the address of the motel where Bear is staying. Next, make me a reservation at the same establishment for three nights. It concerns me that I will be using my ursine investigator's taste in sleeping accommodations, but time constraints leave me no other alternative in the matter. Finally, book me on the next flight from Reno to Las Vegas and rent me a car at the airport. From there I will have to drive myself to the arid hinterland of Needles, California."

TWENTY-EIGHT

Bear—Needles, California

The Sox weren't on TV so I watched Oprah until Flo got back from her tailing job. Oprah wasn't bad. She gives the people in her audience all kinds of cool stuff just to come to her show, but I wouldn't want that Dr. Phil dude taking out my appendix real soon.

The door opened, and the minute Flo walked in she started to burn my ass. "Every time I come through that door you're sitting on your ass in front of the TV. Is that all you do while I'm doing all this work?"

"Glad to see you too, Babe. We've got to change our plans. I talked to Pinky and we only have a couple of days to come up with the name of the guy that killed Brady Blackstone."

"How about Harold Haffner? Just give his name to Pinky and we can go back home."

Dr Phil finally left and Oprah introduced a good-looking redhead that didn't get along with her mother.

"Bear, answer me."

"It's not that easy, Babe. The Gym Guy told me that Haffner's got a lose screw; he says it's short-term memory loss. Called it Antifreeze Ambrosia, or something like that."

"What?" Flo grabbed the laptop, keyed in a few words, and read some crap off the screen. "I think you meant Antegrade Amnesia. What's that got to do with Haffner not being a good suspect for Brady's murder?"

"According to the Gym Guy, Haffner doesn't remember the shit he did yesterday. How's Willow going to hang a murder rap on a dude if he can't remember if he killed or kissed Brady Blackstone?"

"Well . . . there's got to be a way to . . . damn it, that's Willow's problem. I've had it with this hellhole of a town. I want to go back to Carson City."

"Hold on. All we've got to do is find Haffner's motive, I mean a whopper of a motive, and then him being crazy won't stop Willow from taking him to trial. Once he's in court, the whole mess will be up to a judge to figure out if his brains are too scrambled to give him the needle."

"Forget that. I can't stand anymore of this incessant heat. Damn it, we've been on a wild goose chase since Oakland. I vote we go home."

This was the perfect time to tell Flo about the possible bonus money and that Pinky would fire my ass if I didn't finish the job, but the redhead, a real babe, sitting next to Oprah was about to tell everybody why she hated her mother.

"Damn it, turn that TV off and let's check out of this dump."

I hit the mute button but kept an eye on the redhead. "Babe, Pinky offered me a bonus if we can come up with a name in a couple of days."

Flo frowned. "We both know Pinky Delmont, and that bastard doesn't throw money around without a good reason. How much is the bonus?"

Should I tell her the real amount? Damn, I was starting to think like Pinky. "Five thousand."

"I'll bet he's getting a bunch more, like fifty, or even a hundred thousand."

She was right, I thought, but I'd bet he was getting more like half a million. "Babe, he's probably getting a lot more money, but worrying about that won't get us the extra cash."

"So if we stick around for a couple more days we'll make five thousand on top of your salary and expenses?"

"Sort of, but there's one more little thing."

"What?"

"Pinky told me I can kiss this job goodbye if I don't come up with a name."

Flo glanced around the room—at the fancy black velvet painting over the bed—the big screen TV— the pool out the window— all the cool things she had in her life that would go away if I got fired. "Okay, I change my vote. What do we do next?"

"We have to go back to the gym and find out what's inside of Haffner's locker."

"Sounds good, but what'll you do if Haffner walks in and sees you?"

"I told you. He's got that ambrosia thing. He won't remember me."

Flo shook her head. "I hope you know what you're doing."

Dr. Phil came back and sat down next to the redhead. I'd seen enough of that dude so I hit the TV power button.

We walked downstairs to the office. The dude behind the counter gave me a gym pass and we headed back to the gym. I walked in the door with Flo and followed her over to a room, watched her switch on some fancy machine and start to walk. Just watching her started my heart pounding. A couple of guys behind her stopped looking at the TV and stared too.

I said, "I'm going into the men's area. I'm not expecting Haffner, but if he comes in, get off that moving-floor thing and knock on the door three times."

"Whatever."

The men's area looked about like I expected it to. Near the far wall there was a hot tub. On the right there were three doors. Two were open and they led into small wooden rooms, like the pictures I'd seen of those Swedish hot boxes where people go to sweat. Left of the hot tub there was a row of showers. Behind me, against the wall, was a line of lockers.

I found the locker labeled Haffner and felt pretty proud of myself when I saw the brand of lock matched the key I had carried in my pocket since I found it taped under Haffner's desk in LA. The key opened the lock. I pulled out about a four-inch pile of papers and sat down on a wooden bench.

But before I could figure out what the first sheet was all about, a low voice growled from behind me. "Slowly, very slowly, set that paper down and put both your hands up or I'll blow a fist-sized hole through your thick skull."

TWENTY-NINE

Bear—Needles, California

My stomach was tighter than a bull's ass at fly time. I set the paper down.

The second the sheet hit the bench, a high-pitched laugh bounced off the tile walls.

"Fooled you again, Bear!"

Damn it, that was the Gym Guy's cackle! Now I was really pissed. That crazy bastard had threatened to blow my head off for the last time. I jumped up, grabbed his wrist, and pulled a 38 special from his hand.

"Hey, don't get mad. I figured you'd—"

"Gym Guy, if you ever point that damn gun at me again I'll stuff it up your butt so far you'll have to open your mouth to pull the trigger. Got me?"

He was shaking like a leaf in the wind. "Yes."

I squeezed his wrist tighter. The fingers on his hand started to turn dark red and tears popped out of his yellow eyes.

"Tell me that again, loud and clear, so I'm sure you heard me."

"I . . . I won't ever point my gun at you . . . ever again."

I let go of his arm and the tears slowed down.

I said, "You're getting to be a giant pain in the ass, but that's something I'll get to another day. What the hell are you doing here?"

He shook his hand a couple of times. I think he wanted to be sure it was still connected to his arm. Then he said, "After you asked me the name of the lock on Haffner's locker, I figured you must have had the key, and if you had a key, you'd be hightailing it down here—"

"Okay, that's enough. Now get out of my sight. I've got work to do."

I sat down and started to read the top sheet.

He said, "But I've got some information that I think you'll pay big bucks for."

"You've already screwed me out of two hundred, and besides, I told you to move your sorry ass out of here."

"I'll tell you everything I know for another hundred."

Damn, he wasn't going to leave me alone. I was about to grab the bastard by his feet and hands, like he was a young calf, spin him around a couple of times and throw him out of the locker room, but then I asked myself what would Pinky do? He wouldn't use his muscles, he'd use his brain, and he sure as hell wouldn't give him a hundred bucks. Pinky would figure out a way to screw the bastard and get the information. "Gym Guy, I won't give you another buck, but I'll buy everything you're selling for two cases of beer."

"Jesus, have you forgotten? I'm a sick, and broke vet from Nam."

He stared at me and I glared back.

"Okay, I'll settle for five cases."

"Two, and that's my last offer."

For a second I thought the sad sack was going to break down and cry. But then he said, "Bear, you're a tough negotiator. Okay, it's a deal, but I get to choose the beer. Did I ever tell you that I hate light beer?"

"Nope."

"Can't stand it. I'll drink anything but light beer." He cackled.

"Okay, what kind of beer do you want?"

"Newcastle Brown. That's a marvelous brew from the north of England. The aroma of—"

I said, "Cut the commercial. Okay, I'll try to find Newcastle Brown, but I'm not spending much of my time looking in this desert burg you call a town."

"The liquor store near the river carries Newcastle Brown. Bear, you know me. I wouldn't ask you for something—"

"Damn it, cut the bullshit and tell me what I just bought."

"Harold Haffner is my uncle."

I had to admit that was a surprise. "Is your last name Haffner?"

"Yes. My dad's name was Arnold, Uncle Harold's younger brother. My mom divorced my dad years ago and moved to Denver. After the divorce my dad started to drink and he died in a car accident a few years ago."

"Sorry to hear that about your folks. So what's your first name?"

"Larry. Larry Haffner."

"Now I understand why you knew that Harold Haffner was losing it. I'm not an uncle, but if I had to ask my nephew's name every day, I'd really have something screwed up in my cockpit."

"So now that I've confessed, will you tell me what you and that hot babe are really doing in Needles?"

He might clam up if I told him I was trying to set his uncle up for the murder of Brady Blackstone, so I manufactured a little bullshit on the fly. "I represent the Nevada State Department of Revenue Service, based out of Carson City. That hot babe is my associate and we are investigating a complaint that your uncle, as the Controller for the Brady Blackstone Tour, didn't pay the State of Nevada some entertainment taxes that should have been paid before the tour left Nevada."

"Huh?"

"Larry, I tried to cut down on all the technical crap so you'd understand me. What I said was that your uncle owes my state a shit-pot full of money."

Larry said, "But Uncle Harold's lost his marbles and I think he's damn near broke. Hell, you ought to see where he lives."

"I've been to the house and that brings up another question. There was a cute blonde at the house and she drove a red Porsche."

"Nice boobs?"

"That's her. Who is she?"

"My cousin Donna. She was one of those surprise kids. You know, the ones who are born nine months after a twentieth anniversary cruise in the Caribbean."

I said, "So let me get this straight. Harold Haffner has a daughter and her name is Donna?"

"Right."

"So what's the name of the blonde who drove the red Porsche that was parked in the driveway at the Haffner place?"

"That's Donna."

"I'm confused. She told me her name was Betty."

"That's a woman for you. Trust me, her name is Donna."

"And her father, Harold, can't remember shit."

"Right again, but now it's my turn to ask a question. How's the State of Nevada going to get the back taxes if my uncle's really broke?"

"We're sure he's hiding some assets."

"But if those assets are really hidden, poor old Uncle Harold won't remember where he put them."

"So now we're down to why I'm buying you two cases of Newcastle Brown. Sit down, grab a couple sheets of this paperwork and let's see if we can figure out where he stashed the loot."

My first page was full of worthless crap about a dude named Fred Harvey.

I said, "How long did you say you've lived in Needles?"

"All my life, except for that time in Nam, of course."

"This first sheet's all about a guy named Fred Harvey. Is he a local guy?"

"Bear, you're putting me on, right?"

"Nope."

"I thought everybody knew that Fred Harvey was a big time hotel and restaurant tycoon during the railroad boom."

"What railroad boom?"

"Jesus, where did you go to school?"

"Graduated from Elko High. Why? Hey, are you making fun of my—"

The door to the men's area popped open and Flo stuck her head in. "I've been watching a soap opera while I walked on that damn treadmill and now the show is over. Are you finished in here?"

Larry jumped up. "Bear, are you going to introduce us?"

I mumbled, "Larry, this is Flo. Flo, this is Larry."

Flo smiled. "Pleased to meet you."

I growled, "Larry Haffner."

I heard Flo suck some air. "Did you say Haffner?"

"Yup."

Larry jumped toward Flo and stuck out his hand. "Pleased to meet you. Bear tells me you are chasing my Uncle Harold because he didn't pay some kind of entertainment tax in Nevada."

She glanced at me, and then she said, "Right. That's why we've been baking inside this town-like oven for nearly a week."

Still holding out his hand, Larry said, "You don't like Needles?"

"It's okay if you like to sweat a lot. Bear, for the third time, can we go now?"

Larry bowed real low, like he thought he was one of those old-time knights, or something. "Your partner and I were just discussing the history of Needles and Fred Harvey, the man famous for his Harvey House restaurants and hotels along the southwest railroad system."

With more than her usual layer of nastiness, Flo said, "Oh, that Fred Harvey."

Larry smiled. "I was damn sure you'd know who I was talking about."

I grabbed up all the papers. "Flo, what time does Haffner come in here each morning?"

"His daily routine puts him at the gym every morning around 11:00, plus or minus thirty seconds. Why?"

"That means we've got all night. Let's take this paperwork back to the motel. You've got that little laptop computer if we need to look anything up. I took a quick scan at the top page of this crap and it doesn't make any sense to me, but maybe you can come up with—"

Larry started to run around the men's area in circles waving his arms and yelling, "That's it! Bear, I could join you and Flo and help with the paperwork. Remember, I'm Uncle Harold's nephew. All we have to do is stop by the liquor store by the river, purchase my two cases of beer, and then we can head to your motel to continue this discussion."

Suddenly he stopped running, grabbed Flo's hand, and his fingers started to work up her arm. "I'd invite you back to my place but the interior rooms of my abode are undergoing a complete renovation at the moment."

"Larry, let go of her arm."

His yellow eyes flashed bolts of lightning at me. I think he was pissed that I'd caught him rubbing her skin.

His hand pulled away like he'd been stung by a bee. "Right. Flo, does your laptop at the motel have access to the Internet?"

"Of course! Our motel has wireless."

Larry said, "I generally access the Internet through the library computer system, but it's against the law to drink beer in the library. Sometimes I sneak one in by wrapping a can in a newspaper, but the head librarian has gotten wise to that trick. What I'm trying to say is that we'll need access to the Internet so I can bring your partner up to speed, so to speak."

At that point I was pretty sure Larry was conning me, or trying to get close to Flo. With him you could never be sure, but I was getting desperate. Pinky needed a name and all I had was Harold Haffner, a man who couldn't tell what he did an hour ago, much less if he killed a dude last month. As my Pop used to say, 'A bird in the hand was a hell of a lot better than the damn nest made of straw and shit'.

Flo said, "I don't—"

I said, "Okay, we'll all head back to our motel, but Flo doesn't drink beer. She takes an occasional glass of red wine. I'll stop along the way and buy a couple of cases beer, but it won't be Newcastle Brown, and I'll throw in one of those big boxes of burgundy for her."

The dark storm brewing behind Larry's glowing eyes simmered down a touch. "My good man, you're a scholar and a gentleman."

An hour later, while Flo fiddled with the computer, and me and Larry were just starting on our second brew, I heard a knock on our room door.

I looked through the little peephole. Shit, Pinky was standing there. That's all I needed.

I opened the door and tried to act casual. "Boss, why are you here?"

"Because I can't trust you to find my man." He pushed me aside and said, "And who is that cretin sitting on the bed drinking a can of beer?"

"Him? Oh that's Larry. We're all trying to figure out where Harold Haffner hid his treasure so he can pay the back taxes he owes the State of Nevada." I winked at Pinky a bunch of times.

Pinky frowned. "Back taxes? What the hell are you talking—"

For a smart dude, Pinky doesn't pick things up very fast. I pushed him back into the parking lot and closed the door. Leaning against the hood of my truck, I said, "Pinky, you have to cool it. I just told you that Haffner owed back taxes because I didn't want Larry to know that we're tailing Haffner because we think he murdered Brady Blackstone."

"I see. You told a calculated fabrication in an attempt to prove your hypothesis. My boy, I am impressed. You have come a long way in a short time. Now go over everything again. What makes you think that Harold Haffner is our man?"

Larry opened the door and tossed me a fresh beer.

I pushed Pinky toward the pool. "First, I found out that Harold was hiding a key under his desk in Los

Angeles. Second, he was supposed to be a sharp guy who tells other people how to invest their money, but the bastard lives like he's broke. We've been tailing Harold Haffner since we got to Needles. So far, we know what he does and when he does it, but what we don't know is why he's doing it. Third, to make things messier, Larry, he's the guy who tossed me the beer, comes along and tells me that Haffner's lost his short term memory, it's called Ambrosia something."

"Antegrade Amnesia. I am aware of the illness. It is endemic among Alzheimer patients. Are you trying to tell me that Harold Haffner has Alzheimer's?"

I thought for a moment, "Shit no! Do I look like some kind of a doctor? But I know if he's really lost his marbles, you're going to have a tough time convincing Willow to swap him for Jack Spurlock."

"Now I understand some of the reason for your lack of progress, but why is everyone sitting around your motel drinking beer?"

"Flo's drinking red wine."

"Bear, I have had a very long day so please do not test my patience any further. You still have not explained why you are involved in all this frivolity?"

"Oh that. We're looking for information on a dude named Fred Harvey. Old Harold was hiding a stack of paperwork in his gym locker—I had the key, so I lifted everything and brought the stack back here. This is the cool part. The first page was all about some kind of a deal with that Harvey dude."

"Will Haffner miss the paperwork?"

"No, he won't be back to the gym until tomorrow morning and we'll be done by then."

"So beyond consuming enormous quantities of beer and wine, what was your plan to solve the ambiguity toward Fred Harvey?"

"Flo's looking the name up on Google to find out what the hell he has to do with Harold Haffner. Boss, while we wait for her to finish, grab a beer and go through the paperwork to see what you can figure out."

"Is the beer imported?"

"Nope. It's the cheapest crap I could find."

"I note that Flo is imbibing a red wine."

"Yup."

Before he asked his next question I guessed that Pinky was thinking over Flo's taste in wine.

"Did Flo's wine come in a bottle?"

"Nope. It came in a box about the size of two six packs of beer."

"I will take you up on your offer of a beer. However, make sure the can is ice-cold. My taste buds will need to be as numb as possible while the foul liquid slides past my tongue."

THIRTY

Pinky—Needles, California

I pushed my way past Bear and entered his room, an area I was sure looked similar to most of the cheap motel rooms that have spread like a creeping fungus along the byways of America. The wall of cinderblock on my left sported a piece of trailer-trash furniture, euphemistically called an entertainment center, while the majority of the remaining square footage was taken up by a king-sized bed.

I spotted a door and prayed that it led to a bathroom. "My good man, after I spend a penny I will be ready for that beer."

A moment later I exited the bathroom. Bear handed me an ice-cold can of beer with a flavor so non-descript that the brand should, and will remain nameless.

"Thank you. Now, I think it would be best if I take the paperwork back to my room where I can work in peace."

"You could work in my room with all of us, Boss. There's plenty of room on the bed next to Larry."

I glanced at the stranger that Bear had called Larry. He looked relatively normal, and for most of Bear's acquaintances, that was a step up. However, there was something odd in the way his head was carried on his neck. His skull was perched straight, and then, for no obvious reason, it lolled slightly, as if the large cranium lacked a solid attachment to the spinal column. I glanced at Larry's eyes. They were the color of egg yoke and seemed to glow ever so slightly.

I said, "No thank you. I am a touch tired from the long drive."

As I crossed the threshold, the she-witch known as Flo, who had been hunched over a laptop, called, "Nice to see you, too."

The first time I had met Flo Sonderlund was less than a year ago. Her aggressive attitude toward my person had annoyed me then and continues to aggravate me to this day. However, Bear is an adult and I am positive he must receive some sort of massive compensation for him to continue their relationship.

I arrived at my room, opened a second beer, and started to scan through the stack of papers. It took me no more than ten minutes to discover a key sheet. I grabbed the phone and called Bear's room. "Get over here at once."

"Why? Are you ready for another beer?"

"No!" I glanced around the drab room I had to endure. "Wait, I have changed my mind. Bring me one, but be sure it is ice-cold."

"Want me to bring Flo and Larry with the beer?"

"No! At the conclusion of your female friend's previous visit to my abode I had to refinish the top of my marble dining room table at considerable expense. I cannot imagine what possible destruction she could do to this bomb shelter you call a motel room, but I am taking no chances."

Bear's voice dropped to a whisper, "Boss, I don't think I should leave Larry alone with Flo. He's pretty horny and before you got here I caught him grabbing her—"

"Please, spare me the lurid details. Bring him along if you must, but I will hold you responsible for his actions."

Before I finished unpacking my suitcase there was a knock at my door. I opened it. There stood Bear, Larry, and Flo, and she was carrying a large box under her arm.

Bear said, "Flo thought you might like some wine."

My throat constricted at the thought of the swill contained in her wine-in-a-box. "Thank you, Flo, for your kind thought, but I believe the beer, as bad as it is, will suffice."

Flo walked past me, placed the box on the bathroom sink, and proceeded to fill her plastic cup from the spigot. "Whatever." She pushed past me, sat down on the only chair and opened her laptop.

Bear said, "Okay, Boss, what'd you find?"

I handed him a small stack of paper and said, "These are Limited Liability Partnership documents. The name of the company is El Garces and the—"

"Shit, that's the same name as the restored railroad station in downtown Needles."

The strange man who went by the name of Larry had had the audacity to interrupt me. I turned my attention to him. He was the sort of human being that I would avoid making eye contact with under normal circumstances. However, with two million dollars hanging in the balance, these were not normal times.

"Sir, I assume you have a last name?

"Yes I do."

I could see that Larry came from the same mold as Bear. "And that name is?"

"Haffner."

"And you are related to Harold Haffner?"

"Yup. He's my uncle."

"Fine. What can you tell me about El Garces?"

"How much do you want to know?"

"Everything."

Larry Haffner popped a new can of beer. "Okay. Way back, in the late eighteen hundreds, a guy named Fred Harvey built a shit-pot full of good restaurants along the Atchison, Topeka, and Santa Fe Railway. By the turn of the century he had eighty-four joints and one of the best was located in Needles."

I said, "And that restaurant was called El Garces?"

"Wrong, but you should get an extra point for trying." The man let out a high-pitched cry that sounded like the scream of a captured rabbit being carried off by a raptor. "The original building burned down and it was replaced with a concrete one called El Garces. Today, that building's a tourist attraction in Needles. Every year the local school kids go there on a field trip. Hell, even I went there when I was in the third grade."

I made a mental note to avoid asking for Larry's input on future questions and said, "What we need to know is why would Harold Haffner form an LLP called El Garces? Perhaps the next document I hold before you will provide some insight. According to the original filing the officers of the partnership were as follows— Donna Haffner, Chairman and CEO—Harold Haffner, Chief Financial Officer. Who is Donna Haffner?"

Larry said, "That's easy. She's Harold's daughter."

Bear said, "Pinky, this is the funny part. She told me her name was Betty, and—"

Flo said, "Do you mean to tell me that Betty-the-blonde's real name is Donna?"

Bear said, "Yup. Larry just told me—"

I slammed my fist down. "Ladies and gentlemen, cease your inane babble. Bear, is the fact that this woman's name was Betty important to accomplish our goal?"

"I don't think . . . maybe, Boss, to tell the truth, I don't know."

I said, "But we do know that Donna Haffner is Harold's daughter, and she's the CEO of a LLP called El Garces. Now keep your mouth shut until I request more input from you."

Bear said. "Right."

I said, "So there is a limited partnership—"

Flo said, "Pinky, if you'd stop jumping all over Bear and listen to me I could give you some background on the El Garces name."

Listening to anything Flo had to say was abhorrent to me, but her input had to be more productive than Larry's, or Bear's, so I opened my charm floodgates toward Bear's bimbo. "Flo, a modicum of background would not hinder our pursuit."

Her eyes scanned the laptop screen as she spoke. "It seems that Fred Harvey was a real innovator. He hired women, paid them well, gave them free room and board, and they became known as the Harvey Girls. It sounds to me like Harvey treated his employees better than a certain short attorney from Carson City who will remain nameless."

Bear said, "Flo, you promised me that you were going to try to be nice to Pinky."

She sighed. "Right, I forgot." Her eyes shifted back to the laptop screen. "Harvey died in 1901. The company was tied to passenger railroad traffic and as the years passed both businesses dwindled. In 1968 Amfac Corporation bought out the company and later Amfac changed its name to Xanterra. I've checked all the search engines on the web, and except for the town of Needles, there's no mention of El Garces."

Keeping the sarcasm out of my voice as much as possible, I said, "Thank you, Flo, for that valuable information." I waved the third document. "This sheet indicates that the El Garces LLP was involved in a massive project, more than a hundred million dollar project to be exact. The paper mentions a hotel, casino, and a major restaurant that would bring back the old Harvey Girl concept. Also, the original LLP document shows Donna and Harold Haffner, et al. For the non-legal folks in this room, the term et al means there are other partners involved in the deal."

I hesitated for a moment to let my last words sink in. "Also it is important to note that the LLP documents were signed less than six months ago."

Larry said, "So what's et al and the dates got to do with anything?"

Bear said, "I think I know about the date. Larry, when did your uncle start to ask you your name every day?"

"Don't know exactly. About a year, no maybe a half a year ago."

I said, "For a moment, put yourselves in the place of Donna Haffner. You are partners with your father in a deal worth more than a hundred million dollars and your father is losing his grip on reality. What would you do?"

Flo stood up. "If I was Donna, I'd grab my investment and run to the nearest exit."

I said, "Flo, that is an interesting, but I fear flawed solution. About what I would expect from a woman of your ilk."

The she-witch jumped up, tucked her laptop under her arm, grabbed her box of wine and stomped out of my room.

Bear said, "Boss, that wasn't very nice. Flo was just trying to help out and answer your question."

Larry said, "Hold on, Bear. I don't know the man very well, but this time I agree with Pinky."

I smiled. "Larry, those are the first intelligent words I have heard you utter since we met."

Larry frowned. "Hey, what kind of a crack is that?" He reached under his loose shirt and pulled out a 38 special. He screamed, "I don't give a shit if you are a high powered attorney. You take that nasty crack about my intelligence back or your brains will be splattered all over the walls of this room."

I was ready and able to challenge the man, but before I could confront the quickness of Larry's trigger finger, Bear jumped between us. "Hey, Larry, I thought we agreed you'd keep that thing in your pants."

"I promised you, Bear, not this chicken-shit lawyer."

Bear said, "Boss, I think this would be a good time to apologize."

"I agree. Larry, I don't know what came over me. In the brief time we have known each other, you have become an integral part of this team, adding true gems of wisdom to the cause, so to speak."

Larry stared into my eyes, as if he was not sure I had actually apologized. Then, he tucked the pistol back into his belt, grabbed another can of beer and flashed me a smile, a grin that indicated to me that he had missed at least two decades of regular dental check-ups.

THIRTY-ONE

Bear—Needles, California

I forgot to tell Pinky about Larry's little problem with big guns, so I hustled Larry out of Pinky's room before he could draw down again. As I said, Pinky's a damn good lawyer, but once his mouth gets into gear anything could happen.

Back in our room, I calmed Flo down, poured her a fresh glass of wine and turned on the TV.

I said, "Larry, I think it's past the time for you to go home."

"But there's a few cans of beer left."

I moved him toward the door. "Go home, damn it!"

He grabbed the last two cans and shot through the door faster than I can spit a watermelon seed.

Flo tossed down her wine and said, "So what's the story about Betty-the-blonde?"

"Huh?"

"I'll bet you knew her real name all the time."

"Babe. It's exactly like I said before. Back in Oakland she told me her name was Betty."

"Humph."

Sometimes there's just no understanding Flo. I hung around a while just to be sure Larry had really gone, and then I headed back to Pinky's room.

"Boss, you've got to be careful around Larry. He's a Nam vet and has a short fuse."

"That, my boy, is an understatement."

"Okay, what's next?"

"As I see this case, we are one step away from an airtight suspect for the Blackstone murder. If Harold Haffner is not competent, that leaves us with Donna Haffner."

"I forgot to tell you this before, but she was the same broad who showed me around backstage in Oakland, and she was driving the red Porsche I tried to follow out of LA."

He gave his are-you-kidding-me look. "And is there a reason that you did not feel those facts were salient to this investigation?"

"Come on, Pinky, I just went through this pissing match with Flo. IN OAKLAND I DIDN'T KNOW SHE WAS HAFFNER'S DAUGHTER!"

"Calm down my boy, and listen to me. That woman had access backstage. I am beginning to think that Donna Haffner holds the key here. Do you know where we can find her?"

"Nope, but I know where the Haffner house is and I saw her there once."

"We need to pursue this line of inquiry immediately."

I said, "Does that mean you want to go to the Haffner house now?"

"My boy, I am pleased to note that your comprehension of the English language has improved."

We headed to my pick-up and in a few minutes we were parked in the same spot I had used a few days ago to watch the place.

Pinky said, "I see what you mean. The Haffner domicile has seen better days. What is next?"

"We'll need to get closer to see if Donna's car is parked in the driveway."

The setting sun made a line of pointy hills to the south glow, sort of like a set of shark's teeth on fire. A couple of minutes later the sky was dark. A light came on inside the Haffner house.

I said, "Okay, before we go, we need a plan. I think we should—."

"And why must we always use your plan?"

Pinky could charm a jury out of their clothes, but he was totally worthless outside of a courtroom. "Boss, I know the lay of the land so we need to follow my plan this time."

Pinky said, "For the moment, I will accede to your demands. However, if your local knowledge does not give you the edge you claim, then we will stop and renegotiate."

I was pretty sure if I punched him in the mouth I'd be out of a job, so I relaxed my fist and said, "Okay. We're both going to walk by the house sort of casual like. We can't look right or left, only straight ahead. As we pass the driveway I'll glance to my right and check out the garage. If we both look that direction at the same time we'll look weird so you keep staring straight ahead. Now, if the car's parked outside, like it was the last time I was here, we'll know she's home. If not, she's—"

"Come, come, my boy, you are not talking to a child. I understand the exercise. Let us be off."

Pinky's little legs took about one and a half steps for every one of mine. In fact, he was damn near having to run to keep up. We passed the house. When I turned my head to see if the car was there, Pinky stopped and started to walk toward garage. I grabbed him around the waist and carried him back to my pick-up.

He was sputtering when I set him down. "Damn it, Bear! Carrying me back to the truck was not part of the original plan."

"But you turned and walked down the driveway. Boss, we were lucky it was so dark nobody spotted us. Don't you ever listen?"

"Humph. As you so aptly pointed out, it was too dark to see clearly."

"But that wasn't part of my plan."

"Let me say that I agreed to disagree on that section of your plan. What is next?"

"Okay, her car wasn't parked in the driveway so I guess that means she's not home, and if she's not home, we could nose around the garage."

"What are we looking for?"

"Boss, we went through this once before. We're not looking for anything special, we're just looking. That's why it's called nosing around."

"How will we know if we have found it?"

"Jesus! Just clam up and stick close to me."

After waiting a few minutes for the sky to turn completely black we left the truck to try again. When we reached the garage I found a door on the side toward the house. I turned the handle and it wasn't locked. I pushed the door open and a damned siren went off. I threw Pinky under my arm again and ran both of us back to my pick-up.

We watched as someone inside the Haffner place shined a flashlight beam back and forth around the garage door.

I said, "I hadn't planned on that."

Pinky said, "There must be something valuable inside that garage. However, if you are correct and Harold Haffner is non compos mentis, he will soon turn off his flashlight and go back to sleep."

We sat there in the dark and waited to see what Haffner would do next. My heart jumped as I spotted a female figure running from the house to the garage. When the garage door opened, a red Porsche backed out and visions of my high-paying job disappeared along with the taillights into the gloom.

"Boss, our investigation could be toast."

"Don't just sit there. Follow her, damn it."

I glanced out the window. There was a quarter moon. Back when I was a kid, during Easter vacation, I'd help my Pop look for lost lambs on nights like this. "I'll follow her, but you better buckle up tight 'cause I'm not going to turn my headlights on."

Pinky jumped like he'd grabbed the bare end of a plugged in electrical cord. He squeaked. "Are you sure that is a good idea?"

"We'll be okay . . . as along as another car doesn't come along."

THIRTY-TWO

Bear—Needles, California

I gunned the engine and stayed a good quarter mile behind the Porsche. Needles was a small town so following a car's rear lights was a lot easier than trying to tail someone on the crowded LA freeways in the daytime.

After a minute we were in the desert. I dropped back far enough to keep the red lights in sight, but not close enough to be seen. Suddenly the Porsche's stoplights came on. I hit the brakes hard.

Pinky said, "Why did you do that?"

"Because she stopped."

"But we are in the middle of nowhere."

In the darkness I could just barely make out the shape of someone getting into the passenger's side of the Porsche.

I said, "She just picked someone up."

"I do not see a house. Who would live out here?"

I said, "I'll bet my next month's paycheck it's Larry." Son-of-a-bitch, I thought. So Donna and Larry are working on this thing together.

"Larry? Who is . . . you don't mean that creature with the terrible dental work who pulled a gun on me back at the motel?"

"The same dude."

Pinky leaned forward and stared at the moonlit desert as my truck rolled near the spot where the Porsche had stopped. "Am I missing something? Where is Larry's house?"

I slowed. "Get out and look down. Underneath the road there's a dry wash running into a culvert. That's where Larry lives."

Pinky shook his head. "About what I would expect from that creature."

I hit the gas and soon the Porsche's rear lights came into view. We headed back into Needles, wandered around some streets, and when the Porsche's left turn indicator started to blink, I said, "Pinky, see if you can pick up the name of the street we're on."

Pinky said, "I just missed the sign. It is too dark."

Jesus, dragging him along was worse than working with Flo. Sometimes she was a pain in the ass and complained about almost everything but at least she had a good pair of eyes to go along with her other good parts. Pinky? Except for his money, and the job he gave me, was just an endless pain in the ass—without any of the good parts.

I said, "Hey, do your part. I'm doing all I can following the Porsche."

"Bear, don't snap at me. Would you rather I drive so you can watch for signs?

"Oh sure, I'll pull over. We'll switch drivers. Of course by that time the Porsche will be long—"

The wail of a siren and a flashing red light stopped me cold. "Oh shit, that's all we needed."

I pulled over and looked in the rearview mirror. All I could see behind us was the reflection of the cop's headlights. "Pinky, we could be up shit creek without a paddle. No matter what the cop says, keep your mouth shut and let me handle this."

A voice came from the back of my truck. "Move your hands to the door and don't make any sudden moves. My partner and I have our weapons drawn. Driver, we will wait as you open your door and exit the vehicle. After the driver has left the vehicle I want the passenger to do the same as the driver. Once the passenger is outside the truck, anyone else in the vehicle will exit."

I opened my door, raised my hands, but before I could get my feet out, Pinky said, "Bear, I am positive they are bluffing. This is the United States and I will not allow a common law enforcement officer to use his jack-booted Gestapo tactics on me. Their actions represent an unconstitutional invasion of my rights. I am going to remain inside this truck until that officer gives me a good explanation of why—"

"Pinky, if you were here all by yourself, I wouldn't give a damn if you sat there until the cows came home, but those cops aren't going to know that you're the only really dumb guy in this truck and I'm not ready to get shot. I'm leaving the truck now and don't you say another word. Do exactly what they tell you to do or after they shoot both of us dead, I'll figure out a way to come back from the grave and kick your ass from here to Sunday."

Pinky hesitated, and then said, "All right, I will exit the truck as the officer demanded, but only because you give me no alternative."

After the cops patted us down and took our driver's licenses, me and Pinky stood spread-eagle outside my truck as an occasional car slowed down to see what was going on.

The big cop said, "Mr. Zabarte, according to these driver's licenses you and Mr. Delmont are both from Carson City, Nevada. That's about three hundred miles north of here. Tell me, why are you cruising around Needles without your headlights on?"

I said, "Oh my God, I forgot to turn them on. Officer, it was just a dumb mistake on my part. Your town has such bright street lights I didn't even notice."

Pinky sort of pushed his way between the big cop and me. "Officer, it is obvious to me that you have wandered into a legal area beyond your normal capacity. My name is J. Pinkus Delmont. I am northern Nevada's most sought after attorney, and as such, I feel it is time to warn you that—"

The big cop pushed Pinky away. "Pipe down, Shorty. Mr. Zabarte, assuming that you did forget to turn your lights on, you still haven't told me what you gentlemen are doing in Needles."

That's when I got lucky. Over the cop's shoulder I spotted a sign that said we were 14 miles from The Avi Resort and Casino. "Officer, we were on our way back to the Avi Resort, the hotel where we're staying tonight. My

207

lawyer friend and me had read about the historic El Garces building here in Needles. He's been a big Fred Harvey fan all his life, like I'm a Boston Red Sox fan. His house is filled with all sorts of old railroad crap. Ain't that right, Pinky?"

Pinky stared at me for a second, like I'd lost my marbles, and then he finally caught on. "You are correct. Officer, you are blessed with a truly significant structure in your fine town, one that actually puts Rome's Pantheon to shame."

I heard the radio in the cop's car squawk. The big cop stayed with us while the shorter cop walked to his car. The big cop said, "So what do you think of the Avi?"

I didn't have a clue so I faked it. "It seems like a nice place."

My cell phone buzzed. "Can I answer it?"

The big cop nodded.

"Bear, where are you?" asked Flo.

"Flo, we'll be back at the hotel shortly."

"What hotel are you talking about? We're staying in a motel."

"I know that. We'll be back soon."

Flo said, "Are you with Pinky?"

"Yes."

Voices from the cop's radio filled the air.

"Who was that talking?"

"A cop's radio."

"A cop! My God, what sort of horrendous situation has Pinky gotten you into this time?"

"It's nothing. I forgot to turn on my headlights and the local cop pulled us over."

"Are you fooling around with that blonde again? I don't believe you. Put the policeman on the phone."

I handed the big cop the phone. "She wants to talk to you."

He took the phone. "Hello."

He listened for a second, then said, "Yes, ma'am. My partner and I were—"

He listened some more. I could have told him straight up that Flo was a motor mouth, but sometimes it's better to let a guy figure out that sort of thing on his own.

"Ma'am, I have to—"

"Yes, ma'am. That's—"

"Ma'am, you don't understand. My partner and I have a specific area we cover. We can't drive —"

He looked at me, his eyes begging me to bail him out.

I nodded and reached for the phone.

He handed it to me like it was it was a bomb about to explode. "Flo, the cop had to leave to catch a bank robber."

"Bear, I told him—"

"Babe, I'm sure you told him more than he wanted to hear. We'll be home soon. Bye."

The big cop shook his head, and let out a whistle. "Thanks for the rescue. You know, I've never been to the Avi myself. I like the joints a few miles further north on the Laughlin strip. You know, you can't beat the price at those strip hotels. I mean for as little as twenty bucks a night you can get a great room that includes—"

The other cop yelled, "We have to go."

The big cop handed over me and Pinky's driver's licenses. "Being that you're from out of state, I'll let you go this time, but turn those headlights on and keep them on."

I said, "Right, officer. I'll do that."

Me and Pinky got back in the truck.

He said, "We lost the Porsche because of those damn cops."

"Yeah, but at least we found out two things—the car was heading north, towards Laughlin, and driving with your headlights off is against the law. What we need to figure out is what are Donna and Larry up to."

Pinky said, "More important than that is what we are up to? My good man, a great amount of money, a veritable financial windfall for both of us, depends on our

209

ability to escort Harold Haffner through the portals of the Carson City jail in less than thirty-six hours.

"Okay, let's head back to the Haffner place. Donna's gone and the old guy doesn't know shit from Shinola, so we can nose around."

Hoping we'd avoid the same cop car, I kept to the back roads on our drive back to Haffner's place. I parked the truck on a side street and in a couple of seconds we were walking up the front steps of the house.

"Pinky, be careful. This front porch is pretty shaky."

"I will use extreme caution. However, before I move another step I need to understand why we are standing at the entrance to the Haffner abode."

I said, "Just follow my lead."

I rang the doorbell. The porch light came on and Haffner stuck his head out.

"Yes?"

I sort of pushed Pinky away, and said, "Good evening, Mr. Haffner. I stopped by a couple of days ago and we talked about replacing your front porch. I told you then that I'd come back in a few days to check out your garage."

Haffner looked me up and down and shook his head. "I don't remember that, but I don't remember anything very well these days. Are you sure?"

"Positive. Now I've brought a member of my crew with me so we can be sure my bid on the job will be correct."

He looked over my shoulder at the night sky. "Can you do a good job in the dark?"

"We work better at night."

"I wish you'd wait until my daughter returns."

"When do you expect her?"

Haffner's face went blank. "I don't know. She said something about checking the construction project."

"What construction is that, Mr. Haffner?"

His eyes lit up. "My new hotel."

"Oh, you have a hotel?"

"No. At least not yet, but my daughter tells me that the hotel will be finished any day now. Yes, I remember now. That's what my daughter is doing, checking on the progress of the construction. She checks it out almost every day."

I said, "That's good, Mr. Haffner. Now my partner and I need to look inside your garage."

He frowned. "I don't think that's a good idea, but I can't remember why."

Pinky pushed me to one side and said, "My good man, do you store any valuables in your garage?"

He scratched his head. "It's possible, but I don't know for sure."

I could see that the poor bastard was as bad off as Larry had told me. I felt sorry about what we were doing—and then I remembered the five thousand bonus. I said, "If you did, your garage would have an alarm. Lots of people put alarms on their garages to protect their valuable stuff."

"You could be right. Say, how about a beer?"

Haffner turned and we followed him into the kitchen. I noticed a new switch mounted on the wall by the back door. It sat just above the light switch. Haffner opened the refrigerator, stood for a minute, and then said, "Why did we come to the kitchen?"

"You're getting us a couple of beers."

He thought for a second. "Right."

He pulled out two cool ones and then hitched his pants up. I noticed his zipper was open and there were wet stains around the fly. "I'm sorry young fella, what were we talking about?"

I took the beers. Handed one to Pinky, and said, "Thanks."

Haffner said, "You're welcome. Now if you'll excuse me, I think I have to pee."

He walked down the hall and left Pinky and me standing alone in his kitchen. I walked to the back door and flipped the alarm switch off.

Pinky said, "Let us make haste. Time waits for no man."

"Hold on. Haffner seems like a nice guy. Do we really have to turn him over to Willow? And don't forget, we're in California. What about that extra-inning thing?"

"I believe the word you are striving for is extradition. Do not concern yourself with that little detail. I have a plan to solve that minor problem. But back to your original question, 'Do we really have to turn Haffner over to Willow?' My boy, we do if I am to collect my fee from Lucinda Blackstone and if you are to receive my generous bonus. Now let us—"

"Boss, there are times when I think what we're doing is wrong, and this is one of those times."

"Bear, if you are going to stand there and struggle with the morality of the situation, go right ahead. However, if I enter that garage alone, I will interpret your lack of resolve as your way of informing me that you have forfeited your five thousand dollar bonus."

The bastard had me by the short hairs and he knew it.

I said, "Damn it, you can't get rid of me that easily."

Pinky took a sip of his beer. "So be it. Let us proceed."

I opened the same garage door that had set off the alarm, and this time nothing happened.

Pinky said, "I like the lack of sound."

"Me too."

It was really dark inside, so I felt around the door jam. My fingers brushed a light switch. An overhead florescent tube flickered on. Leaning against the garage wall stood a six by six sign. The signboard looked like it had been mounted on two posts. I saw screw holes on the side and deep indentations on the backside where the nuts had tightened the bolts. A couple of the painted letters were chipped, the edges were a bit scruffy, like the sign had been out in the weather for a while, then taken down and stored in the garage.

COMING SOON
THE EL GARCES HOTEL AND CASINO
FEATURING THE BEAUTIFUL HARVEY GIRLS
APPEARING SOON IN LAUGHLIN'S NEWEST AND
LARGEST SHOWROOM
THE BRADY BLACKSTONE THEATER

I said, "What the hell—"

"My boy, I would be willing to risk my Lucinda Blackstone fee on my next statement—Brady Blackstone was one of the partners legally known as et al."

I took a big swig of beer. "Boss, I bet you're right 'cause I know how much you'd hate to lose that fee."

"That is correct."

"Okay, so you'll lose your fee if you're wrong, but I still don't know who else might be part of et al, and what this sign has to do with Haffner being a murder suspect."

"I apologize. I forgot with whom I was speaking."

There were times when keeping up with Pinky's brain made me feel like a dumb shit, and that was usually about the same time I tried hard to keep from smashing him in the chops. But my Pop had taught me that because I was a big kid, I had to learn to keep my temper. In my head I counted, One—two—three, and then I said, "Boss, slow down and explain things for this dumb son of a sheepherder."

"First, Harold Haffner was the CFO for Brady's national tour. At some point, my guess is a month ago, Brady figured out his main moneyman was losing his touch with reality. Not a good omen for a national tour that grosses more than a hundred million a year.

"Second, The El Garces partnership papers were signed six months ago, prior to Haffner's illness becoming obvious. Now, if I have guessed correctly and Brady is one of those et al partners, he would have invested a very large sum of money with a man who, as we have just witnessed, is non compos mentis. Once Brady discovered his investment in the El Garces partnership was at risk, he would have confronted Haffner. That was when

213

Haffner devised his nefarious plan to kill Brady. My boy, don't you see it? Haffner had to kill Brady or he would stand to lose everything he had worked for."

"I still don't get it. You think Haffner murdered Brady because—"

"Because Brady destroyed Haffner's vision of immortality if he pulled his money out of the El Garces partnership. Trust me, you can pilfer a man's food, you can even take away his source of revenue, but if you destroy a man's dream, you risk pushing that man over the edge. Once you do that—"

A female voice cut through the air. "Shut up and don't move. I'm holding a double-barreled shotgun and it's aimed at your backbones. The shotgun is loaded with slugs. According to my cousin Larry, from this distance one of those slugs would blow a hole the size of a football through your chest. Both of you put your hands in the air and then slowly turn around."

I was beginning to not like Needles. This was the fourth time that somebody had pointed a gun at me and it was getting old, but before I could do anything, Larry Haffner's insane cackle bounced off the walls of the old wooden garage. That did it. That crazy Nam vet had really pissed me off.

I growled, "LARRY!"

THIRTY-THREE

Bear—Needles, California

Donna screamed, "What's wrong with you two? I said turn slowly and stick those hands up, or I'll shoot."

I'd been stuck in this kind of mess before and I was pretty sure that most dudes holding a gun didn't have the balls to pull the trigger. That was with most dudes, and Donna wasn't a dude, so I didn't have a clue what the hell a broad would do. I reached up, almost high enough to grab the rafters, and slowly turned around.

Standing a few feet away was Larry and Donna, and sort of helping to hold up the barrel of the shotgun was Donna's right boob. I gave Larry the stink-eye.

Larry said, "Don't get all pissed off, Bear. I know I promised that I wouldn't point a gun at you again but this is a whole new game." He cackled like he was a kid again, opening presents Christmas morning. "I'm not holding the shotgun and we just caught you and your shyster friend breaking and entering into my uncle's garage. Most cops would understand if Donna shot you both."

Pinky said, "My good man, I take umbrage at your accusation."

Larry frowned. "Huh!"

Pinky said, "Bear and I did not break and enter into this building. We walked through the side door and we entered the garage under the direction of Harold Haffner, the owner of this rather ramshackle structure."

Donna said, "Poppy told you to come in here?"

I said, "You got it, Babe. Your dad asked us to find him a screwdriver. Now point that damn gun somewhere else before it goes off and something really bad happens."

She glanced at Larry.

He shrugged.

Donna's eyes darted back and forth between me and Pinky. "Keep your hands up. I've got to think this through. Larry, I recognize the big guy from Oakland when he was snooping around the show, but the little one is new to me."

Larry said, "Him? He's some kind of a lawyer."

She said, "Okay, big boy, you've got ten seconds to tell me why you're sneaking into my father's garage before I blow a hole through your chest."

Pinky started to lower his arms.

Donna jerked the barrels of the shotgun up. "I told you to keep them up."

Pinky's hands shot up. "My dear lady, we represent the Nevada Tax Board. According to our records, the Brady Blackstone tour left our state without paying two hundred and twenty-seven dollars in back entertainment tax."

As much as Pinky is a pain in the ass, I had to admit that he was pretty good in court—like when he had to shade the truth to get his guy off, but nobody in their right mind, and that included Donna and Larry, was going to fall for his line of crap that the state of Nevada would have two guys run around California for three weeks for a couple of hundred bucks.

I bumped Pinky with my hip. "Miss Haffner, my arms are getting real tired. I promise I won't make any quick moves. Would it be okay if my partner and me lower them?"

Donna shook her head, and then she glanced at Larry. "Cuz, how did you know the little fart was a lawyer?"

I said, "Please, Miss Haffner, my arms!"

She said, "Okay, but I have my finger on the trigger so move very slowly."

I lowered my hands as slow as I could. "Thank you. Now, Miss Haffner, the tour actually owes the state of Nevada much more than two hundred and twenty-seven dollars. There's a lot more to this than a couple of—"

She said, "Thank you. It's about time someone started to tell me the truth for a change. I knew there had to be more than money involved here. Okay, go ahead. What's the real reason you're here?"

I didn't have a clue what to say next so I stalled for time. "See, Pinky. I told you she'd never fall for that line of crap. Go ahead, tell her why we are really here."

Pinky stepped out, put his hands behind his back, and started to do his circling thing as he talked, like he does in court. "Miss Haffner, my associate was correct. There is more involved here, much more, but I need to consider how to construct my explanation so that a layman, or in your case, a layperson, will truly comprehend the situation. At present, the authorities consider the tragic death of Brady Blackstone as murder—a death caused by a person, or persons unknown. However, Nevada's equivalent of OSHA, commonly referred to in our state capitol as the Industrial Accident Department, feels otherwise. In the view of my department, Blackstone's death could be construed as an industrial accident, and as such, the Blackstone tour would be subject to major penalties including fines that could reach as high as seven hundred and fifty thousand dollars."

Donna and Larry both sucked air once their brains did the math. Like I said, Pinky was something to behold once he got on a roll.

Pinky said, "Miss Haffner, now that you know why we are here, do you have any questions?"

Before she could answer, the door opened and old Harold stood there. Normally that would be a bad thing for me and Pinky, 'cause if Harold still had all his marbles, Donna would ask him if he really sent the two of us into the garage for a screwdriver. He'd say no. Donna would shoot us both, and Larry would bury us in the backyard. But as I said, the remembering part of Harold's brain was working about as good as a sieve holds water.

But right now, the old fart had more problems than his ambrosia thing. Harold Haffner, a guy who took care of millions of other peoples bucks, stood in the doorway wearing one black shoe—no sox—and nothing else. The dude was as naked as a newborn baby. Trust me, there's not much in this world that looks worse than a naked old fart wearing one shoe. There was a sunburned vee below his neck that pointed to a chest of rib bones and down to his tiny shriveled up thingy. He was a hell of an example why old dudes shouldn't walk around without clothes.

He looked around and smiled, like it didn't register in his noggin that his daughter was holding a shotgun on me and Pinky. "Sweetheart, I just made us some ham sandwiches for lunch. I cut up some of those dill pickles you like and opened a jar of the giant green olives with the garlic cloves stuffed inside." Harold stopped talking, like he just realized there were more of us standing in the garage. "You can invite your little friends if you want. We have enough ham and bread and I can always whip up a few more sandwiches."

Donna sobbed, "Oh, Poppy." Then she handed the shotgun to Larry and ran to the naked dudes side.

Larry waved the shotgun in my direction.

I said, "Larry, put that damn thing down or I'll tie you behind my truck and drag your worthless ass all the way to the Nevada border."

Larry said, "Come on, Bear. Don't go showing me your bad side. How do we know that Pinky's telling the truth?"

Donna took Harold's arm and said, "Let's go, Poppy. I'll take you in the house before you catch a cold."

Pinky moved to her side and said, "My dear, would you allow me to assist you?"

Tears were tumbling from her eyes. "Thank you."

With Pinky on one side and Donna on the other, they guided Harold out of the garage.

Larry cackled. "Good riddance. The old bastard's worthless."

"Larry, we all know you're nuts, but even a total fruitcake knows better than to make fun of an old fart who doesn't know he's naked and can't tell the difference between dinnertime and a picnic lunch."

THIRTY-FOUR

Pinky—Needles, California

Donna pushed the old man and guided him toward the kitchen door.

I followed, avoiding, as best I could, contacting the bony vestige ahead of me.

When I was a boy of eight, my elderly grandfather slipped and fell as he exited from his morning shower. I heard his cry and ran to his side. I will never forget the sight of him lying on the tile, a writhing, naked body of pale skin and bones. My grandmother rushed in and pleaded with me to help her lift him off the floor. I loved my grandfather, but the thought of touching his wet, cold skin revolted me. I screamed and ran from the room.

As Donna steered her father up the three stairs that lead to the kitchen door, Harold began to list toward my side.

Donna cried, "Hey, give him a shove toward me. He's about to fall off the stairs."

I quickly pulled out one of my Irish linen handkerchiefs, laid it on my right palm, closed my eyes, and pushed his bare buttock.

Once inside the kitchen, I rushed to the sink, threw the handkerchief away, and scrubbed my palm with soap. While I dried my hands, Harold spotted the plate of sandwiches. He grabbed a chair and started to sit down at the table.

A moment before his naked gluteus maximus touched the wooden chair, I cried, "Mr. Haffner, I know it's nearly bedtime but might I suggest a short nap? I find a brief rest before a busy night picks me up."

He jumped up. "An excellent idea, young man. Would you care to share a beer before I lay down?"

"No, thank you. I will have one with my ham sandwich."

I followed Donna as she guided her father down the hall to his bedroom. After she covered the old gentleman's nakedness with a blanket we returned to the kitchen and sat down at the table.

Donna said, "Thanks again."

"My dear, as a gentleman, I could do no less. Now, I think we need to talk about what you must do before your father wakes up."

Donna poked at a ham sandwich and frowned. "I don't understand. What do you mean, must do?"

"My superior in Carson City, a truly wicked woman who goes by the name of Willow Stone, has made it her personal vendetta to collect as much money as she can from the Blackstone tour. I feel she believes that a successful conclusion to this case will give her a boost up the next rung of the governmental ladder. I tried to explain to her that your father was having a major competency issue but she refused to take my word concerning his difficulty. My dear, I have an idea that will resolve your father's desperate dilemma but it will require your complete cooperation. I will place a call to my superior and explain to her that your father is in no condition to travel all the way to Carson City. I can tell you right now that she will not believe me. Then I will suggest that Ms. Stone fly to Laughlin. We could drive your father that short distance and meet her at the airport. Willow, as cold and calculating as she is, would instantly recognize your father's condition and finally realize what I have been telling her is correct. At that point, I am positive my superior would back off from her fool's quest."

"I don't understand this tax problem."

"My dear, all you need to understand is that until this Nevada tax problem is resolved, your father's financial stability, and his professional reputation are hanging at the edge of a cliff, if not doomed."

Donna slumped in her chair. "Excuse me, but I don't even know your name."

I offered her my hand. "J. Pincus Delmont. However, my friends, and I trust I can include you in that group, call me Pinky."

"But, Pinky, we're in California and Nevada's another state. What can they do to Poppy?"

"I've been through a similar situation. A few years ago a traveling circus, a company based in Florida, came through Carson City. One of their elephants sat on an employee. It was obvious to all that the circus was involved in an industrial accident. However, before my department could complete its investigation into the case, the circus management decided to leave the state, just as your Blackstone tour did. My partner and I were sent to Florida. Four months later, Ms. Stone's insatiable demands had depleted the circus' assets to an extent that the business was forced into bankruptcy. Trust me, my superior will petition the court in Carson City to put an immediate lien on all your father's Nevada assets, and that will include the El Garces LLP, the very partnership in which I believe you hold the title of CEO. In my humble opinion, the state of Nevada has the power to destroy your father. And, I fear, his financial destruction could easily take down you and your cousin."

Donna frowned. "So you know about the hotel?"

"My dear, that is my job, and I believe you will discover I am very good at my job. For example, we know all about your proposed hotel."

Donna's eyes darted around the kitchen, as if she was seeking an escape from reality, or about to burst into tears. "How did you find out about the hotel?"

"For starters my partner and I saw the sign in your father's garage."

Donna stood and headed toward the refrigerator. "I could use a beer. How about you?"

"That would be nice."

She opened two bottles and sat down. "The sign you saw was a big deal a couple of months ago, but when

Brady found out what was happening to Poppy's mind, he demanded Poppy return his investment. Without Brady's money, the hotel deal fell through. Those two signs use to sit on our property at the south end of the Laughlin Strip."

I took a sip of the cold liquid. "A desirable location I am sure."

"The best. We would have the newest hotel on the strip. Poppy used to tell me that El Garces would make money faster than we could bank it."

"An admirable goal. Now, just between you and me, you said that Brady demanded your father return his investment. However, you neglected to say if that transaction was ever completed."

Donna hesitated for a nano second before swallowing her beer. It was too short a time for the casual spectator to notice, but I had not become the best defense attorney in northern Nevada without honing my observation skills to a fine edge. I said, "The reason I felt duty-bound to ask is that Ms. Stone will expect a detailed accounting of all your father's financial transactions for the past twenty-four months. Come to think of it, considering your father's mental condition, how did he take care of his business obligations during that time?"

Donna set her bottle down and leaned close. "Pinky, I've worked with my father since I received my MBA. Two years ago I noticed he started to miss little things, like due dates, or he was late for a client meeting. That was the point when I moved in to take over Haffner Investments."

"Did he object?"

"At first he did, but as the days went by, he became less and less aware of what was going on."

"How long has Harold, or you for that matter, been the financial guru for the Blackstone tour?"

"Four years. At first, it was fun. You know, the glamour of show business and all, but the last year was hell."

"Why was that?"

She flashed me that look women give when a question starts to tread on dangerous ground. "I think it's time to call your boss and set up our meeting at the airport. While you make the call, I'll check on Poppy."

The moment she left I grabbed my cell phone and called Willow.

"Pinky, where are you. I've been trying to call you—"

"Willow, I have the man who actually killed Brady Blackstone in my custody."

She hesitated. "Who is it?"

"The Blackstone tour controller. His name is Harold Haffner. He was involved in a partnership to build a hotel with Brady in Laughlin. After the project started, Brady changed his mind and demanded his money back but Haffner had spent all of Brady's money. Willow, it was Haffner, not Jack Spurlock, who rigged the chair so the fail-safe device did not work, thus killing Brady."

"And you have all this evidence?"

"I do. Bear and I are in Needles, California and—"

"Bear's with you? Damn it, there's still a warrant for his arrest, and you promised me that you didn't know where he was."

"I realize that my dear, but—"

"Pinky, hold on."

I waited for a moment.

"Okay, I'll catch a ride south on one of the state's Highway Patrol planes and should arrive at Laughlin inside two hours. After going over your evidence, and deciding whether your suspect is the real thing, I'll call the jail in Carson City and tell them to release Spurlock. Then I'll determine if you will face charges for contempt of court for not turning Bear over to me. Are we square on that?"

"Willow, do what you must. In fact, you could place me in a public pillory as long as you would stop by every day so I could listen to the melodious sound of your voice."

"Stop that! There's a rumor floating around town that you will receive a huge sum of money if you can get me to spring Spurlock, so don't try and pull anything shady. Pinky, your evidence had better be as solid as a rock."

"Not to worry, my dear. You will be provided with a veritable mountain of solid granite—so much so that your pilot will have trouble lifting his aircraft off the ground." After Willow hung up, I left the empty kitchen and walked through the darkness toward the garage. Suddenly, I stopped and considered my situation. I was in deep trouble and my position was getting more desperate by the second. Regardless of what I had told Willow, I did not have a mountain of evidence. In fact, a molehill was closer to the truth. However, to keep the millions within my grasp, I had to hand over someone to Willow Stone in a few hours and if that simple act forced me to expand the truth and go beyond the known information in this case, so be it!

For a moment I stared at the stars in the sky above, then I pulled out my cell phone and called the motel.

"Hello. Please connect me to Mr. Zabarte's room."

Impatiently, I counted ring after ring, and finally, "Hello."

"Flo? Pinky here. I need —"

"Let me talk to Bear. I don't like him running around the—"

"Woman, cease and listen to me. I have a —"

"Not interested. Call me back after Jeopardy's over."

"Flo, I—"

"Pinky, stop blabbering and answer this. What is Das Rheingold?"

I paused before responding and considered the fact that Flo had finally drifted over the edge of reality. "Excuse me, what did you say?"

"Das Rheingold, and I answered correctly."

"Woman, I still don't understand what you are talking about."

She said, "Are you slipping? I told you I was watching Jeopardy. The answer was—Richard Wagner's first opera in his Ring Cycle. The question was—what is

Das Rheingold, and it was a Daily Double question. Pinky, when I get to be a Jeopardy contestant, and I get a Daily Double opportunity, I'll take the big risk and make it a 'True Daily Double.'"

"Flo, I am very tired. In fact my mental and physical reserves have reached the point of empty. Could we return to the beginning of this phone conversation?"

"Sure, the show's in a commercial break. Where's Bear?"

"He standing inside the Haffner garage and staring into the wrong end of a shotgun, but do not worry, the man holding the other end of the weapon is that misfit, Larry Haffner."

"And where are you?"

I sighed. "Is that item of information important to our conversation?"

"It is if you plan on continuing this discussion."

"I am standing between the Haffner garage and the kitchen while I converse with you on my cell phone."

"And why did you call me?"

What a bitch! "Damn it, Flo—"

"Don't push me, Pinky. Bear and I have been on the road for weeks—living in crappy motels—eating greasy-spoon food. We've done everything humanly possible to come up with the phony murder suspect you need for some reason. Now ask me nice, or I'll hang up and watch the final minutes of Jeopardy."

God, I could not conceive how Bear, or any man for that matter, could come up with a viable reason to spend more than five minutes with that woman. However, at that moment I needed her to do my bidding, so I forced a happy lilt into my tone, "Flo, how would you like to make five thousand dollars?"

"I'm all ears."

If everything else fails, offer the woman money. Why had I not thought of that first? I must be tired. "Go to my room and collect the paper work off my bed. I did not get all the way through the stack and I need to find out if there is any physical evidence tying Brady Blackstone to the El Garces deal."

"Sounds interesting, but what happens to the five thousand if I don't come up with a tie between Brady and El Garces?"

"The five thousand dollar bonus remains in your custody regardless of your success, or failure to make the connection."

"And I'm supposed to trust you?"

"That is correct."

"Where's Bear? I should run this deal by him."

"I told you. At the moment he's involved with Larry."

She paused, and her moment of hesitation assured me of her acquiescence. A female of Flo's ilk would never turn down an offer that included a princely sum of cash.

"I'll do it, but I don't have your room key."

"I'll call the owner and tell him to give you a key to my room."

"I love Jeopardy, and Alex Trebek even more, but five thousand bucks is a pot-full of money. Pinky, you've got yourself a deal."

THIRTY-FIVE

Bear—Needles, California

After a lot of arguing back and forth, Larry set the shotgun down. Me and him had just agreed to bet a case of beer on who'd win the upcoming three game series between the Red Sox and the Yankees when the door opened and Pinky waltzed in.

"Bear, it is imperative that we return to the motel immediately."

"What's up, boss?"

Pinky glanced at Larry and then back at me.

I guessed that was Pinky's sneaky way to tell me that he didn't want to say anything in front of him. I said, "Larry, my boss has something important to tell me and he doesn't want you to listen in."

"Oh! I understand! I'll go into the kitchen and get myself a beer."

After Larry left, Pinky said, "I knew I could count on your subtlety to handle a delicate situation."

I heard a light bump come from the door. I put my finger to my lips, quietly moved across the garage floor, and snapped the door open. There was Larry, leaning with his ear where the door use to be.

"Damn it, Larry, I told you to clear your sorry ass out of here."

"Right. I just stopped to tie my shoelaces."

"Damn it, you're wearing flip-flops. If I have to tell you one more time, I'll whip your ass!"

I watched Larry run to the house, and then I returned to Pinky. "Okay, Boss, what's the scoop?"

"I just called Flo and hired her to scrutinize the documents that remain in my room."

"Ah . . . what did you say you wanted her to do?"

"I told you! Scrutinize the documents—review the volume of paper I left in my motel room to look for hard evidence—something I can present to Willow when I hand over Haffner."

"Boss, this might have slipped by you, but there have been times when Flo's been a tough broad to deal with. How much are you going to pay her?'"

"Bear, the exact remuneration will remain between your female friend and myself."

"Shit, Boss, you know she'll tell me if I ask her."

"My good man, I have no control over what you and that She-Witch do, or discuss, when you are alone."

"Then tell me."

"Not until you tell me why what I pay Flo is so important to you."

"Jeez, Boss, I'm the dude you hired to do your investigations. If Flo helps me out once in a while that's something between me and her."

Pinky said, "My God, over the last year you have become a chauvinist and a misogynist. My boy, I'm proud of you. Under these newfound circumstances, I will tell you. I made a commitment to Flo that I would pay her the princely sum of five thousand dollars for her efforts, and, as you know from past experience, I follow through on my obligations. I also recall an agreement between us for an identical sum, as a bonus to you, once Willow agrees to release Jack Spurlock from jail. My boy, that totals up to the grand sum of ten thousand dollars for the Zabarte household. Not bad for the son of a Basque sheepherder, who a brief eighteen months ago, was facing twenty-years to life on a second-degree murder charge."

Pinky always had to remind me that he had me by the balls and he knew it. But that didn't mean that I had to agree with every damn thing he said. "Okay, go ahead and pay her, but don't ever go behind my back and make a deal with my woman again."

Pinky flashed his evil grin. "I believe I can agree to that. Now let us make haste. I am scheduled to meet

Willow at the Laughlin Airport, with Harold Haffner, hard evidence in hand, in less than three hours."

I opened the garage door and bumped into Donna.

She grabbed Pinky's arm. "Poppy's sleeping. I'm not sure it's a good idea for us to meet tonight with your boss at the airport."

Before I could ask Pinky what the hell Donna was talking about, he said, "Tomorrow will not work, my dear. The deal I worked out with my superior expires in less than three hours."

Still wondering what Pinky was up to, I noticed a shadow move in the darkness at the far corner of the house. I listened to Pinky, but kept my eyes glued to that spot.

Pinky said, "I will return in thirty minutes. Please have your father dressed and ready to travel. Tonight's meeting will be his final, and only chance to take this deal."

Donna squirmed.

As my eyes got used to the dark, I could make out a head, then an arm, in the shadows.

Donna said, "How do I know I'm doing the right thing?"

Pinky said, "You will just have to trust me, my dear."

Donna sighed and stared at her feet for a second. I felt sorry for her. I was pretty sure her dad wasn't Brady's killer, but Pinky had told me more than once that was not my problem. My job was to find Haffner for Pinky. It was his job to turn the poor bastard over to Willow. It was Willow's job to figure out if she wanted to prosecute Haffner for Brady's murder.

Donna said, "Okay, I'll have him ready when you get back. But, Pinky, I'm going to hold you personally responsible for his well being."

Pinky said, "And so you should, my dear. You know you can count on me."

Donna spun around and went into the house. I grabbed Pinky's arm and whispered, "Don't look now, but we have company."

Pinky started to turn. I held his shoulder and locked him in place. "Jesus, Boss, what is it about 'don't look now' that you don't understand."

"Let go of me."

"I will when you promise me that you won't turn around."

"Fine, I will remain in this position. Now who, or what, is behind us?"

I thought about Larry and how he keeps turning up everywhere I go. "My guess is it's Larry. Let's head back to my truck. I've got an idea."

"Bear, we must return to the motel post haste. I have important work to—"

"Is that what you were talking about with Donna? Boss, what do you have up your sleeve?"

"Bear, take me back to the motel at once or—"

"Sorry, but my idea won't take more than fifteen minutes."

"If it takes you more than that, you will be off my payroll, and, I assume, you will return to your old position of supplying alcohol for the habitual drunks of Carson City."

That wasn't a pretty picture so I drove as fast as I could to the gym. As far as I knew, Larry didn't own a car, so there was no way he could have walked, or run to the gym and arrived before us.

We lucked out and found a parking place close by the front door. I pushed Pinky ahead of me through the gym door.

The guy behind the desk said, "You dudes got a member number?"

I said, "I'm staying at the motel down the street. I was in here a couple of days ago and my friend moved into the motel today."

A couple of cute broads walked in. The guy behind the desk glanced at the two babes, and said, "What are

231

you dudes waiting for? Get your butts inside and start working up a sweat."

I grabbed Pinky and dragged him into the locker room.

Pinky said, "Stop pulling me around. Now tell me, why are we here?"

I walked toward Haffner's locker. "When I was here the last time, I was so happy to find that Haffner's key matched the lock on his locker I didn't stop to look at anything else. I knew once we—"

Pinky jumped up onto the bench, I guess so we could be nose to nose, and said, "Bear, I demand you cease your verbal diarrhea and listen to me. You have dragged me to this questionable place of business where normally sane people pay good money to sweat, a notion that I, as a true gentleman, have never been able to comprehend. Now you compound the situation by continuing to talk in riddles. Return me to the motel at once."

I checked out the lockers near Haffner's locker. All but one had their doors open and I could see they were empty but there was one that was locked with a Master lock, just like Haffner's.

I grabbed the lock, and said, "Boss, my guess is this is why we're here."

Pinky smiled. "Ah, now I understand. Did you also find that key?"

"Nope, but I have a way in. Stay here. I'll be back in a second."

I ran out of the locker room and glanced around the gym. It was pretty empty. The two babes who had followed us in were both working on machines to build up their boobs. As far as I could see, their boobs were just fine the way they were. I flashed my pearly whites in their direction and headed to a rack of barbells. I grabbed up a twenty-pounder and ran back to the locker room.

Pinky said, "What are you going to do with that—"

I lifted the barbell and smashed it into the locker. The Master lock didn't open, but the wooden door shattered into a pile of kindling.

I set the barbell down. "Boss, if you ever need to buy a padlock, it should be a Master. Those babies are damn near indestructible."

Pinky pushed the splintered wood aside. The locker was full of paper, just like the Haffner locker. But this stuff looked a little different. Pinky sat down and started to shuffle through the stack. Then he stopped and handed me a booklet. It was the installation and operating instructions for the chair lift that Brady rode to his death. The booklet opened at a dog-eared page, and surprise, surprise, it was headed—Dead Man's Brake.

"Boss, I think we found something important here."

"My boy, I would say you've come up with my mountain of evidence."

"I agree, there's some bad shit here, but we need to slow down. I don't think this locker belongs to Harold Haffner."

"I am sorry, but your conjecture is not relevant at this point. I required hard evidence. My boy, in your hands, you hold the blueprint that Haffner used to convert Brady's spectacular entrance into his final act.

"I can see that, but I don't think this is Harold's stuff, and if I'm right, Harold didn't kill Brady—the dude who uses this locker is the murderer."

Pinky glanced at his watch. "My boy, your conjecture is both time consuming and academic. I needed hard evidence and you have found it. The determination of Harold's guilt or innocence will be decided by the courts."

"But if you can give me another twenty minutes I'm pretty sure I can deliver Willow the real killer."

"But I do not have twenty minutes. Now drive me back to the motel!"

At that point I wanted to tap Pinky's head with the iron barbell to see if I could shake loose something other than the dollar signs that lived inside his skull. "I think that the only reason we're running out of time is you're pulling some sort of con to collect a pile of money from Lucinda Blackstone."

"And I challenge you to tell me how that desire constitutes an impropriety on my part."

"Boss, I'm not sure what you just said, but if you asked me if I think you're doing something sneaky, my answer is yes!"

"Then I suppose we agree to disagree."

"Cut the crap. I'll bet that somehow you've conned Donna into turning her father over to Willow."

"Bear, you are skating on thin ice here. A short time ago Mabel challenged me, and as you well know, that woman is history. Are you willing to risk everything you have—your highly paid position as my investigator—your personal relationship with Flo—to continue this line of questioning?"

"What's Flo got to do with this?"

"My boy, do you think that a woman of Flo's obvious charms would remain in a relationship with a common bartender? I think not. In fact, I would give her no more than a week before she would return south to her cadre of male friends in the City of Angels."

The thought of getting by without Flo, and losing her great body was the worst thing I could think of, but my mom, and my pop had brought me up to do the right thing. There was that one bad time in my life when I killed that dude, but that didn't really count. He started it. All I did was finish it.

I waved a barbell over Pinky's head, and said, "Boss, job, or no job, Flo, or no Flo, I won't let you send an innocent man to prison, and that's my final word."

Pinky's eyes followed the heavy barbell as it barely ticked his nose. He blinked a couple of times, like he was afraid I might get closer the next time. "My boy, I am proud of you. Over the last few moments, I administered to you my famous Delmont integrity test and you passed with flying colors. We both know that I, as a sworn officer of the court, would never partake in an endeavor where the freedom of an innocent man would, or could, be placed in jeopardy." Pinky glanced at his watch. "Now tell me, if not the sickly Harold Haffner, who do you think murdered Brady Blackstone?"

"Let me think for a second. We're sitting in a men's only locker room, so that means Donna Haffner's in the clear. That leaves good-old cousin Larry."

"You mean the yellow-eyed cretin who lives under a road in the desert?"

"That's right. Now all we've got to do is find him."

"My boy, knowing how much you want to retain your lofty investigative position, I have complete confidence that you will. However, before you go any further on your quest, please return me to my room."

"Why?"

Pinky said, "While you wander about the desert attempting to apprehend Larry, I need to sit down with Flo and review what she discovered. Trust me, my boy, the two of us will patiently wait for your return."

THIRTY-SIX

Bear—Needles, California

Pinky keeps telling me that I'm nothing but a dumb-shit, Basque bartender, and he's right most of the time, but I'm not dumb enough to fall for his last line of bull.

I said, "Okay! But if I drop you off at the motel, you've got to promise me that you'll wait for me there with Flo. I'll be back inside ten minutes."

"Of course I will wait for you. Why would you even pose the question? Are we not equal partners in this investigation?"

"And you won't steal a car, or something stupid like that, and do what ever it is you are scheming to do?"

"My God, Bear, what must I do, or say, to regain your trust?"

I didn't have an answer to his question. All I knew was, if I moved real quick, I was pretty sure I could get to Larry's culvert before he got there. I also knew that if I had to drag Pinky along, I might not make it in time. But, if Pinky wasn't with me, I wasn't positive he'd wait for me at the motel.

I said, "All you have to say is, Bear, I promise I'll wait for you at the motel."

"My boy, you will find me waiting for you there, just as sure as there are stars in the night sky."

That was probably as good a promise as I could expect from Pinky. "Okay, we've got a deal."

We returned to my truck and I punched the gas. When we reached the motel, I pulled the truck into the parking place in front of my room. I guessed Flo must have seen my headlights because our door popped open and she stuck her head out. Before I killed the engine, Flo was all over me like salsa on a chip. "Bear, it's about time you got back. Where have you—"

Pinky opened his door and jumped out. "If you will excuse me, I will go inside and leave you two lovebirds to conclude your domestic discussion."

I popped the truck into reverse. "Sorry, Flo, got to go and catch a bad guy. Pinky will explain everything."

Before she could say a word, I hit the pedal and the rear wheels peeled rubber. Inside of a few seconds I was heading out of town. I knew that Flo was already pissed at me, and leaving her with Pinky wasn't going to make her any happier, but there were times when a guy had to do what a guy had to do.

I wasn't positive that Larry would head to his place, especially when his home was a shitty culvert in the desert, but home's where most guys head when the shit hits the fan. And if Larry did go home, how would he get there? And what route would he take?

Okay, if I guessed he walked, he would take the straightest line, and that would mean he'd end up on County Road Seven. Did Larry have any other way of traveling? None that I knew of, so I took the road that paralleled County Road Seven until the wash that lead to Larry's culvert flashed by the left window of my truck.

Desert towns were generally wide-open spaces without hills or rivers to interrupt straight lines, so most roads were laid out on a mile, or a half-mile grid. I kept my eye on the odometer and a half-mile after the wash I came to a crossroad. I turned left. A half mile later I turned left again and pulled my truck onto the shoulder. I shined a flashlight at the road sign. I was on County Road Seven, about a half-mile south of where Road Seven crossed over the top of Larry's culvert. Feeling damn proud of myself I killed my lights and drove about a couple of hundred yards short of the culvert. I pulled my truck off the road as far as I could and started to walk toward the culvert. About fifty feet from the wash I slowed down to make sure I wouldn't trip or make any noise.

Once I stood above the culvert I stopped and listened. Everything was quiet and I could see the opening below me was dark. I scooted down the embankment, made my way to the opening and felt my way to Larry's chair. Before I could sit down I heard the noise of a car approach on the road above. The car stopped.

I ducked out of the east side of the culvert and hid behind a big bush of sage.

I listened to Larry slide down the west embankment and walk into the culvert. He lit the Coleman lamp and then, after a couple of minutes, I heard a bunch of grunts, like he was doing some heavy work. I guessed he was trying to move the couch because that was the only thing inside the culvert big enough to make him work hard. Then I heard a weird sound. I moved close to the metal wall of the culvert and peeked around. Larry held a shovel and he was digging a hole where the couch used to sit.

I could have jumped him right then and dug up what he'd buried, but if I waited a couple of minutes, I'd find out what was so important and Larry would do all the hard work.

Then I remembered the car on the road above us. Larry had left it there, and I knew he wouldn't leave the car sitting there forever. Whatever it was he was digging up, he was going to take it to that car once he pulled it out of the ground.

I took one last peek. He had set his shovel down and popped the cap on a bottle of beer. What he was digging for was deep enough to take at least one beer's worth of time, and if I knew Larry, he'd never stop at one brew.

Slowly and quietly I backed away from the culvert. When I was about fifty feet clear of the digging sounds I walked as fast as I could through the rocky desert to my truck. I climbed in and waited. Then I got lucky. A sliver of moon popped out from behind a cloud. In the pale moonlight I could just make out the rear end of an old Cadillac. I'll be damned! Larry was driving Harold's car. I wondered if Donna knew it was gone? The clouds rolled back and dark returned. I sat back and waited for Larry to finish digging up his buried treasure.

THIRTY-SEVEN

Pinky—Needles, California

Flo, obviously upset at Bear's treatment of her in the parking lot, slammed her motel room door. "Pinky, I'd be willing to bet you a thousand bucks that before Bear met you, he was a good person. I don't like what you've done to change my man!"

"You are correct, my dear. Your boy friend was the perfect gentleman except for that minor incident where he smashed a man's head into a solid brick wall." I knew better than to waste my time and energy arguing with Flo's convoluted logic, so I changed the subject. "Now, do you have any idea where the phone book is hidden?"

Flo glared at me and shook her head. "It's in the drawer under the phone, you dork." Then she said, "Why do you need a phone book?"

"Not that it is any of your business, but I need to find out if this backwater burg has a car rental agency. I ended up with a tiny compact in Vegas and now I require a much larger vehicle."

"Hell, you don't need a phone book. Take my SUV. It's the big silver boat parked in front of this room."

I said, "You have an SUV?"

"I needed the SUV to follow Harold Haffner every day. Come to think of it, you might as well use the damn thing since you're already paying for it."

For a moment my mind contemplated what other hidden expenses the dynamic duo had incurred during their extended vacation in the golden state. However, if Flo was telling the truth, and there was an SUV waiting outside the door, my present problem was solved. "And I am sure you did an exemplary job of following Mr. Haffner. Now, time is of the essence. Where are the keys?"

"In my purse. But hold on, you owe me five thousand bucks first. Don't you want to see what I found in the paperwork?"

In my haste to turn Harold over to Willow, I had nearly forgotten the task I had assigned Flo over the phone.

"Of course I am interested. But time constraints will only allow a brief perusal of the facts. I have to pick up Harold Haffner, and deliver him to the Laughlin Airport in an hour."

"Who are you delivering Harold to?"

"Willow Stone."

"Why?"

"For the murder of Brady Blackstone."

"Come on, Pinky. We all know that dippy old fart didn't kill Brady Blackstone."

I glanced at my Rolex. "My dear, I am not the least bit interested in your opinion concerning the guilt, or innocence, of Harold Haffner. A short time ago I made a verbal contract with you where I agreed to pay you five thousand dollars to peruse the paper work in my motel room. You need to understand that you have three minutes to show me what you found, or our deal will be null and void. That means—"

"You're talking to a college graduate, damn it. I know what null and void means, you bastard. Okay, sit down and I'll show you the two items that you'll find very interesting."

I did as I was told and Flo handed me a document. It was a photocopy of a bank statement. The statement showed that Brady Blackstone had transferred forty million dollars into the El Garces partnership account.

I said, "Good work, this is just the sort of evidence I was looking for. Anything else?"

She said, "I know you consider me an ignorant woman, but if you liked the last item, the next one I turn over will make you dance with joy. It is a copy of a letter from Brady to Donna demanding the return of his forty million dollar investment."

I scanned the letter and the She-Witch was correct. That document, along with the bank statement could, and would, be accepted by any District Attorney as hard evidence of a motive for murder.

"Flo, I take back what I said earlier. You more than earned your fee."

"I hate to be the sour lemon in the punch, but I don't think you noticed that Brady sent his letter to Donna Haffner, not Harold."

"My dear, all I ask is that you cease pointing out the obvious. How I use, or choose not to use these documents is my concern. Now, I am leaving to pick up Harold Haffner."

"Not without me. I wouldn't miss this show for anything."

I leveled my sternest look at Flo and made a grab for her purse. "I think not."

To my surprise, Flo moved with the quickness of a nimble gymnast." "Buster, if you want the keys then you will have to take me with them."

"Good point, but if you come with me, you must follow my ground rules."

"And they are?"

"Until I return you to this motel, you will speak only when spoken to, as if you have reverted back to your petulant childhood. Agreed?"

"Don't worry about me. I'll just sit in the backseat and watch the DVD's I didn't get to watch before I stopped tailing Harold."

We arrived at the Haffner home and drove up the driveway to the kitchen door. Donna, as promised, had Harold dressed and ready to go. I carefully tightened a seatbelt around my million-dollar prize and invited Flo to join him in the backseat.

She climbed in, and with her usual sarcastic tone, asked, "Did you want me to read the old coot his rights?"

Positive I could not stomach a full day with this woman, much less an ongoing relationship, I marveled at

242

Bear's forbearance. "Please sit down and remember our agreement. Do not speak unless you are spoken to."

"Whatever."

Donna, who had either missed or ignored Flo's cryptic remark, climbed into the SUV next to me.

While I drove the twenty miles to the Laughlin Airport, Donna seemed agitated. A state that I assumed was caused by pondering what could possibly happen during her father's meeting with the head of Nevada's Industrial Accident Department. Meanwhile, Harold and Flo sat behind me transfixed watching that dreadful Gene Kelly movie, "<u>Singing In The Rain</u>".

We crossed the Nevada state line and a few moments later reached the point where I could see a glow on the horizon created by the Laughlin Strip of high-rise hotels and casinos. Suddenly, Harold let out a primal scream. "STOP! STOP THE CAR AT ONCE! WE'VE ARRIVED AT EL GARCES AND I WANT TO SHOW MY LADY FRIEND MY NEW HOTEL!"

I slammed on the brakes. The wheels locked. Blue-gray smoke floated up from the pavement.

While the tires skidded on the asphalt, Flo cried, "Stop the car, Pinky. The old coot has unbuckled his seatbelt, opened the back door, and he's about to fall out."

As the vehicle stopped, Harold tumbled out the door and ran off into the darkness.

Donna cried, "Poppy." Before I could say a word she jumped out and followed him.

Flo sat on the back seat and laughed. "That was pretty cool. I hope you have an alternative plan, counselor."

I grabbed my cell phone, dialed Willow's number and took a couple of deep breaths. "Willow my dear."

"Pinky, where are—"

"Sweetheart, I am a couple of minutes late because I blew a tire about a mile south of the airport and there is no spare in this rental. Would it be possible for you to commandeer a vehicle and meet me here? You can't miss me. I am driving a large, silver SUV and I am parked on the shoulder of the highway heading north."

"Are you okay?'

"I will admit there was a moment when the vehicle lunged violently to the right, that my life flashed before my eyes, so to speak. However, everything is under control now."

"Thank God. I'll tell Detective Conner to rent a car and we'll be there shortly."

"Thank you, my dear. I knew I could count on you."

Flo leaned close to me and said, "Not bad, but your line of crap to your girlfriend will only work for five to ten minutes. What are you going to tell her when she gets here now that your man has flown the coop? Pinky, I derive enormous satisfaction to see you sitting here hoisted on your own petard. Looks to me like you have come up with another flawed plan."

I turned and glared at the female sitting in the back seat. Her expression was impassive, but her tone and words indicated to me that she was mocking my brilliantly conceived strategy to conclude the Blackstone case on a positive note. However, with Harold Haffner wandering aimlessly through the black night, I did not have the time, or the inclination to allow my spirits to sink any lower.

"Flo, as you had agreed upon earlier, you will speak when spoken to and not before. Now, sans further discussion, you and I will sit here and wait. There is always the possibility that the delusional Harold Haffner will return before Willow arrives."

THIRTY-EIGHT

Bear—Needles, California

I hunkered down and waited for Larry to finish his digging. After about ten minutes, the Caddy came to life, and without my headlights, I followed Larry from a distance to the Haffner place. The house was dark and that seemed a little weird to me, but maybe Donna and Harold had gone to sleep.

Larry pulled into the driveway and I stopped about a hundred yards away. He got out and knocked on the kitchen door and tried to open it. Then Larry's short fuse popped and he kicked the door a couple of times. Finally, he got back in the Caddy headed toward downtown Needles.

I was ready to follow the loony bastard all the way to Canada, but I was pretty sure he was heading to the road to Laughlin. I had to back off because that was the intersection where the Needles cop had pulled me and Pinky over for driving without headlights. I got away with that once, but even a dumb cop from Needles wouldn't let me cruise through his beat without headlights a second time.

I pulled over to the curb, counted to fifty, turned my headlights on and punched the gas. The Caddy was long gone by the time I turned left onto the road to Laughlin. Damn, Larry was nowhere in sight. I hit the pedal harder—sixty—then sixty-five and still no Caddy. The second I cleared the city limits of Needles, I slammed my foot all the way to the floor and got my old pick-up to ninety-five before I spotted the Caddy's rear lights up ahead. Other than Laughlin, I didn't have a clue where he was going, but in my gut, I was damn sure that he would take me to Brady's killer. A couple of miles south of the

Laughlin Strip, the Caddy disappeared over a rise. Before I hit the top of the hill I slowed, pulled off the road, and stared at the highway below. What I saw looked like one of those weird Eye-talian movies that Flo dragged me to all the time. You know, those black and white films where a fat woman falls in love with a midget—or a brass band marches through an old village and the tuba's toots are off-key—or a broad with big boobs flashes a bale of dark hair hanging from her arm pit—you know, one of those off-the-wall, Eye-talian movies that Eye-talian director Phil Eeny makes.

Just then the moon came out from behind a cloud and the Caddy skidded to a stop about five feet from a silver SUV at the SUV and then stared off in the direction of the Colorado River. In the bright moonlight, to the east of Larry, I could make out a big empty area, maybe four or five football fields worth of leveled dirt that ended at the edge of the river. Just before the clouds ducked behind the moon and it got real dark again, I spotted two figures wandering around the middle of the leveled area. I killed my headlights and started down the hill. As I got closer to the SUV, I saw it was Flo's rental. I couldn't see anyone sitting inside because it had those cool windows that didn't let you see through them. Flo told me she had to have them because she didn't want to let Haffner see her if he noticed she was following him. Damn it, I thought, I knew better than to trust Pinky to wait for me at the motel.

As my truck rolled to a stop, I watched Larry sling a backpack over his shoulder and walk toward the dark field.

I jumped out and tried to figure out what Pinky would do in a pickle like this, where everything was starting to turn to shit. Hell, he'd lie like an oriental rug, that's what he'd do.

I yelled, "Hey, Larry, I've got a couple of extra beers in the back of the truck. What do you say we sit down and have a cold one?"

I didn't have any beer, but Larry didn't know that. He stopped, turned around, and walked back toward me. He slipped the pack off his shoulder and set it on the ground. "Sounds great, Bear. I've had a tough night and wrapping my lips around some of the good stuff will help clear away the sweat I got from digging that big hole in the ground."

"What big hole are you talking about, Larry?"

He wiped his forehead with a hand covered with dirt. "Ah . . . hole? . . . there's no hole. No hole at all."

"What's in the pack?"

Larry looked down, like he'd forgotten all about it. "Oh that. Nothing important."

"Why's it covered with dirt?"

"Well . . . it was buried. I dug it up and—"

"Larry, I can see it was buried. What I want to know is why did you bury it?"

He reached down and grabbed the pack. "Bear, I like you, and you're a damn fine drinking buddy, but I've really got to skedaddle. Got to find Donna and finish some important business."

Suddenly, Pinky jumped out of the driver's side of the SUV and blocked Larry's way. "Larry, you can confide in me. What does your cousin Donna Haffner have to do with—"

Larry's yellow eyes narrowed and I watched the fingers of his right hand tighten into a ball. "Get out of my way, shyster. Bear's okay because he's my drinking buddy, but I don't trust you as far as I can throw you. Now move away or I'll punch your lights out."

Pinky took one look at Larry's cocked fist, and I guess he figured the dude wasn't bluffing. He jumped back into the SUV and disappeared behind the dark glass window.

About that time, Flo hopped out of the backdoor of the SUV. She acts like I'm not standing there and says, "Larry, if I recall, you had something important you wanted to talk to me about. I have a feeling it was

247

something we should discuss in private. How about you and I go back to the motel."

Larry smiled. "Gee, Flo, that's a great idea. First I have to find Donna. After I'm finished with my business, and if it's okay with Bear, we can head back to your room."

This was definitely weird. Larry was sort of asking my permission to fool around with my woman, but he was a total nut case. If the thought of getting naked with Flo for a few minutes kept him from losing it, I'd agree to just about anything at this point.

I said, "Larry, I'm still waiting to find out what's inside the backpack?"

The grin Larry had pasted on for Flo faded away. "Wouldn't you like to know?"

I said, "Yup. That's why I asked."

His eyes were glowing and sweat rolled off his forehead, like there was a red-hot wood stove burning inside his head. "Bear, just between you and me, there's no money inside."

I said, "Then if there's nothing in there, why did you bury it?"

Flo glared at me. "Excuse me, but I believe Larry and I were having a private conversation. If you can't stop butting in, then I'll have to ask you to leave."

"Okay, Babe. I'll clam up."

Flo was doing a great job of stringing Larry along, and I trusted her, but I wasn't a hundred percent sure she was playing a game. There were lots of broads out there who didn't care if their wagon was hooked to a yellow-eyed wacko as long as he had a pile of money.

Flo said sweetly, "Larry, I'm sure you and I will have a lot of things to talk about back in that motel room."

All of a sudden, Donna ran into the beams of the Caddy's headlights and stopped cold when she saw Larry standing there. While she tried to catch her breath, I watched her gaze drop down to the backpack, then her eyebrows sort of jumped, like she was really surprised to see it sitting there.

She said, "Larry, what are you doing here?"

"You weren't home like you said you'd be. I guessed you'd come to the property. When I spotted Flo's SUV by the side of the road, I figured that you were with her."

Donna said, "But we agreed that you'd wait for me at the house."

Larry said, "Hey, don't get pissed off at me. I'll head back there as soon as we —"

That's when a big, black Dodge, heading in the direction of Needles, pulled off the other side of the road. The headlights were set to high and shined directly into my eyes. The passenger door opened and a silhouette with a damn good shape got out. "Bear, where's Pinky?"

Jesus, it's Willow! "He's sitting in the SUV."

"How come I can't see him?"

I said, "It's got those cool windows you can't see through. Flo wanted that kind so Haffner couldn't spot her while she was following him."

"That's a lot more information than I needed, but thank you."

She walked across the road and just before she reached the SUV the driver's door opened and Pinky popped out. "Willow, my dear. It is good to see you."

Willow stuck her head inside the SUV and said, "Damn it, I just flew a couple of hundred miles because you promised me that you had the man who murdered Brady Blackstone. Where's your suspect?"

"Put your hands up, Zabarte." A hard voice came from the Dodge that Willow just left.

Shit, it was Ice Conner! I reached for the stars.

"Now hit the dirt and spread-eagle."

I dropped to the ground. A little rock dug hard into the left side of my face. I crossed my fingers and hoped he wouldn't start shooting.

Willow said, "Detective Conner, I have everything under control."

"Ma'am, I don't want to disagree with you, but that man on the ground is Bear Zabarte, the same man who struck me in Carson City while I was investigating the

249

Blackstone murder. He has an outstanding warrant for obstruction of justice and I am going to take him into custody."

Pinky said, "Detective Conner, I recommend you calm down and—"

"Ma'am, it's obvious to me that Pinky has been harboring Zabarte."

Willow said, "I agree but first—"

Ice barked, "Pinky, Flo, and you two standing by the SUV, on the ground."

Willow said, "Detective Conner, I believe you are over reacting. First, we have—"

I opened my right eye a crack and saw Flo was still standing, like she thought what was going on between Ice and Willow was a TV show.

Without moving anything but my lips I whispered, "Damn it, Flo, do what he told you to do. That's Detective Ice Conner. Remember? He's the cop that shoots first and takes names later."

The voice said, "This is your last chance. Everybody on the ground."

Flo, Donna, Larry, and Pinky hit the deck.

With the left side of my face pressed in the dirt, only the right side of my nose was free so I had some trouble grabbing enough air. Sweat poured off my forehead and into my eye making my eye sting and everything look sort of blurry. Then it hit me—Forget it. Ice was going kill me in a second, so my breathing and eye problems were nothing to worry about.

I whispered, "Flo, can you hear me?"

"Yes," she sobbed. "Is he going to shoot us?"

"Don't cry, Babe. You'll be okay. He's after my ass." But I was pretty sure I was blowing smoke. Ice couldn't shoot me in the back and leave any witnesses.

Willow said, "Detective Conner, stop this at once."

"I will as soon as I get the cuffs on Zabarte."

I spread my arms and legs wide apart and listened to Conner's shoes crunch the sand as he walked toward me.

For some weird reason, all I could think about was the last time I camped out with my Pop. We were about fifteen miles southwest of Elko. I had collected an armload of Mesquite and built a fire. Pop was mixing some cornmeal and—"

Ice smashed the heel of his shoe on the side of my face and stomped down. "Zabarte, you're under arrest for obstruction of justice. Now, make a move so I can blow your head off."

I was a lot calmer than I thought I'd be, considering I was about to die, but mostly I was worried about what was going to happen to Flo after that bastard shot me.

Ice leaned over and whispered, "And because you've really pissed me off, the first one's going straight into the gut. I've heard that's a slow, ugly way to die."

About then I picked up the sound of some feet shuffling through the sand. Then I heard, "Welcome to El Garces, the finest hotel, casino, and spa in the great state of Nevada."

That's all I needed. Crazy old Harold had joined the party.

Harold said, "Why is everybody laying on the ground? Is this a new game? Can I play?"

"No, Poppy, you can't play now." I couldn't see Donna but I heard her voice.

If I moved a finger Ice would shoot me, and if I didn't move a finger, he'd shoot anyway, so what the hell, I had nothing to lose. I blew some sand away from my mouth. "You've got it, Harold. It's a new game and we're having a barrel of laughs. Come on over here and lie down next to me. I'll explain the rules."

He did and I had to close my eyes when he pushed his naked butt a few inches from my face. Dying was one thing, but having Harold's boney ass the last thing I saw was a horrible way to go.

Willow said, "Pinky, is that naked old man the one I'm taking back to Carson City?"

"Yes, it is he. Trust me, the man was fully clothed when we left his home in Needles. I can not comprehend where—"

Donna said, "If you let me stand up, I'll get something to cover him up and—"

Ice yelled, "Everybody, clam up. Zabarte, as I told you, you're under arrest for obstruction of justice. Come on wiggle your ear. The State of Nevada will be a better place once I put away another Basque half-breed."

Willow said. "Detective Conner, did you just use an ethnic slur? I will not tolerate that sort of talk under any circumstances. We are here for one reason, to take Harold Haffner back to Carson City. Now forget Bear and find something to cover up Mr. Haffner."

Donna said, "I thought you were here to make a deal with my father?"

Ice leaned closer and whispered. "Zabarte, I don't know what sort of con you and that shyster are trying to pull, but it's not going to save your ass. And forget Willow, she can't help you." The barrel of his gun pressed hard against my temple. "I'll just tell her that you bumped into me and my weapon accidentally discharged."

That was when a weird picture came into focus between the dirt and the bottom of Ice's shoe. I saw Larry reach for his backpack, like he was going to get up and go for a hike.

Without a word, Ice turned and fired a single shot into Larry's shoulder. The gunshot echoed in the night.

Larry's body jerked a good six inches off the ground when the bullet hit him.

Flo and Donna screamed.

Pinky cried, "Oh, my God."

I knew if I moved any part of me, the next piece of lead would have my name on it, so I just lay there, face squashed into the dirt, and watched the blood leak out of a small hole just above Larry's armpit.

Willow cried, "Detective Conner, you just shot that unarmed man without any provocation or warning!"

Ice lifted his foot off my face, ran to Larry's side and shoved his pistol into Larry's belly. "Maybe you saw something different, but I was positive the bastard was going for his weapon in here." Ice picked up the backpack, turned it upside down and shook hard. A little book hit the ground, and nothing else.

"Detective Conner!" Willow's voice was tough and cold, like she could all of a sudden lift a five hundred pound barbell with one arm. "From my viewpoint the man was, and remains, unarmed. Step back from the victim and turn your weapon over to me."

Ice stared at Willow like he just figured out that maybe they weren't on the same side anymore.

Willow stood tall and said, "Detective, you are immediately suspended from duty pending an investigation into this incident."

Ice said, "Come on, Willow. We both saw that scum reach for his backpack. We both were positive that he could have a weapon hidden in there. I had to shoot him—out of self defense."

"Detective Conner, there are two quick ground rules you need to understand. Number one, never again address me as Willow. My title is Deputy District Attorney Stone. Number two, the man you shot did not, I repeat, did not show a weapon much less have one hidden in his backpack. As an officer of the court, I will testify to those facts concerning your despicable actions during a formal hearing when we return to Carson City. Now hand me your badge and your weapon, or you will risk facing additional charges."

I had to say this for Willow, she had guts. Not many people faced up to Ice Conner that way and lived to tell the tale. But you need more than guts when a bad cop has the drop on you. That's when you need the good guys to come charging in to save your butt, like one of those old John Wayne movies where he's about to get scalped and the dudes in the blue uniforms come riding over the hill with one of them blowing on a trumpet. In this case the cavalry was a Sheriff's car that just happened to cruise by.

The cop car screeched to a stop. Two uniformed deputies jumped out and one yelled, "Everybody freeze. You, with the weapon in your hand, lay it down on the asphalt and back away."

Even Ice Conner knew when someone had the drop on him. He set his police special on the road, raised his arms, and stepped away.

Once Ice's itchy trigger finger moved away from his gun, I jumped up. My face hurt where Ice had stood on it, but I didn't care because I was still breathing.

Then Harold stood up and brushed a bunch of dirt off his bare butt.

The deputy who had the drop on Ice scrunched up his face. "Jesus, what an ugly sight. Harry, get me that old army blanket we have in the trunk."

They wrapped the blanket around Harold and then noticed Larry sprawling on the ground and heard him moan. "What's wrong with him?"

I said, "Just before you got here, the dude with the gun shot him."

"Harry, I guess we got lucky. Hell, if we'd stopped for coffee and doughnuts like you wanted to the bastard would have killed them all and we'd be filling out forms for a week."

The Sheriff started to put the cuffs on Ice when Willow stepped forward. "Officer, my name is Willow Stone. I'm the Deputy District Attorney for Carson City. The man you are cuffing is a Detective with the Carson City police force." She handed the deputy her card. "I have the detective's pair of cuffs and can handle everything from now on."

The deputy gave Willow a long look. "Ma'am, I'll have to run this by my Captain first." He walked back to his car and grabbed the mike of his radio.

Larry moaned again."

Harold suddenly threw his arms in the air and the army blanket hit the ground. "Welcome friends to my El

Garces Resort, the finest hotel, casino, and spa in the great state of Nevada."

The deputy jumped out of his car. "Jesus, can't somebody wrap a bungee cord or a rope around that old fart? Ms. Stone, my captain checked out your story and everything is good. The detective is now your responsibility. And you can keep the blanket for the old guy."

"Thank you, officer. Do you have a card? I want to write a letter of commendation for your file. You and your partner did excellent work tonight."

While the two deputies and Willow played kissy, kissy, I got up and Flo rushed over and held onto me like she was a tired swimmer in the deep end of the pool.

Donna ran to Larry and checked his wound. "People, listen to me. We have to get my cousin to a hospital. Larry, are you strong enough to get into Poppy's car?"

"I don't think so. My right side is going numb."

The deputy said, "We can run him up to Laughlin General. It's only a couple of miles away."

"Thank you, officer. I'll grab Larry's backpack and follow you in the old Caddy."

Willow said, "Everybody, slow down. Pinky, you ride in my rental car with Haffner. That leaves Detective Conner."

I said, "I can drive him to the airport but then I've got to go back to Needles to check out of our motel before me and Flo start back to Carson City."

Willow shook her head. "I must be losing my grip. I am actually considering turning a dangerous, rogue cop over to an accused felon who has a warrant out for his arrest."

Pinky said. "My dear, I believe it's time we discussed that outlandish obstruction of justice charge you filed against my boy a few weeks ago. After observing Detective Conner's outlandish behavior over the past hour, I think that Bear Zabarte deserves a reconsideration of that charge."

Willow shook her head. "I'd like to, but I have too much on my plate at the moment. I'll review Bear's obstruction charge once I return to my office."

Pinky said, "That's not good enough. Bear is as innocent as a new born baby, and you know it."

Willow smiled. "I wouldn't go so far as to call Bear innocent, but I'll agree to drop the charge. Now are you satisfied?"

Pinky said, "Thank you, my dear. Now, as we had discussed previously, I am officially turning Harold Haffner over to you for the murder of Brady Blackstone. Please call your office and demand the authorities release my client, Jack Spurlock."

Willow said, "Pinky, cut the crap. Are you sure he killed Brady? The old fart can't tie his shoes much less rig Brady's chair."

Pinky said, "Trust me my love, have I ever failed you?"

Willow shook her head. "This is not the time, nor the place to recount the numerous occasions that has occurred. Bear, take Detective Conner's handcuffs and place them on his wrists."

"Yes, Ma'am. Always happy to help out."

Ice's lip curled, "Bear, when I get out, and I will get out, your ass is mine. You'll be sitting by the pool, walking down the street, sleeping in bed, but sooner or later I'm going to blow a big a hole in that empty head of yours."

I closed the cuffs as tight as I could. "Willow, I'll take Ice in my truck and follow you to the airport."

The Sheriff's car turned around. Donna sat in the Caddy by the side of the road. Pinky had fired up Willow's rental and I ran a heavy rope through Ice's cuffs and one of the stake holes in the truck bed. With any luck he'd freeze his ass off before we reached the airport.

That's when Flo punched me in my arm. "Damn it, Bear, what the hell am I suppose to do? I have to turn in the SUV rental in Needles."

"Babe, join the wagon train. Once I dump Ice off, we'll both go back to the motel and celebrate."

"I guess that'll work."

We went off in a line, the Sheriff's car, Willow's rental, my pick up, Flo's SUV, and bringing up the rear was Donna driving the big, old Caddy.

THIRTY-NINE

Pinky—Laughlin, Nevada

Willow's vehicle had not traveled a half mile when my cell phone rang. It was Bear.

"Boss, stop the circus train. Donna's disappeared."

Was there nothing he could accomplish without my guidance? "What do you mean, disappeared?"

"Gone! Flo just called me and told me that Donna wasn't behind her any more. I'm going to turn around and see if I can find her. Hold on a minute. Boss, you don't seem to care if she disappears."

"My boy, you are correct. Donna Haffner's not my problem. I can see the airport runway, and once we are there, Willow promises me that she will call her office and tell them to release Jack Spurlock. You will receive your bonus and I—"

"Boss, put Willow on the phone."

"Why?"

"Because I'm going to tell her that Harold Haffner didn't kill Brady."

"If not Harold, who?"

"My money's on Donna. Now put Willow on the phone or I'll tell her all about that babe I caught you with about six months ago."

"Bear, I don't see how—"

He growled, "Put her on the phone."

I handed Willow the phone. "My dear, Bear wants to converse with you."

"Bear, what is it?"

She listened for a minute and then hung up. "He told me you're conning me. His exact words were, 'The naked old fart in the back seat couldn't kill a fly if you gave him a cannon.'"

I said, "My dear, there are times when you have to take what Bear tells you with a grain of salt."

She said, "And how about the part where he said, 'The real killer is either Larry, or Donna, or both. Larry's in the cop car in front of you, but Donna has vanished. The cops can keep an eye on Larry at the hospital. I need you to turn around and follow me and Flo. We've got to catch that blond bitch before she disappears into the desert.'"

"As I previously stated, what that ex-bartender tells you and—"

Willow flashed her headlights. "Pinky, call Bear back and inform him I'm going to follow his instructions to the letter."

The Sheriff's car in front, responding to the blinking headlights, slowed and Willow pulled along side. "Deputy, we seem to have lost a member of our group. Again I ask for your assistance. Please continue to the hospital, but rather than drop off the wounded man in your backseat, keep him under surveillance. He may be part of a conspiracy to murder."

The deputy chuckled, "Did he murder anyone I know?"

Willow gave the deputy her sternest glare. "I believe you do. The man who died was Brady Blackstone."

The deputy's face paled. "Are you telling me that son-of-a-bitch killed my favorite singer? Don't worry ma'am. We'll make sure your suspect remains in his hospital bed. All I ask is you save me a seat when they give him the needle."

"I'll do that, Deputy."

Willow turned the Dodge around and we headed back toward Needles.

Obviously outnumbered, I called Bear's number.

"Hello, Boss."

"Willow and I agree to your request for assistance. We'll be by your side in a few minutes. I do have a question for you. What are you going to do about

Detective Conner who is handcuffed to the bed of your truck?"

"I guess he'll just have to tough it out."

FORTY

Bear—Laughlin, Nevada

I was happy Willow was coming. She was a lawyer, but I knew I could trust her to do the right thing as compared to Pinky, who would do anything as long as he made a buck.

I called Flo's cell. "Catch up to her yet?"

"Yes, and the Caddy seems to be slowing down."

"Babe, keep her in sight but don't get too close. Stay back a couple of hundred yards. We don't know what that broad will do when cornered."

I was going ninety when my truck popped over a hill and there was Flo's SUV by the side of the road. About a hundred yards ahead sat the Caddy.

I got closer, stopped the truck and ran to the SUV. "Are you okay?"

"Hell yes. I'm just sitting here like you told me to. Now what are we going to do?"

"We aren't going to do anything. You're going to get in my truck and keep an eye on Ice. I'm going to walk up to the Caddy. When I get there, fire up my truck and drive slow, I mean real slow. If I wave you up, keep coming. If I don't, hit the brakes and wait for Pinky and Willow."

Flo frowned. "Do you think she's dangerous?"

"Do Eye-talian's eat spaghetti? Hell yes she's dangerous. Donna and Larry are in this together. What really scares me is she let the cops take Larry away like she'd never met the guy. And she let Pinky turn her own father over to Willow for a murder she committed. Shit, that broad would eat her young if she thought it would help her get away."

"Okay, you've made your point. So be careful out there."

Bright moonlight came and went as I walked toward the Caddy. To tell the truth, I didn't have a clue what I was going to say once I caught up with Donna, but that didn't turn out to be a problem. The Caddy was empty. No Donna. No Backpack.

When the moon wasn't stuck behind a cloud, I could see pretty good. But when the clouds covered the only light, I could barely make out my hand a foot in front of my face.

I jogged south for fifty to a hundred yards. The desert floor fell away, and by the time I stopped, the flat dirt was about ten feet below me. I looked and listened to see if I could pick up Donna's movement.

Suddenly, below me, maybe twenty-five yards away, I heard some snapping and cracking noises, like somebody, or something was trying to push through a line of scrub.

I yelled, "Donna, I'm up on the road where it's sort of safe. You can keep on bumping around the desert in the dark, but whatever you do, don't sit down. There are all sorts of critters out there, like rattlesnakes and scorpions and they do their hunting at night. Trust me, you might not see them, but they see you."

I sat down on the road and guessed I wouldn't have to wait long. Donna was pretty fit for a broad, but sitting on her butt all day, staring at a computer screen, wasn't the best training for a nighttime hike across the desert to Needles.

I yelled again. "Hey, it's up to you. You'll probably die out there, but who knows? In four or five years a Boy Scout troop might stumble across your skeleton, or you can take your chance with me. You may not know this, but a couple of years ago I was up on a second-degree murder rap and I got off. Giving up sounds a lot better to me than dying of thirst or a scorpion bite, but that's your choice. I'm calling Flo and she's going to pick me up. See you in Hell."

I heard more crackling noise below, but this time the crashing moved in a circle, like she wasn't sure what to do next.

"Donna, like it or not, you've only got two ways to go. With me, or walking the ten miles back to Needles."

The moon slipped out from behind a cloud and it was like someone flipped on the lights. Donna stood at the bottom of the embankment, not fifteen feet from me. She started to scramble up. Then the clouds covered the moon again and she stopped. I couldn't see her and crossed my fingers that she wasn't packing a gun. I jumped toward the spot where I last saw her and got lucky. I wrapped my arms around her waist. We rolled down the rocky slope to the desert floor and crashed into some kind of scrub. I banged my elbow real bad but held on to her like she was a lamb that me and my Pop were trying to dock. I lifted my two hundred pounds off Donna's hundred and twenty, saw she wasn't moving, and grabbed my cell to call Flo. A few seconds later I saw the headlights of the truck stop on the road above me.

I heard Flo jump out.

"Down here. On the passenger side, below the road."

Flo said, "I can't see you. Are you okay?"

"I'm good, but Donna has seen better days."

I lifted the limp body up, staggered up the steep slope, and checked for signs of life on Donna's face in the truck headlights.

Flo cried, "Jesus, I know she murdered Brady, but did you have to kill her?"

As I started to set her down on the asphalt, Donna coughed a couple of times and grabbed a hunk of air.

"She's okay. I just sort of knocked the wind out of her."

Flo said, "That's good news."

Donna grabbed my arm. Her eyes darted around like she was looking for a way out of this mess. "Bear, Larry killed Brady. I didn't do anything except transfer some dollars from one account to another."

"Donna, that's for the courts to decide. By the way, why did you stop driving? I figured once you opened up that old Caddy, you'd be a hundred miles short of the Mexican border by now."

"That was my plan, but I ran out of gas."

"That happens fast when you only get eight miles to the gallon." I carried her to my truck. "Flo, we need to head back to the hospital where the cops took Larry."

Donna, when I said her cousin's name tried to break loose again. "Bear, put me down at once. I told you Larry did it. Don't you understand that I'm not part of the Blackstone murder? Now take me to a gas station. I'll pick up a gallon and you'll never see me again."

She was small, but was as hard to hold onto as a sack full of feral cats. "Look, it doesn't make a damn bit of difference to me if you did it or not. That's up to Willow to decide. I think we can all fit on the front seat. Even a murderer shouldn't have to ride in back with Ice."

As I pushed Donna between me and Flo, Ice yelled, "I'm hungry and cold. What the hell is going on?"

"Sit down and shut up or I'll drive faster and then you'll freeze your ass off."

While we headed back to Laughlin, I made a call to Willow. "You can turn around again, I've got Donna."

"Good work. See you at the hospital. The deputy tells me we can't miss the place. All you have to do is follow the signs."

Ten minutes later, with me holding onto Donna, we met Willow, Pinky, and Harold, who was still wrapped in his blanket in the hospital emergency room. The cops had put Larry into a small room. He was stretched out on a bed with a tube pushing some watery looking stuff stuck in his arm.

Willow said, "Okay, all I need to find out is who killed Brady Blackstone?"

Pinky started to walk in circles, that thing he does when he's going to talk a lot without saying anything. "I can take it from here, my boy."

I was pretty sure Pinky didn't have a clue of who did what. I handed Donna over to one of the deputies. "Let me handle this, Boss."

I walked over to Larry who was lying on the bed. His face had faded to the color of the sheet that covered his legs. "Larry, before you say a word, you need to know that Pinky's the best damn lawyer in northern Nevada, and sometimes he works for free if his client is a deserving Nam vet. Right, Pinky?"

"Why yes, pro bono work ranks high on my to-do list once I take into consideration the service record of my client."

Larry said, "Bear, believe me, I didn't have anything to do with Brady's—"

I reached for Larry's bandaged shoulder and pushed hard on a little strip of tape that looked like it was coming loose. He squealed like a puppy that just had his tail stepped on. "Larry, before you say any more, you've got to know that me and Pinky cleaned out your gym locker and found all the crap you had stuffed in there. Like the instructional booklet for Brady's chair-thing. And then there was that dog-eared part in the booklet that explained how a dead-man brake works. Come on dude, I may look dumb, but I'm not stupid. I'm pretty sure that Donna was the brains behind this deal. She knows how to do books, fiddle with numbers, that sort of crap, but I'd bet you a case of beer she couldn't figure out how to screw up a dead-man brake in a million years. We all know that you're the member of the Haffner family who's good with his hands."

The anger that flashed through Larry's yellow eyes switched to fear when I reached for his shoulder again.

Willow said, "Larry, before you say anything, you have the right to—"

"Forget that rights crap. I'm tired and ready to confess. Donna told me she'd give me twenty-five percent of the pot to rig Brady's chair, but you've got to understand, we had to kill the bastard! He wanted his total investment back, and he didn't care that Donna had already spent half of it buying and grading the property, paying the architect, and all that other crap. Brady's forty million dollar investment was down to half so we couldn't pay him back the full amount. I'm sure by now that you've heard that Brady was one mean son of a bitch. God knows what he'd do to us once he figured out that he'd lost twenty million. Hell, we had to kill him before he killed us. Donna came up with the idea, and I rigged the dead-man brake on the chair."

While Larry stopped and downed a slug of water, I backed away from the bed and stood between Donna and the door, just to be sure she wouldn't try to slip out now that she'd been fingered for Brady's murder.

Larry continued, "That stupid shit, Jack Spurlock, was supposed to test the dead-man button every night, but the night Brady died, Donna found him backstage and gave Spurlock a little something to do that was a lot more fun at the time, if you get my drift. Once Brady was dead, I guess old Spurlock didn't want Lucinda, that's his girlfriend, to find out he had been pushing Donna's buttons instead of the one on Brady's chair."

Pinky said, "Willow, I believe the confession you just heard should be more than sufficient to release my client from incarceration."

Willow sighed. "I agree, but what I was looking for was justice, not a financial reward. Tell me, is there anything in this world that you desire more than money?"

Pinky smiled. "Yes. More than anything, I desire you, my love, and I am ready to continue this discussion concerning our relationship, after you make the call to your office."

Willow took her cell phone out and walked away so she could talk in private.

Pinky pulled his cell out like he wanted to be sure everyone heard what he said. "Good evening, this is J. Pincus Delmont calling. My client, Jack Spurlock, is now being released from the Carson City Jail . . . Yes, I understand that you will have to verify that fact, but the moment you have completed that task, please note that he is being released with," Pinky glanced at his watch, "A full six minutes to spare. I will expect the agreed upon sum to be deposited into my account by close of business tomorrow. Thank you, and if you ever have future considerations in northern Nevada, please call me."

I whispered to Donna. "I knew you were a cold-blooded bitch, but I can't believe that you'd let the State of Nevada give your father the needle for Brady's murder."

"Hey, you saw how sick Poppy is. There's no way he'd stand trial for Brady's murder. My hope was that by the time the DA figured out his mental condition, I'd be on an island somewhere in the Pacific."

The deputy put a pair of cuffs on Donna and said, "Ms. Stone, I'll contact you as soon as your wounded suspect is ready to travel."

Willow said, "Thank you, officer."

I grabbed Donna's arm and we all walked out of the hospital.

When Flo reached my truck she screamed, "Bear, he's gone!"

Pulling Donna with me I ran over to my truck. The rope I had looped through Ice's cuffs was hanging there and Flo was right, the bastard was gone. "Son-of-a-bitch, I yelled. "While we were inside the hospital he used the sharp metal on the truck bed to cut through the rope. Willow, that was dumb of me to tie him up like that."

Willow sort of slumped, like she was really tired or something. "That's okay, I'll alert the Sheriff."

I shook my head. "But you've got to do more than that. He'll just turn up in another backwater town like Carson City, get another badge, and start shooting some innocent crooks."

"He can't get very far running around in those cuffs."

"Not good enough. That bastard will figure out how to get out of those cuffs inside of thirty minutes. I know I would."

Willow said, "As soon as I get back to my office, I'll put out an APB in Nevada, Arizona, and California."

I looked Willow straight in the eye. She had prosecuted me during my second-degree murder trial. Hell, we had been friends for years, but this was the first time I'd ever stood up to her.

"Willow, I know I'm just a stupid Basque bartender, but you don't understand how dangerous that bastard is! I'll agree with your APB, but only if you add Oregon, New Mexico, Colorado, Wyoming and Idaho to your list."

She nodded and gave me a tired smile. "I'll do that, and thank you for finding the real killer."

I handed Donna over to Pinky. "Willow, are you going to need any help getting this broad back to Carson City?"

"I believe between Pinky and the handcuffs we'll make it. It's been a long, but productive night. Bear, I don't know about you, but I'm exhausted."

I put my arm around Flo. "Me too. Have a good flight."

Flo reached up, put her thumb on my chin, and turned my head. "Hey, there's a trickle of blood running down your face." She pulled out a little rock that Ice's shoe must have squished into my cheek.

"Ouch!"

"Stop acting like a baby."

"Babe, I need to check with Pinky on a couple of things before we go back to the motel."

"Take your time."

The grin on her face told me that Flo was hot to trot. I turned to Pinky. "Boss, before you leave, me and Flo are heading—"

"Before you do that we need to discuss the future. I have a few simple tasks for you to perform while I fly back to Carson City with Willow."

"Fly back? What about the rental car you left back at the motel? Where're you going to sleep tonight?"

He glared at me. "The answers to those questions are a part of the duties you are about to perform."

"But what about your clothes?"

"Bear, that question makes me ponder why I lifted you out of the primordial ooze at the Old Globe Bar." Pinky shook his head, like you do when you see a three-legged dog trying to run down a cat. "My boy, feel free to take notes. One, go to my room, pack my bag, and check me out of that rattrap motel. Two, return the SUV you rented in Needles. Three, follow that woman while she drives my rental car back to Las Vegas. After those simple duties are completed, you can return to Carson City. Do you understand, or should I go over the list a second time?"

I waited for a second, not sure if I should punch Pinky or go back to tending bar. But I growled, "Just give me your room key. I'll see you in the office in two days and you'd better have the ten G bonus ready to hand over."

"Do not fret about your bonus, my boy. You earned every dollar and the cash will be waiting for your return."

Pinky, holding tight to Donna's cuffs, said, "Willow, we are ready to go now."

I walked up to my truck and kicked the front tire so hard that I thought for a second I'd broke my big toe or something.

Flo said, "What's the matter?"

"It's just Pinky. That bastard knows I saved his ass again and—"

"Bear, forget Pinky. In fact, you might want to walk over and wish him a permanent fond farewell."

"Huh?"

Flo reached down into that grand canyon between her beautiful boobs and pulled out the little book that fell out of the backpack.

I said, "Jesus, how did you end up with that?"

"I guess you could say it just jumped off the desert sand while everyone was watching the deputies arrest Detective Conner."

I glanced around. Willow was talking with Pinky and nobody seemed to notice me and Flo standing there.

"What do you say, Bear? Should we look inside?"

Before I could open my trap, she read the first page. "It's a Swiss bank account book, and just like Larry said, the balance is a touch over twenty million." She smiled. "According to a note at the bottom of the page the bank requires a special password to access the account."

"I'll bet that means nobody but Donna or Larry can get at the loot."

Flo flipped to the last page and gave me a little kiss. "That's what most people would think, but look here, written on this back page is one word—Needles2ElGarces. I'd be willing to bet you a cool twenty million that's the password."

Except for Flo, and now me, no one was thinking about the dumb little book that fell out of Larry's backpack. Next week, when Willow got Donna talking, the book would become a hot item, but right now it was as cold as a well-digger's ass.

Flo tucked the bankbook back into that soft, warm place between her giant ta-tas. "It looks to me like the book is ours."

My head spun. Twenty million could take us a lot of places real fast, but then I remembered what the inside of a jail cell looked like.

Flo said, "Earth to Bear, did you hear me?"

"Jesus, give me a minute, I'm thinking."

I knew what she was asking. I liked money as much as the next guy—and twenty million was a pot full of cash—but a couple of seconds isn't much time to come up with a guaranteed plan. Maybe if she gave me a day, or a week, I might come up with a workable scam, but once we kept the bankbook, and drove back to Needles, as far as the law was concerned, we'd be as guilty as Donna or Larry.

I looked straight into Flo's baby blues. "We've got to turn it over to Willow."

"I figured we'd have a week before Willow realized the book was missing. By that time we could be—"

"Babe, have you ever spent a night in jail?"

"No. Is it that bad?"

"Trust me, it's not worth the gamble."

"Not even for twenty million bucks?"

"Nope."

Flo sighed, "I suppose you're right."

"Babe, I'd never do anything that would put you in jail."

"That's really sweet in a weird sort of way. Bear, I hope you understood that I was just stringing Larry along when I told him I'd go with him back to the motel."

"I knew. Would you mind if I reached down and pulled out the bank book so we can give it to Willow?"

"Sounds good to me."

My fingers did the walking for a minute or so of happy searching. Actually, I bumped into the book right off, but I was having too much fun to stop. Finally I dragged it out, and handed it to Flo. "After we give the book to Willow are you ready to head back to the motel?"

"Almost, I have a couple of quick questions, but they're for Donna."

Shit, what was she up to now? "Go ahead, I don't think Willow would mind."

Pinky and Donna were standing by Willow's rental. Donna was crying, like she just figured out she was up shit creek without a paddle. With the sand, pieces of scrub stuck in her hair, and sweat, the blonde broad looked like she needed to be run through a car wash without a car.

I yelled, "Hold on, Pinky. Flo has a couple of questions for Donna."

We ran to the car. Flo pulled Donna away from Pinky and said, "Donna, one thing confuses me. Why did you skim money off the top of the food allowance for the tour?"

Donna stopped crying and brushed the sand from her face. "And what makes you think I did?"

"Cool it. I found the two sets of books you hid inside the computer Solitaire game. So why steal chump change when you had twenty million hidden away in a Swiss bank?"

Donna's shoulders drooped, and for a second, she looked almost as old as her dad. "I'd been juggling funds for years trying to cover up for Poppy's problem. The tour was one of Poppy's good-sized clients but he had others and all their accounts were screwed up. I had to grab all the cash I could to cover up what he had done, or . . . "

Flo put her arm around Donna. "I understand. I would have done the same for my father. But why didn't you use some of the forty million Brady gave you for the hotel investment?"

"If you knew Brady you wouldn't have asked that question. There was no way that I'd risk co-mingling any of that bastard's funds to pull Poppy out of his mess. I figured I could hold everything together with the food allowance scam until the hotel was built. Then I'd sell Poppy's share to cover all his debts and let him retire with his reputation intact."

Flo leaned closer, so she thought I couldn't hear. "Donna, one woman to another, why did you tell Bear your name was Betty when you met him in Oakland?"

Donna blew some of her blonde hair from her mouth. "I panicked because I was afraid he had figured out that Brady's killer wasn't sitting in the Carson City jail. Why is that important?"

Flo whispered, "Just between us, in Oakland, or anywhere else, did the two of you do anything that I should know about?"

"What do you mean . . . oh no . . . Bear was a perfect gentleman."

Whew! Donna could of dumped me down a hole that I'd never be able to climb out of. Hell, for a murderer, she wasn't all that bad.

I joined their little huddle. "Donna, maybe you can hook up with Pinky's offer of free legal stuff for Nam vets when you're looking for a lawyer."

Flo said, "Bear's right. Pinky's a bastard, but he's still the best attorney in northern Nevada." Then she pulled me toward Willow. "Bear and I just found this bank book. You know, this could be where Donna and

Larry stashed the investment money they took from Brady Blackstone."

Willow stared at Flo's hand. "That looks very similar to the item that fell out of the backpack. But how did it get here?"

I said, "I don't think that's as important as the fact that Flo's turning it over to you."

Willow scanned a few pages and her eyes started to blink real fast. "Wow. Twenty million dollars, and anyone who had the password could waltz into the bank and take it all out."

Flo said, "Check the back page. It's only a guess, but I think some fool wrote the password there."

Willow closed the bankbook and said, "Thanks to both of you for all you did tonight. I owe you a dinner and then some when you return to Carson City."

I smiled. "You're welcome. My vote is for the High Roller All-You-Can Buffet at the Nugget."

As we walked back to the truck, Flo rubbed some of her best parts against my back. "Bear, I'll give you my personal thank you when we get back to our motel room."

"Babe, I bet there's a casino less than a mile away. Hell, with our bonuses we're ten big-ones richer. Let's hit the first one we come to and I'll buy you a bottle of the best red wine they've got in the joint."

All of a sudden, she stopped rubbing and gave me her nasty glare. "Hold on. With everything that's gone on, I forgot that you left me alone with that miserable little Napoleon tonight. Don't assume a bottle of the best red wine in the casino will get you off the hook. No matter what happens to us in the future, don't ever leave me alone with Pinky again!"

Damned if she wasn't hell on wheels. I pulled her close. "You've got my solemn promise, Babe. I'll never leave you alone with J. Pincus Delmont again." And then I sort of mumbled, "In Needles, California."

Flo's head turned and she glared at me. "Did you say something about Needles?"

"Just that it's a hell of a town. Now let's find ourselves some grub. I'm starving and it's been a hell of a long time since we got naked."

Flo's nasty look was replaced with a grin. "That would be nice."

"Which part, the food or the naked part?"

"Both, you fool."

FORTY-ONE

Pinky—Carson City, Nevada

It was nearly ten when I walked into my office. The night had been long, with the flight home, and a glorious period of bliss with my favorite ex-wife. This morning, after we woke, we lingered over a perfect breakfast of hot bran muffins and my private blend of gourmet coffee.

The first sight of Lu standing by her desk, dressed in a sheer white blouse, reminded me how brilliant I was for hiring her sight unseen.

She smiled. "Good morning, Pinky."

"Good morning to you, my dear. Any messages?"

"Yes, quite a few. First, there are five from a woman by the name of Mabel. During our last phone conversation she claimed that—"

"Throw those offending pieces of paper into the trash. And if that traitor ever calls again, tell her that I have nothing, I repeat, nothing to discuss with her." After a moment to recover my bright outlook on the day, I said, "And what about the remaining messages?"

Lu handed me the stack of notes. The top one was from Lucinda Blackstone. Her call had come in ten minutes prior to my arrival.

I said, "I'll take care of this one immediately. Now, before I forget, I want you to cut two checks for five thousand dollars. One for Bear, and one for Florence Sonderlund."

"The same Flo that's Bear's girlfriend?"

"That is a strong possibility, but I discovered long ago that attempting to keep track of Bear's social life is more than I can cope with. And now, my dear, if you will be so kind as to bring me a fresh cup of coffee, I will retire to the comfort of my inner sanctum."

I sat down and dialed Lucinda's number.

"Ah, Pinky. It's been a while since we last talked. You may not be aware of this fact, but the demise of my husband has turned me into one of America's richest women. If you have any future contact with Brady's killer, or killers, please express my sincere appreciation."

"I will take care of that. Now, is there anything else I can do for you? I have been out of my office for a few days and I have an extremely large backlog of work to accomplish."

"Do you recall the suite I stayed in when we first met?"

"Yes, you were ensconced on the top floor of the Nugget Hotel, a short thirty miles from Carson City. Why?"

"It just so happens that I'm in that same suite, sitting on a couch, sipping a glass of Veuve Clicquot Champagne, and I'm completely, and totally alone."

I sat back and considered the obvious innuendo. The last time I had conversed with Lucinda, at a sidewalk cafe in Quebec City, the bitterness behind her words informed me, in precise terms, that she did not care to see me again.

I said, "Alone with a bottle of Veuve Clicquot. That should be the title of a best-selling novel."

I buzzed Lu.

Lucinda said, "Pinky, if I look to the west I can see the hotels of Reno, and those magnificent Sierra Nevada mountains are thrusting, I repeat, thrusting up into the blue sky."

"I am familiar with the view, my dear. Trust me, those peaks have been thrusting for millions of years."

Lu walked in. I gently covered the transmitter on my phone, and said, "What does my calendar look like for the rest of the day?"

Lu said, "You have two court appearances, one at two-thirty and the other is scheduled at three."

I signaled Lu to remain in place and pulled my hand away from the transmitter. "Lucinda, as you requested I am returning your call. Do you have an urgent legal need? I am at your disposal but trust you understand that I am a very busy man."

She chuckled. "I'm sure you are, and occasionally you actually slip in a touch of legal work."

I said, "Excellent, I think I can fit in a brief meeting to discuss any legal concerns. The only caveat is that I must be back in Carson City before two."

"Counselor, that's only a couple of hours from now. I'm not sure that will give us enough time. From my perspective, it could take closer to five hours of consultation for me to deplete my pent-up legal needs."

"Just a moment."

I covered the transmitter again and said to Lu, "I don't need to know what you do, or how you do it, but I will require a one day postponement on my afternoon court appointments."

She stared at me for a moment, as if she were trying to determine the depth of my perfidy. Then Lu said, "I'll do my best."

Once Lu had discreetly left my office, I uncovered the transmitter. "Lucinda, you are in luck. I have managed to clear my afternoon calendar."

She laughed. "Why am I not surprised?"

Suddenly, Lu rushed back into my office and stood across the desk.

Again I moved my hand over the transmitter, and snapped, "What now?"

"I'm sorry to interrupt, but Willow's waiting for you on line two. She wants to know if you can break away for lunch around one?"

"Tell her, no, and that I am on the phone and will talk with her later."

It was obvious from Lu's expression that my latest request had exceeded her ability to cope. I took my hand off the transmitter. "Lucinda, I apologize, but duty calls. Would you be so kind as to hold on for a moment?"

Lucinda said, "Pinky, I've waited much too long to give up now. Besides clipping bond coupons, and watching the stock market, what else would I do during a northern Nevada morning?"

"I thank you for your forbearance, my dear."

I hit the hold button and then the button for line two. "Sweetheart, I am on a phone conversation with an important client at the moment. Could I call you back?"

"Who's the client?"

"My dear, you know that I cannot divulge that information to you. Now, what can I do for you, my love?"

"After last night, I had hoped that we could get together for lunch to discuss a . . ." Willow's voice trailed off, as if she wanted to continue, but could not bring herself to finish.

I said, 'To discuss what my sweet?"

"I know this sounds crazy, but I was considering a possible reconciliation."

I glanced at line one. The light continued to flash.

I said, "My dear, there is nothing on this earth that I would rather do than have lunch with you. However, I have an afternoon commitment with one of my most valued clients in Sparks."

Willow said, "So what happened between us last night meant nothing to you. The enticement of a client's retainer still holds sway over our relationship."

"I disagree with your conclusion, my love. As you well know, an attorney/client relationship can be, at times, a very tenuous situation. I must go to Sparks to cement that relationship, so to speak."

Willow said, "Forget this phone call. In fact, I don't know what came over me. Normally, I'm not a woman who lets impulse direct her life."

"Please, my dear, slow down and give me another chance."

During the conversation between my ex-wife, and myself, Lu stood quietly, as if she were weighing her need of a job against a woman's desire to tell another woman the truth. I immediately recognized her situation, as one of those rare moments where I would be able to determine the level of trust I could place in my new secretary.

Willow said, "No, erase from your memory what I just proposed. I must have been crazy to think that we could have—"

I said, "Darling, I am sorry, but I have a client waiting for me on another line. Is there anything more I can—"

I heard a click as line two went dead. I shifted my finger over to line one.

Lu cleared her throat, and said, "If you'll excuse me, I have those court appearances to change."

It looked as if Lu and I were going to get along just fine.

I pushed the button. "Lucinda, I apologize for the interruptions. As I said, I have been out of touch for a few days and—"

"Counselor, I do understand. Just tell me when we are getting together."

"I will be knocking on your door in less than an hour."

"Now that sounds more like the Pinky Delmont I know. Let the games begin."

Now that you have completed the latest Pinky and the Bear adventure, continue on to learn the inside story of how to design and construct a world-class cover for less that a thousand bucks.

AUTHOR'S NOTES

You'd think that once an author finished the final sentence of a book, he or she would be done and generally, you would be correct.

However, in the case of *The Big Show Stopper*, completing the writing did not give me the satisfaction of popping a bottle of champagne and celebrating.

For my last two novels, my son, Hugh, was kind enough to use his artistic and graphic expertise to design a "killer" cover. His only request? Send him a copy the completed manuscript. He would read the latest Pinky and Bear adventure and then come up with an idea. As he had done in the past, Hugh sent me his first idea, and as before, his initial concept was perfect.

So what was my problem with Hugh's brilliant concept? The cover included an image of a smashed guitar. No problem there. The guitar looked great, but there was one small drawback. The image of that copyrighted smashed guitar was going to cost me one thousand dollars and that was about nine hundred and ninety more than I had planned to spend!

After mulling the problem over for a few moments I had a sudden brainstorm. The solution to my financial dilemma could be stated in one word, eBay!

I called Hugh and asked, "If I shipped you an old guitar would you be willing to smash it and take a picture for the cover?"

He responded with what sounded like a destructive glee, "Sounds like fun."

Now you would think that picking up a worthless guitar on eBay for twenty to twenty-five dollars would be a no-brainer, but let me be the first to tell you that in the murkey world of defective guitars, we would both be wrong.

The first day I checked eBay, one seller in southern California, had listed approximately fifty defective guitars, so I put in a low-ball bid on the first one. Being an experienced and very clever bidder on eBay, I figured that twenty bucks had to be a bid big enough to snag a guitar that didn't work. I mean get real, the instrument couldn't make music so beyond smashing it into smithereens, what good was a defective guitar?

Well, I found out my twenty-two dollar final bid wasn't enough because I lost the first guitar to someone who bid fifty cents more. Then I was out-bid again on the second, the third, the forth, fifth, sixth, seventh, and on and on, and each time I cranked up my final bid fifty cents to a dollar.

By this point I was beginning to panic. I had reached thirty-three dollars on my final bid. the stock of fifty defective guitars stock had dwindled to a final few, and I still didn't own a faulty guitar.

I threw caution, and my budget, to the wind and placed a final bid of thirty-seven dollars on one of the last three defective guitars. This time, lady luck was on my side. I finally owned my very own malfunctioning guitar.

I had my purchase shipped directly to my son and then waited for the results.

Here's what happened after FedEx made their precious delivery.

A moment before Hugh strikes the fatal blow

The instant before a defective instrument goes to guitar heaven

The photo studio/morgue before the cover shot

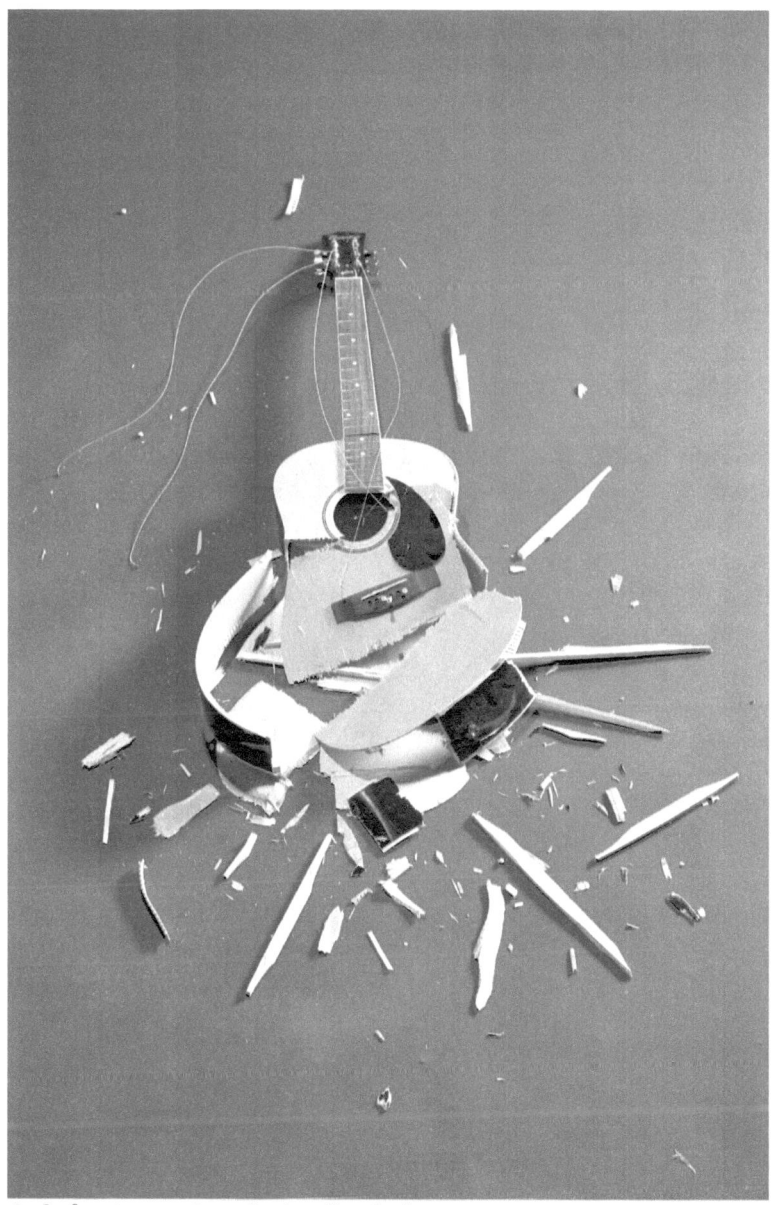

A defective guitar in its final glory

So now you know the rest of the story of how to get an exceptional book cover for less than a thousand bucks.

The total cost?

One defective guitar purchased via auction off ebay, shipping included—Thirty-seven dollars.

One case of wine, plus shipping—one-hundred and thirty-five bucks.

The final cover?—Priceless.

The notes on this book would not be complete without going over a few memories concerning my immersion backstage at a 2006 concert in Oakland featuring one of America's top concert performers.

As the other backstage guests wandered about staring at the musicians, I was more interested in the 'load-in/load-out schedules posted on the walls—or the logistics concerning the feeding of the crew—or how the stage crew, all dressed in black, moved on and off stage like nearly invisible dancers, to be sure the star had the right guitar at the right moment.

Before the show began, we were warned to wear the soft, plastic earplugs that were handed out before the first act hit the stage. During one number, I was dumb enough to pull the earplugs out of my ears and rapidly reinserted the devices. The brute force of the sound beating at my body was a bit like being tossed about by a giant wave while body surfing. The power of raw sound is amazing, if not a little frightening, and besides, if the noise became too loud, I could pop back stage for another beer and a handful of chips. Get real, what's a little hearing loss compared to picking up the background material needed to write *The Big Show Stopper*?

That pretty much concludes my notes on *The Big Show Stopper*. If you have any questions, drop me a email and I will do my best to answer each and everyone.

The third Pinky and Bear adventure will be released next year. I would be happy to read a chapter of the unpublished novel to any book club who purchases *The Big Show Stopper*.

And don't forget to spread the word on *The Bloody Birthright*, and *The Big Show Stopper*, to your friends, fellow book readers, or anyone who has $14.95 just dying to jump out of their wallet or purse.

Until next time,

Ken

August 24, 2010

www.kendalton.com